DRAWN TO THE MEAN

A Marley Dearcorn Novel

JESSICA McCLELLAND

COLD RIVER STUDIO
NASHVILLE, TENNESSEE

Published by Cold River Studio, Nashville, Tennessee

First Edition: 2012

Printed in the United States of America
ISBN 978-0-9848044-8-1

Above and beyond, Dad, above and beyond.

DRAWN TO THE MEAN

CHAPTER 1

"**M**arley, you had better come down here," said a quiet voice on the phone.

I rolled over with the receiver pressed to my ear and tried to read the clock beside the bed. Nothing was coming into focus.

"Wendy?" I asked.

I'd answered the phone purely on reflex, hoping I had guessed right about who was on the other end of the line.

"Yes. It's Wendy. I really think you should come down here… right now."

I sat up in bed, trying to see what time it was. The digital clock wasn't cooperating with me. Then I felt the soft satin sheets between my fingers and heard the gentle tick of a stately grandfather clock in the hallway. This wasn't the ranch house.

"What time is it?" I asked. My hair was tangled around the phone, and it took three attempts before I managed to brush it aside.

"About five."

I rubbed my eyes and fiddled with the lamp switch on the bedside table. When it clicked on everything snapped to life around me.

I'd somehow managed to wiggle to the center of the king-size bed during the night, and finding the outer edge of the massive thing had taken a concentrated effort. That, plus navigating the herd of throw pillows mounded at the headboard, had slowed me down considerably.

"Is everything all right?" I asked.

Well, of course everything wasn't all right. Nobody called before five a.m. unless everything wasn't all right.

"No," said Wendy. She sighed. Then she sobbed.

Wendy had moved into my father's little caretaker's cottage about the same time I'd gotten shot. Six weeks ago, now. Since she was my closest neighbor here in the isolated valley in Killdeer, Montana, and I'd moved out of the cottage to help her during her terrible divorce, I felt responsible for her. She called often with minor troubles, or if she needed to talk. But five in the morning?

"Wendy, did the pipes freeze up again?" I asked.

"No," she said between sobs.

Oh boy.

"Can you give me a half an hour?" I asked. I had been divorced too. I knew how tough it could be on someone. And the pain usually hit you at inconvenient times.

"You better bring your dad with you," she said.

That didn't sound good.

I flipped the covers off, slid out of bed, and my feet touched the lush Persian carpet. The floors were nice and warm.

Well, Leif Gable's house was always warm. He'd built it to withstand frigid temperatures, and even in December it was toasty inside. It didn't hurt that the house had three fireplaces.

"It's the furnace, again, isn't it?" I said. I tucked the cordless phone under my ear and started to grope for my jeans. My father and I had been fighting with that old furnace for weeks. He was probably wide awake at the ranch house just down the road from Wendy and probably hoping for some sort of disaster so he wouldn't be so bored. Calling him at five in the morning was the best way to reach him anyway, before he left the house and vanished into the pastureland surrounding the ranch.

"No, its not—it's not the furnace," Wendy said. She tried to stop sobbing. It sounded like a prairie dog with the hiccups.

I finished pulling on my jeans, and I sat back on the tall four-post bed.

"Wendy, it's all right. I understand how you must be feeling right now."

"No, Marley. I really don't think you do," she said.

It was my turn to sigh.

I let my eyes drift around the master bedroom, taking in the tasteful and beautiful décor while I tried to think of what to say to Wendy.

Leif and Virginia Gable had lived in this big house for only a few years before Virginia had gone a little bit crazy, had an affair, and gotten herself a cozy relationship with a bottle of pain pills so she could escape the doldrums of rural Montana life. Needless to say, Leif had divorced her after he realized how unhappy she had been living in a town with a population smaller than the average shopping mall on a busy Saturday. But at the moment Leif was stuck in Washington D.C. until the divorce was final, and since December in Montana could be a terrible time to leave a house like his empty, he'd hired me to be the live in house sitter. I was still pinching myself that I'd managed to snag such a fantastic job.

Since personal experience had taught me that having a husband serve you with divorce papers could turn the world upside down, I was sympathetic to Wendy's situation. "I know things have been pretty hard on you lately, Wendy. But, honestly, there isn't anything going on right now that you can't handle just fine."

"There is a dead Indian kid on my deck," she said.

I closed my mouth. It fell open again as the information sank in.

"A dead kid…on your deck? Are you sure?" I asked. This was definitely one of those times it was important to be very clear about things.

"Yes. I went out to plug in my car so it will start, and there he was. Just, lying there."

"Are you absolutely certain he's dead?" I asked. "Did you call an ambulance? He could be passed out, or he could be hurt."

"No. He's dead," she said.

"How do you know for sure?" I was fumbling with my socks, cramming my feet into them as fast as I could while still holding on to the phone.

"I know for sure," she told me.

I'd worked at the Montana Fish and Wildlife branch office in Helena for nine years. Part of the job was regular first aid training. I knew just enough to help someone with basic medical emergencies.

"Did you check him for a pulse? Did you try to see if you could get a response from him?"

She finally stopped sobbing. "I don't need to do that."

It was early Tuesday morning. Although it wasn't likely, maybe the poor kid had gotten lost and was suffering hypothermia.

"I'm going to tell you how to check for a pulse. It's not that difficult," I said.

"There is an arrow sticking out of his chest."

I nearly tripped going down the long staircase and grabbed the handrail, my mouth hanging open.

"How much of the arrow is sticking out?" I asked.

There was a pause. "About half."

Sitting down sounded like a good idea, and I eased onto the edge of a step. "Okay."

"I called the sheriff," she said. "He should be here in a minute.

What should I do now?"

"Wait for him to get there, then stay out of the way," I said. "I will be there as quick as I can. I've got to hang up now, Wendy. But you won't be alone for very long. We will all be there soon."

I hung up the phone and pulled myself to my feet. It wasn't easy, but I managed to find my boots and tug them on, locate my car keys, and keep my presence of mind long enough to slip into my heavy coat and go out to my little black Honda.

Bad memories were crowding my mind. The previous fall, not six months after I'd come back to lick the wounds from the unexpected loss of my job, a string of bad events had unfolded in my tiny hometown. The aftermath of a terrible storm in Killdeer had led to my discovering my closest neighbor dying on his kitchen floor, and I'd been helpless to save him. Since I hadn't been able to leave well enough alone, somehow it had become my personal mission to find out what had really killed him. All the snooping had led to my getting shot, and hearing the desperation in Wendy's voice was bringing back the memory of that horrible event.

As I climbed into my car, I purposefully did not look towards the backyard of Leif's house. That had been the place it had happened. The place I had been shot by someone I had trusted. The last thing I needed right now was a vivid visual reminder, so I kept my head down and turned the key in the ignition.

My Honda sputtered to life, some sort of black cloud shot out the back, and I drove down the tree-lined road towards my father's ranch. I drove too fast, my little car bouncing along the washboard road, the back end hopping to the side as it lost traction. The rows of aspen and lodgepole pines dashed by in a blur, but I couldn't seem to keep my foot from pressing the pedal down too hard. I dodged the potholes by memory and in a few minutes was pulling up in front of the ranch house.

When I climbed out of the car, my father was already standing on the porch. He had probably seen my headlights. A cup of coffee was clutched in one hand, and he had missed a button on his green flannel shirt. He took a sip, steam curling around his ears.

"Pipes freeze again?" he asked.

"Wendy's in a bit of trouble. We need to go," I said.

My father paused for only a moment. Then he pitched the rest of his coffee over the side of the porch rail, went inside and came back lacking his coffee cup but with a coat. He wordlessly climbed into the passenger seat of my car and didn't bother buckling his seat belt.

I threw the car into reverse, and soon we were headed down the road, past the thousand acres of rolling hills and pastureland that made up the ranch, and towards the western-most edge of our property.

"It's that damn furnace again," my father said, glaring at the windshield. "I knew I should have replaced it."

"Um, no. It's not the furnace," I told him, wishing very much that it were. I shifted gears.

"She have bears again? I think I'll get her a locking trash can today down at Farm and Ranch Supply. I'm telling you, Kiddo, it's all these people feeding the deer that bring 'em around. You mark my words, someone's going to get hurt one of these days and then people will all complain to the Fish and Wildlife office that they should have done something. Well, bears go where the food is," he said, irritated.

"Someone did get hurt. But it wasn't bears," I said.

His eyes scanned the fence line as my headlights shone on the wires. No doubt he was searching for gaps that needed repairing. "Who got hurt?"

"Wendy says there is a dead boy on her deck."

"She sure he's dead?" he asked.

"There is an arrow sticking out of his chest."

My father turned his head back towards the road. "Yep. That would do it."

We didn't talk the rest of the way. I couldn't talk about it anymore, and my father didn't feel the need. But I was stronger for his simply being in the car with me.

We pulled up in front of the little house and saw the sheriff's truck already parked in the driveway. I shut off the engine and started to open my car door when my father laid a hand on my arm.

"Why don't you wait here, Marley? I think you've seen enough action for one lifetime."

I nodded and pulled my door shut. I felt a responsibility for comforting Wendy, but I also wasn't completely sure I could handle seeing another dead person again so soon. It had only been two months since the last time. Maybe it was better to let someone else handle things for a change.

My father climbed out of the car, his lanky arms and legs unfolding awkwardly as he extracted himself from the low seat. He went around to the backdoor so he could avoid the deck and not contribute yet another set of footprints to the crime scene. There was no doubt that Nick Wilcox, the deputy of Killdeer (who happened to have a serious CSI complex), would be arriving any moment to back up the sheriff, and would begin rolling out the yellow tape and documenting every pine needle within a mile of the place.

I sat in the car and kept my eyes down. A quick glance showed me a prone figure was lying at the top of the stairs that led to the front door, but I deliberately avoided focusing on the spot. When Wendy was done talking to the sheriff, I'd be able to go inside to offer her what little support was possible. Preferably after someone had put a sheet over the body.

I rubbed my hands together and watched the picture window over the deck. Every light in the little house was ablaze, the curtains were pulled open, and I could see sheriff Loy Shucraft standing in the small living room, one hand propped on the butt of his pistol. I'd known Loy since high school and I knew his habits. He always rested one hand on the butt of his pistol when he was nervous or unhappy. I imagined that Wendy was on the small couch wringing her hands and sobbing. I think Loy would rather shoot a skunk in the cab of his sheriff's truck than face a crying woman. But he was leaning down, serious set to his jaw, and nodding encouragingly. In other words, he was doing his job.

Where was Nick? I glanced over my shoulder down the dirt road leading back towards Killdeer, but I didn't see any headlights. He should have been here by now.

The minutes passed, and I started to feel chilly. Sitting in the car doing nothing was making me feel utterly useless. Everyone was inside. Shouldn't someone be out here securing the scene?

Then I recalled that Sheriff Shucraft was exactly one half of the entire law enforcement team of Killdeer, Montana, and was currently taking a statement. Until his deputy, Nick Wilcox, arrived, there wasn't anyone else to spare. I knew from experience that the ambulance crew would not show up for at least a half an hour. Parkman was the closest town large enough to have emergency medical crews to send to Killdeer. This could take some time.

I fidgeted, then gave in to my restlessness and got out of my car. Staying beside the Honda, I vowed not to do anything more than keep my eyes open and make sure no raccoons came wandering by to contaminate the area. Not that they would, with the headlights of my car shining away and the porch lights turned on.

I glanced back at the window and saw my father handing a glass of water to someone sitting on the small couch, and assumed he was all over the comforting-of-Wendy situation.

Nick Wilcox was nowhere in sight. The deputy's headlights should have been bouncing towards the house by now, but the road was empty. Not that I was ever terribly happy to see Nick, but at least he knew his forensics. I could imagine exactly what he would do when he pulled into the driveway.

First and foremost, he would check for tracks leading to or away from the deck.

I swept the ground with my eyes and knew right away he was going to be disappointed. It had been an unusually dry December, and virtually no snow was left over from the last storm. What snow did remain was hard packed, and it was impossible to see tracks of any kind. I scanned the ground leading into the trees and saw the same thing there. No visible tracks and hard-packed ground. Thick trees surrounded the house, crowded the driveway, and hid the foothills beyond in thick shadows. The sun wouldn't be up for another three hours. Finding anything in the pitch-black morning would be difficult.

I looked up at the deck, driven by curiosity, and focused on the boy lying there. I could see the arrow shaft protruding from his chest. No wonder Wendy had been able to tell almost at once that the boy was dead and not injured. The arrow was buried deep, almost in the center of his chest. Judging from what I could see of the arrow, it was possible the tip had penetrated so deeply it had gone out the other side. That would leave an open wound for the blood to escape. But when I scanned the ground again I couldn't see any blood. Anywhere.

Frowning, I stepped away from my car and searched the ground carefully. I couldn't see one drop of blood. What could that mean? Had the boy been shot and walked here looking for help? If that were the case, there would be an obvious blood trail.

There wasn't. And considering the position of the arrow, I doubted very much that the boy had survived more than a few moments after being shot. Granted, I knew more about the anatomy of a whitetail deer than a human, but it was pretty clear the arrow was lodged in a fatal spot.

I steadied myself and crammed my hands inside my coat pockets. Growing up on a ranch that hadn't always made enough money to pay the bills, you learned at an early age that a person had to do things they didn't necessarily like. There usually wasn't a cavalry riding over the hill to save the day. Most of the time it was just you and the one or two folks who lived down the road. I'd had a scare a couple of months ago, but I was also painfully aware of the fact that the world didn't always slow down to let you recover from things that were hard to bear. More often than not, the hits just kept coming.

I stopped searching the packed ground and looked at the stairs leading up to the deck. I didn't see anything that resembled blood on the steps, either. Not one smear of blood could be seen at all. Crouching down, I peered under the deck to see if anything had dripped down between the boards to pool on the ground. There was nothing underneath the deck but a fine dusting of pristine, white snow blown in on the light breeze.

So, the only possibility was that the boy had been brought here by someone and dumped. Who would want to do something like that? If you had just murdered someone, why bring the body someplace where other people would see it? Maybe it had been an accident and someone had brought him here looking for help?

I stood up and edged closer to the deck, careful not to step anywhere other than packed ground. When I was a few yards away, the body became visible between the wide slats of the deck rail, and for the first time I could see it clearly. I let out an involuntary gasp.

The young man was dressed for the weather in a quilted flannel coat and warm snow boots. His small form was resting like he'd been laid out on the deck reverently, not like he'd been dropped haphazardly. His arms were tucked at his sides, his legs were straight, not twisted or sprawled. He wore a stretchy blue stocking cap and gloves. But for the arrow penetrating his chest, he looked like he was simply sleeping.

But I hadn't been shocked because of that. I had gasped from the jolt of recognition.

It was Joseph Flies Low, a teenager from Killdeer High School and someone I recognized at once. This boy was no stranger. He was someone I knew.

Someone had killed Little Joe.

The front door opened with a whoosh, and the sheriff was suddenly blocking the light. He looked down at the body and then back to me. His wide face darkened. He was not happy to see me.

"You should have stayed put," he said.

"Little Joe? He was only sixteen years old!" I was heartsick.

"Hun, would you please come inside? It's freezing out here," Loy said. He emphasized the word *please*.

Even with the shock of seeing Little Joe, I was conscious of the fact that for December it was very warm outside. The sun hadn't come up, and yet I couldn't see my breath in the air. Loy wasn't trying to get me in the house because it was too cold outside.

I eased away from the deck carefully and gave Loy a nod. "I'll come in the back."

Loy went inside the house, slamming the door behind him. I took a couple steps, heading around the deck, but I stopped and looked at Little Joe again, weary with sadness.

Joseph Flies Low was a happy Crow Indian teenager, but for his age he was small. He never said he minded being called

Little Joe instead of Joseph, but now I was thinking of all the times I'd addressed him that way, and I was wishing I hadn't. Joe had always struck me as a gentle kid living in a harsh world. He lived in a trailer park just outside of Killdeer all the locals called "the Suburbs," or "the Burbs" for short. His parents were on the Reservation as far as anyone knew, and he'd come to Killdeer to live with his ancient grandmother, Wilma Flies Low, when he was only ten years old. The pair of them were a common sight in the grocery store. Little Joe would lead his mostly blind grandmother through the aisles of the store, carefully placing the items she wanted on the flat push cart and joking with her about her sweet tooth. Glaucoma had robbed Wilma of the majority of her sight years ago, and Little Joe had made up the difference by being her eyes in the world. Who would take care of Wilma now?

I felt my throat tighten at the thought of Wilma suddenly finding herself alone. When I glanced back at the deck again, it wasn't from curiosity, it was from sadness.

Something struck me about the scene. Joe's face was oddly serene. His narrow features and sharp eyes were set in a peaceful expression. He looked like he was simply staring up at the sky, curious about something. He certainly didn't look like someone who had suffered. Maybe he hadn't known he was about to die just before it happened? That was the only explanation I could think of that made sense.

Joe had been taken completely by surprise. His face showed no trace of fear or shock. How could that be?

I looked away, started towards the backdoor and let my eyes drift to the forest, feeling angry and sad at the same time. Then my eyes caught a shimmer from the shadows, and I stopped. Someone was looking back at me from the gloom of the trees.

A startled owl perched on a gnarled branch in a pine tree,

glaring at me. He fluffed his feathers, irritated that I'd seen him. He gave me a suspicious examination, his eyes glowing like tiny mirrors, reflecting the light from the house. He didn't seem willing to linger, and when I didn't move away, he spread his wings and dropped from the branch smoothly, gliding further into the dark forest.

For a moment I felt like a trespasser, a great bumbling interloper who had crashed my way into the calm of the owl's domain. I'd been born and raised in Killdeer, and yet at that moment I felt like an intruder. We'd built homes, stores, and schools, and tried to tame the land here in southern Montana, but I always knew the wild was only temporarily accommodating us. Try as we might to conquer it, or separate ourselves from it, in the end we were simply at the mercy of the wild forces around us.

Killdeer was a tiny community scraping out an existence on the fringes of civilization. Folks had enough to worry about with the weather, the dangers of living so close to the edge of nature and the uncertainty brought on by poverty. And now, someone had fallen victim to violence from one of their own. Something savage had claimed one of us on this night. Little Joe Flies Low was a small and gentle soul. Why did it always seem like the best of us, the most deserving, met with such devastation?

I wrapped my coat tighter around my shoulders, and headed inside.

CHAPTER 2

"This time, I kept my nose out of it," I said.

Irene Baker, my best friend and owner of Killdeer's busiest café, snorted. "That's a first."

We were sitting together in Leif's kitchen, going over the morning's events and sharing our sadness over what had happened.

I sipped coffee from a heavy pottery mug, and then stirred in another teaspoon of sugar. "Has word got out yet?"

Irene ran her hand over the smooth, black granite countertop, thinking. "Not yet. But it will only be a matter of time."

We both fell silent and concentrated on drinking our designer coffee from hand-made mugs, our feet propped on the rungs of bar stools that had been crafted in Italy. Sunlight streamed in through the tall windows, bathing the terra cotta walls with a cheerful glow. It seemed like the weather should match our dark moods, but the bright morning was relentlessly cheerful.

"Of course, Loy had to go over to tell Wilma that her grandson was dead," Irene said. "He stopped by the café afterwards and had some dry toast. I think his stomach wasn't doing too well."

I felt my heart sink. I could only imagine Wilma sitting with Loy, hearing that her only grandson and caretaker had been murdered. "What will happen to her now? She can't drive."

"I think that must be the worst part of Loy's job, telling someone that they have lost family," Irene said.

She rubbed her eyes, her short blond hair tousled from a frantic morning. She'd left the café after the lunch rush had ended at Lil's and had driven over to sit with me for a while. She hadn't mentioned it, but I knew in the back of her mind Irene was here to make sure the shock of seeing Little Joe hadn't pitched me over the edge. I was doing the best I could, without saying it outright, to show her that I was fine. But I wasn't entirely certain I was fine.

"You must have talked to my dad." I was pretty sure he'd prompted Irene to swing by Leif's and check on me. That was my dad, always hovering over me while trying to look like he wasn't hovering.

Irene frowned. "No, your father has disappeared on me. I tried to call him over at the ranch house, but he didn't answer. I forgot the phone number out here at Leif's, and I knew he'd remember it. But I couldn't reach him. I haven't seen him all day."

That seemed strange to me. Usually when there was trouble of some kind my father was careful to be where he could be reached by phone. It was his way.

"Well, he will turn up," I said. "He is probably at the hardware store setting up a pre-emptive strike against the furnace at the caretaker's house. I think the thermo-coupler is going bad."

Irene sat back on her stool and took a long look around the kitchen. She let out a low whistle. "This place is even nicer on the inside."

I had to smile. "Can you believe that Leif trusts me enough to house sit? And he pays me for it?"

Irene shook her head. "Don't sound so surprised. You have a nasty habit of being too hard on yourself, and you need to quit it."

I clamped my mouth shut. She was right, but coming back to Killdeer eight months ago had not been easy on me. I'd been fired from my office manager job at the Montana Fish and Wildlife office up in Helena, and been forced to return home to rely on charity from my father. Since I'd left the small Helena branch office under a cloud of suspicion concerning a criminal investigation that had gone terribly wrong, I'd been filled with self-doubt and couldn't shake the thought that everyone in Killdeer was whispering behind my back. More than likely it was my own paranoia making me feel self-conscious. Small towns could be great places to live, but they could also be hard if you had a sketchy history. Still, I had to admit things had gotten better for me over the last few weeks. I was getting the impression from most folks around Killdeer that whatever mistakes they thought I'd made in Helena were partially atoned for now. Honestly, it had been a horrific experience, but I imagined getting shot had done wonders for my reputation.

Irene and I looked up when we heard a knock on the door.

"Do you suppose my dad has suddenly developed manners?" I asked. He never knocked when he came to see me. He usually didn't bother with that and simply walked in, no matter what house I was living in at the time.

Irene shook her head. "Not a chance. That's not your father."

I left Irene with her coffee, feeling a flutter in my stomach as I went to the huge oak door. I had a feeling I knew who was knocking. I quickly smoothed my strawberry-blond hair, certain it was a complete mess.

The doorknob turned in my palm, and I took a steadying breath. "Hi, Finn."

He stood on the porch, his back to me, surveying the area. He turned to look at me over his shoulder, then took off his signature mirrored sunglasses and gave me a grin that made me blush.

His accent sounded British, but it wasn't. Not even close. "Heya, doll."

Any other man who would dare to call me doll would have gotten a scathing glare in reply. But when Finn said it, I was ashamed to admit it made me feel like a teenage girl with a crush.

"I suppose you just happened to be in this neck of the woods," I said.

"No. I wasn't. I came to see you." His smile had faded and he watched me intently. His pale blond hair looked even lighter against the dark grey sky of winter.

"Do you want some coffee? Irene made a pot, and we…"

"I was just leaving," Irene said. She'd been standing behind me the entire time.

Finn gave her a nod and a smile. "Miss Baker."

Irene giggled and lowered her eyes. Normally she used her sharp tongue to torture her terrified waitresses into submission and drove them like she was a maniac college football coach, but whenever she spoke to Finn she turned into a vapid cheerleader. Finn seemed to have that effect on most women. I could only shake my head at her.

"You call me if you need anything, Honey," she said to me as she squeezed past. She waggled her eyebrows at Finn as she brushed by him.

Finn lacked the shame response, and one corner of his mouth turned up as she sauntered to her little pick-up truck. She drove away, offering me privacy, which was a shocker. Irene loved to be in the middle of things, and the fact that she was leaving without a fight was an unusual surprise. But since Finn and I had been spending more and more time together the past few weeks, I imagined in Irene's mind we were officially dating. In my mind, however, I was still not completely sure.

18

DRAWN TO THE MEAN

When it came to Finn I was never sure about anything. He wasn't an American by birth, having been born and raised in South Africa, and that accounted for some of his quirks. But not all of them.

I stood on the porch for a moment, grinning like an idiot, until I remembered my manners. "Why don't you come inside?"

He shook his head. "Can't. Training."

I noticed that he was armed today. Well, more armed than usual. He normally wore at least one concealed weapon wherever he went. But today he was wearing a shoulder holster with a pistol that was visible and a heavy gun belt holding a second pistol in a hip holster. His signature black pants and black shirt disguised the dark pistol under his arm, a little, but I could see it poking out from beneath his jacket. I wondered what else he was carrying today that I couldn't see.

"You know, I'm not that clear why a weather station needs a full time security agent," I said.

As usual, he pretended I hadn't even asked the question and ignored any comments I made about where he worked. He never talked about his job. Ever.

"I need a favor," he said, flashing his ice-blue eyes at me.

I tucked my hands inside my jeans pockets, feeling my left shoulder protest. My left collarbone was almost completely healed from the gunshot I'd suffered six weeks ago, but certain movements reminded me that I was still a couple weeks away from being back to normal.

"All you need to do is ask," I said. Finn had been the one who had prevented my broken collarbone from becoming a fatal wound. I owed him a great deal.

"There is a pre-wedding celebration in Fable, and I need a date," he said.

"A pre-wedding celebration? You mean, an engagement party?" I asked. Finn had grown up running with the surfing crowd outside of Johannesburg, South Africa. He was sometimes a bit off when it came to American expressions.

"Yes. A party. Would you like to be my date?"

"Sure," I said, feeling a sharp jolt of happiness. Apparently I had advanced in Finn's social circle to the rank of 'date.'

"Good. I will be here to pick you up at six."

"Tonight?" I said, my eyes wide. "That's pretty short notice."

He looked confused. "But, I'm giving you plenty of time to prepare. The party is not for another four hours."

I felt my usual mixture of excitement and exasperation. Although we had been spending time together, very sporadically, for almost two months, I still felt like I knew absolutely nothing about this man.

"It's fine," I said.

He relaxed and checked his watch. I noticed that it had two dials so that it could display two separate time zones.

"I have to go. I would wear something warm if I were you. I am told the party is in a barn."

"So…I probably shouldn't wear my little black cocktail dress," I said, smirking.

"Not unless you want to suffer frostbite," he said. He wasn't joking, and had missed my sarcasm.

A barn party? That was nothing unusual for Killdeer. But it was for December. This was going to be an interesting evening.

When Finn ended a conversation, usually he would simply walk away. He was abrupt to the point of rudeness, but I attributed it to his background and his work.

All I knew about Finn was that he was the chief of security at a new weather station that was located just outside of the tiny town of Fable. It was only a twenty-minute drive from my father's ranch, but when you arrived in Fable you knew right away you had just entered a very different world. The total population of Fable was only one hundred one. Sometimes the residents would change the population number on the green highway sign posted at the entrance of town if someone had a baby or moved away. They did it by adding or subtracting to the number on the highway sign with reflective silver duct tape. A retired couple from Florida had recently moved to Fable, following their dream of living in the woods in a log cabin. Currently the sign read, "103," with the number three stuck on haphazardly with duct tape.

Finn started to descend the stairs, then paused and turned back. He reached out, wrapped one hand around the back of my neck, and bent down to kiss me. I felt my knees wobble. Finn kissed like a predator. When I managed to open my eyes again he was already halfway down the stairs and heading to his Jeep.

He never waved goodbye when he drove away. Finn gave all of his attention to the activity he was doing at that exact moment. I'd never met anyone who was more attuned to his surroundings. I'd also never met a man who was as infuriatingly vague and distant. It was like being in a relationship with a spy.

Was it a relationship? That was a question I still hadn't answered for myself. Whatever it was that existed between Finn and me was tentative, at best. But until he gave me a good reason not to spend time with him, I had made up my mind I would endure the mystery for the benefit of his company. I felt a chill from the crisp afternoon air, and I went back inside. In spite of the morning's awful events, it was easy to smile after a visit from Finn. His presence was oddly comforting. That might have had something to do with the fact that I suspected he was something more than a run-of-the-mill security guard.

Leif's big house should have felt empty with only me rattling around inside the cavernous space. But it was so comfortable, despite its size, that I never felt overwhelmed by it. I busied myself tidying up the kitchen until it was time to get ready for the party. It took a surprisingly long time for me to decide what to wear. My thoughts were scattered and kept drifting back to the image of Little Joe. As much as I hated to admit it to myself, the prospect of having Finn's company for the evening was doing a great deal to sooth my tired nerves. Although my gut instinct was telling me not to get too attached to him, there are some things that simply cannot be helped.

At 6:01 Finn pulled into the driveway. The headlights from his Jeep illuminated the stairs, so I left the porch light off when I locked the house and pulled the front door closed behind me. The house had an alarm system, but I didn't understand how it worked, and so I never attempted to arm it. Since it really was in the middle of nowhere, the chances that someone would ever even manage to find the house, let alone break in, were remote as far as I was concerned.

I climbed into the Jeep, sizing up Finn's choice of clothing and comparing it to my own. He was dressed in black from head to toe, as usual. I'd decided to wear khaki slacks and a heavy, cream-colored wool sweater. Over that I wore a pale grey down jacket. I'd managed to get my stubbornly straight strawberry-blond hair to hold a bit of a curl, and even though my ears were already feeling the chill I refused to put on a hat and spoil it.

Finn didn't smile at me when I closed the door of the Jeep and buckled my seat belt.

"Joseph Flies Low," he said. He stared at me, his blue eyes glittering. "You did not tell me what had occurred when I was here this afternoon."

I could see instantly that he was angry.

"I didn't want to bother you with it," I said.

He slowly and deliberately cut the engine. We were enveloped in darkness.

"You didn't want to bother me," he said.

"I suppose I was trying to forget that it even happened. I didn't want to go over the details again. It was bad enough experiencing it, and the last thing I wanted to do was add another helping of trouble onto your plate."

"Someone disposed of a murder victim on your front porch, and you didn't want to bother me with it."

A whisper of moonlight glowed from a break in the cloudy sky, casting enough light to see his outline, if not his expression.

He stayed still, waiting for me to explain.

Finn's solemn relentlessness could induce a team of pack mules to surrender and cooperate. He sat beside me in complete silence, wearing me down.

"How did you find out about it?" I asked.

"There are 901 people in Killdeer, Marley. How long do ya think a homicide will stay a secret?"

"I wasn't trying to keep it a secret," I said.

He resumed waiting, silent and immobile.

I gave in at last. "Wendy called me this morning just before five. She found Little Joe on the deck when she went outside to plug in her car. I went over there with my father, but really, there wasn't a hell of a lot I could do."

"How long had he been there?" Finn asked.

"I have no idea."

"What *do* you know?" he asked.

"Why is this important? Can't we just go to the party and have a good time?" I asked. I wanted to let it go.

"I need to know possible threats to you," he said.

"Finn, I know you used to be a bodyguard, but I'm not your client."

"No. You are my girl. If there are reasons I should be tuned towards possible risks to your safety, I need to know what they are so I can reduce the likelihood of a dangerous encounter."

I hadn't heard a word he'd said after "*You are my girl.*"

I leaned forward in my seat. "What did you just say?"

"If there are possible threats…"

"No, no. The part about me being your girl?"

It was his turn to waffle. His hands fumbled in his lap for a moment as he tried to come up with a reply. He finally gave up and started the engine of the Jeep. "We are late."

He did a three-point turn and drove us away from Leif's house, suddenly seeming to develop an urge to fiddle with the CB radio. But we had danced around this issue for long enough. I wasn't going to let him off the hook this time.

"Finn, when you say that I am your girl, exactly what does that—"

"It means you tell me important things that happen to you. It means when something out of the ordinary occurs, you communicate it to me," he said.

Communication went both ways, and I was about to point that out but stopped. I didn't want this to become an argument.

"I'm sorry I didn't tell you," I said.

He glanced towards me and gave an apologetic shrug. "I know you still have not fully recovered from what happened this fall. It takes time to get your equilibrium back. Finding a victim of a homicide on your property must have been a shock."

I felt my palms start to sweat from the memory. I wiped them on my kakis.

"You could say that," I said.

He turned the Jeep around a tight corner, gunned the engine, and stared straight ahead. I could tell from his sudden silence this conversation was over.

We drove down the long dirt road that led past my father's ranch and my old cottage, now Wendy's cottage, and then we headed south. The entrance to the road leading to Fable wasn't clearly marked. Unless you knew where it was, on a dark night it would be easy to miss entirely. But Finn seemed to have an innate sense of direction, and he turned at the entrance without hesitation. If I didn't know better I would have sworn Finn was a local. He drove like he had lived in Killdeer his entire life, instead of having only appeared suddenly a year and a half ago.

We followed the twisting road leading up to Fable, the dark trees crowding the narrow dirt track like they were simply waiting for a chance to move in and take over once again. I was surprised to see three other cars ahead of us, their headlights glowing through gaps in the trees. Three cars in Fable could be considered gridlock.

"Watch for deer," I said, out of habit.

"Always."

It was a bit pointless to remind him to be alert.

He drove past a few houses, then slowed down, and began searching for the party.

Fable's houses didn't have any numbers. Occasionally a sign was posted at the end of a driveway that bore the name of the family who lived there. But more often than not, it was anyone's guess as to which address was where. The residents of Killdeer knew better than to randomly drive through Fable unless they knew exactly where they were going and who was inviting them to their home. If you took a wrong turn anywhere in the forested labyrinth of the little town, it wasn't unheard of for someone to greet you with a loaded shotgun and politely but firmly ask you to turn around. People in Fable liked their privacy.

The three cars ahead of us were all turning down the same unmarked driveway, and Finn followed them. A cheerful bundle of balloons, pink and white, dangled from a mailbox at the end of the driveway. The balloons were cold in the December air and had lost their lift. They swirled on the ground in the breeze, drawing circles in the powdered snow. Fable always had more snow than Killdeer. It was close to eight thousand feet, and tucked in a cut in the mountain like a hidden Tibetan village. Well, a hidden Tibetan village populated with trailers and rednecks.

We parked beside the three other cars in a makeshift parking area, forming an uneven row. Several other vehicles were already there, and as we climbed out of the Jeep we could hear music coming from the old barn tucked off the road in the trees.

Finn came around to my side of the Jeep and took my hand. It wasn't an overly affectionate gesture. He was making sure I didn't trip in the darkness.

Two other couples and a single man had gotten out of their cars and were walking together towards the barn. We followed them into the darkness, the dim light from the barn giving us just enough illumination to see the path. I noticed that Finn was carrying a small paper sack in his left hand.

Our little group bunched together, and we filed inside the barn through the tall swinging door. The only light came from a deep fire pit that had been dug in the center of the dirt floor. Most of the barns in Fable were so old and dilapidated, a fire inside one was trouble. Although this structure was ancient, and the boards making up the walls sagged with gaping holes, the chances we would burn the place down tonight were slim. I could see intermittent moonlight from the roof, and I knew the barn was more a suggestion of a building. There were plenty of ways for the smoke to escape, and the fire pit was deep and well tended.

A half-dozen or so guests mingled around the ring of the fire pit. An even mixture of men and women, most of the people in the group wore jeans, hiking boots, and work coats. Not a gathering of the upper crust of Fable. These were valley regulars, like me.

A keg of beer sat on the ground, flanked by two steel tables loaded with plastic cups, several bottles of wine, and what looked like an entire roast pig rested on a bed of cedar planks on a sawhorse table.

A white sheet cake, a few pieces missing, sat on the table behind the wine bottles. It was obviously the engagement cake. Two plastic figurines had been stuck into the frosting on top. A plastic groom, lying on his back, was being dragged away by a plastic bride. It was definitely an engagement party done Killdeer style.

"Finn, good to see you!"

I felt Finn let go of my hand as someone came towards us. He shook the hand of the man who had stepped over to greet us.

"Marley, this is Julian Hartmann. He owns the sporting goods store here in Fable," Finn said as he turned to the side to introduce me.

"Hi, Julian. I'm Marley…"

"Dearcorn," Julian said. "Sure. I know your father. I'm glad you could come."

Julian was an inch shorter than me, unusual because I have never been considered tall. Though he wasn't long in the leg, Julian probably weighed close to 190 pounds. Not an ounce of it looked like fat to me. He had to be close to fifty, but he looked like he could bulldog a Texas Longhorn. His broad face beamed with delight.

"So, when is the wedding?" I asked, shaking Julian's hand. He appeared to be very strong, but he gripped my hand gently.

Finn handed the paper sack he had been holding to Julian.

Julian pulled a bottle of Australian wine from inside, smiled, and set it beside the others on the table with care. He gave Finn a nod of thanks.

"Me and Patty are running off to Sedona to get married," Julian said proudly.

"Nice down there," Finn said with an impressed tone. "Expensive."

"Very," Julian agreed. "You have no idea how tough it is to scrape together the cash for this. But, it's what my Patty wants, so that's what I'm gonna do."

"Who will operate your sporting goods store while you are gone?" Finn asked.

Julian's expression darkened. "I haven't quite got that far yet. Probably I'll close down for a couple weeks. Hate to lose the income, but everybody needs a vacation, right?"

"Small ceremony?" Finn asked.

Julian nodded. "Just me and Patty and the medicine man. She wants to have a traditional Native ceremony. Eagle feathers and incense."

"You wearing a loin cloth, then?" Finn asked, a teasing grin spreading across his face.

"I would if Patty asked me to," he said, coloring slightly. "She said my blue suit would be fine."

"It sounds very nice," I told him. "Smart to have a small ceremony. But, you won't have any of your family or friends there, though?"

"It would be a hassle to fly everyone down and get hotels, pay for dinners, and such. So we thought we'd have a big party now. If I can get all this mess from work sorted out, we want to go down there at the end of the month. Get married on New Year's Eve."

Finn, who had helped himself to a piece of cake, spoke around a mouthful. "What trouble at work, Julian?"

The stout man chuckled and waved it off. "Oh, just kids, more than likely. Someone broke into my store early this morning. The alarm is tied to my telephone so I got there right after it went off, but whoever it was had already got away. They didn't take much. A sleeping bag and a Coleman cook stove. A few cans of chili, you know. Stuff kids would take."

It was suddenly impossible to keep my mouth shut and not ask any questions. It was like I had suddenly developed Tourette's syndrome and couldn't stop myself.

"They take anything else?" I asked. "Like maybe a few arrows?"

Julian thought about it, turning his head to the side. He regarded me with a puzzled look. "No, but I've got so many arrows in stock it would be hard for me to tell unless I took an inventory."

Finn gave me a stern look. He clearly wasn't in the mood to see me poking my nose into any unsolved crimes this evening.

I smiled. "Think I'll get some of that cake."

Julian slapped Finn on the shoulder. "You two have fun. We will be here all night. Some folks can't make it until the shift ends out at Big Bear. So enjoy!"

The Big Bear was a coal mine about an hour-and-a-half drive away from Killdeer. Some of the heartier residents of Killdeer worked shifts at the mine and commuted. Julian must have had a few friends who were among that group.

The other party-goers were milling around the fire, talking loudly and toasting Patty. Patty was a slender brunette who preferred camouflage vests and Wolverine work boots to skirts and pumps. I'd seen her around town but had never associated her with Julian's sporting goods store. She was petite and bright-eyed, and simply adorable. No wonder Julian was so smitten with her. The cluster of friends around Patty were all laughing at her, teasing and going on about shotgun weddings. She was enjoying the attention and took the ribbing gracefully. Two of Patty's younger girlfriends were busy unwrapping a small package with their backs to the rest of the group, giggling. They kept glancing at the fire pit, glancing at Patty, and their expressions were mischievous. Probably unwrapping a game of pin-the-tail-on-the-bachelor.

I took a piece of cake and nibbled it while I thought. What if the break-in at Julian's had something to do with what had happened to Little Joe?

"Stop it," Finn said, bumping me with his shoulder.

"What?" I asked.

"You know what. Thinking. I can see smoke coming out of your ears."

I shuffled my feet. "It just seems odd, that's all, that there would be a burglary the same night someone is killed. That's too much coincidence."

"Have you ever read the daily police blotter for Detroit?" he asked.

"This isn't a city," I said. "Killdeer doesn't have a quota on how many murders it can fit into a twelve month period."

"It's nothing to do with you," Finn said. He had stopped wolfing his cake and was eyeing me. "You had a brush with trouble, but it passed you by, so the best thing to do now would be to forget it."

I dipped my head a little, and then looked up at him with my best Bambi eyes. "All right. That's probably good advice. I'll let it go."

He shook his head, pressing his lips together. "Why don't I believe you?"

Suddenly a loud crack filled the barn, followed by another, and another. The barn erupted with explosions and I winced from the deafening sounds. Before I could move my hands to cover my ears, Finn grabbed my shoulders, pivoted both of us in a mad spin that put him between me and the noise, and drew his pistol. He shoved me to the ground and crouched in front of me, one hand pressed hard on the back of my head.

"Stay down!"

I pushed Finn's arm, trying to lift him off of me, but he had me pinned.

"Keep your head down, Marley."

From the corner of my eye I saw him sweep the barn intently, his pistol raised and ready. He focused on the fire pit, studied it, and just as abruptly as he'd shoved me to the ground, I felt him stand up and pull me to my feet. My head was spinning. What had just happened?

"Are you injured?"

"I think my pride has been dislocated," I said, glaring at him. "We're at a party, Finn. A *party*."

He hastily holstered his pistol, his eyes searching me up and down. "How is your shoulder?"

My face burned with embarrassment. "It's fine. Finn, what in the *hell* was that all about?"

He started dusting off the sleeves of my jacket. "Sorry. Firecrackers."

We both slowly looked around the circle of concerned faces watching us from the fire pit. Every single person in the barn was gaping at us, drinks stalled halfway between hand and mouth, wearing expressions of utter astonishment.

Finn paused, looking at the group with a clenched jaw. Then he wrapped one arm over my shoulder and gave the group a wry smile. "I can't wait to get her home."

A blush ran all the way from the top of my head to the tips of my toes. I wiped the last of the straw off my backside and felt a bit of relief when everyone in the barn started laughing at us. It was much better than having them stare.

"And you're the one who thinks I have a problem," I said.

Julian started clapping, and everyone else in the group followed suit until the entire wedding party was applauding Finn's overreaction. Someone shouted out that he wanted Finn to join his paintball team.

Finn gave my arm an apologetic squeeze, then bent to collect his plate of ruined cake. He tossed it in a barrel that was currently doubling as a garbage can, and when he looked back at me he frowned.

"You have frosting in your hair."

"But luckily that is my worst injury."

He grimaced at my joke. "Sometimes my training kicks in, and there's not a damn thing I can do about it."

"It's not the worst thing to ever happen to me on a date," I said, trying to ease his embarrassment.

I knew that Finn had been shot in the leg while working a job in South Africa a few years ago. Sometimes, when it was a very cold day, I noticed that he suffered a slight limp. But the other wounds he'd gotten that day had nothing to do with his own physical pain. Someone with him had been killed. A woman. Someone he never talked about. I was starting to think he had developed more than a professional relationship with the woman who had died on his watch, and maybe his overprotective reactions were a product of unfinished emotional business.

He already looked about as mortified as a man could look, so I decided the last thing he needed was to have me poking around in his past. He'd talk about it when he was ready.

We rejoined the rest of the revelers, Finn enduring a barrage of jokes throughout the rest of the evening with good-natured humor. When the time crept towards eleven p.m., the shift workers from Big Bear mine began to drift in, and Finn suggested we take the opportunity to say our farewells. We said our goodbyes, enduring suggestive catcalls from the other party-goers. They all seemed to think we were slinking home to finish what we had started on the floor of the barn.

We didn't disappoint them.

CHAPTER 3

In the morning I found myself alone in the big bed, tangled in the satin sheets. Finn had left sometime in the night, as he always did. I had never woken up to find him still in the bed with me. Not once. I mumbled to myself about what it would be like to have a normal boyfriend, then climbed out of bed to start a pot of coffee.

I padded down the stairs in my stocking feet and was about to push through the swinging door to the kitchen when a knock at the front door stopped me. I rubbed my sleepy eyes and changed course.

When I opened the big oak door, I wasn't surprised to see Loy Shucraft standing on the front porch. This was the other ritual I had come to expect—a visit from Loy every morning after Finn and I had spent the night together.

"Are you stalking me?" I asked.

Loy pushed the brown baseball cap back on his head and scratched his thinning hair. "Not today," he said. "Today, it's business."

"Joseph Flies Low," I said. That had to be why the sheriff was standing on my porch at six thirty in the morning.

"Well, not exactly," Loy said.

"You think the burglar from Julian's sporting goods is hiding in my basement?"

He stared at me. "How the hell do you know about that?"

"People talk," I said.

"Marley, can I come in?"

I stepped aside, and we went to the kitchen. He sat on one of the bar stools. "Nice place."

"Very. But in two weeks I am going to start looking for a real job. My shoulder is almost to the point I can start working, and Leif's generosity isn't going to last forever. I need to start drawing a real paycheck again."

I made coffee while we chatted. Loy watched me with a slight smile. I knew he kept tabs on me—and on Finn's visits. I should have been angry, but Loy was an old friend, and he always gave me a lot of leeway when it came to my habit of sticking my nose into his cases, and because of that I gave him a great deal more leeway than I normally would when it came to his unhealthy interest in my personal life. It would take some time, but eventually Loy would figure out our friendship was never going to be anything more than that.

"Have you seen your dad?" Loy asked.

I sat beside him at the tall bar. "No. Not since I left the caretaker's house yesterday morning."

He leaned his heavy arm on the black granite counter top. "If I was to look for your dad, say, because I needed to ask him something important, where would I start?"

I was paying very close attention to him now. "Why?"

Loy put his hand on the butt of his pistol. He was clearly uneasy. "I'm a bit worried about him."

I crossed my arms. "Loy, you had better start explaining."

The burly sheriff swallowed, then gathered his courage and looked me in the eye. "Dean Tisdale is missing."

I thought about this. "And Little Joe is dead, with an arrow sticking out of his chest."

Loy nodded. "And Dean is the only one around your end of the valley who *never* hunts with a gun."

"Dean always uses a bow," I said. That was a well-known fact.

Dean Tisdale was a resident of Fable, the same eccentric little village Finn and I had visited the night before. He had managed to become somewhat of a legend in Killdeer because of his odd behavior. Dean was an avid hunter, but he never carried a rifle or a pistol. Nobody knew why, exactly, but it was his way. He was such a skilled archer that he'd garnered a reputation as a marksman. He didn't own a television or a car, and he shunned the company of people. Well, that was the popular wisdom concerning Dean. That and rumors that he was a cannibal, a paid assassin, and a voodoo priest, all rolled up into one man.

"What's Dean got to do with my father?" I asked.

Loy shifted in his seat. "I went over to the ranch house yesterday to ask Nathan if he had seen Dean around. I know he lets Dean trap bobcats on your place during the season. I thought he might have seen Tisdale, but I couldn't find your dad anywhere."

I stood up, went to the cordless phone mounted on the wall beside the steel refrigerator, and dialed the ranch house.

I let it ring twice. "Hey, Dad," I said, after my father answered. I looked at Loy, my expression hard.

"Hey, Kiddo. What's up?" he said.

"Loy seems to think you disappeared."

My father paused. "No, I don't think I have. I'm right here."

"Uh huh. You seen Dean Tisdale lately?" I asked. I was not very happy about Loy coming over to worry me with his suspicions when he could have simply knocked on the door at the ranch.

"Tisdale? Can't say I have. Last time I saw him was middle of last week when he came by to let me know he wanted to hunt some cottontails in the alfalfa field, and to get my permission."

"You didn't see him yesterday," I said.

My father mumbled. "Well, no. Not yesterday. We were all a bit busy then."

"Thanks, Dad. I'll talk to you later."

I hung up the phone and sat beside Loy.

The sheriff shrugged. "What can I say? I looked everywhere for him yesterday, and I thought you might know where he was."

"You must not have looked in the right place," I said.

"When it comes to Tisdale I don't ever take any chances."

"Dean isn't that bad," I said.

"Marley, do you know how many times that guy has had run-ins with the law? The game wardens have been trying to bust him for years for poaching."

"Dean eats everything he kills," I said. "And he only traps enough to pay his bills. He's no criminal."

"Dean doesn't think he's a criminal. But you and I both know he skirts the line of the law pretty damn close," Loy said.

I looked at my hands. "I know. Poaching is poaching. If I saw him doing it, I would be obligated to turn him in. But, I've never seen him do it."

"Nobody ever sees him do it," Loy said. "The guy is a ghost."

"He's just different than other folks, is all."

"Well there's one thing we agree on," Loy said.

The coffeepot finished its burbling, and I stood up to get a cup. "You think he might have had something to do with Little Joe?"

"If you mean, do I think that Dean Tisdale killed Joseph, then yes. I do."

"Because he was killed with a bow?" I asked.

"Yes. And because Dean disappeared the day after it happened."

I sat down, two cups of coffee in my hands. I slid one over to Loy.

"I'm sorry I worried you about your dad," Loy said, taking the mug from me.

"You had good intentions," I said.

We sipped our coffee, letting our raw feelings smooth out before we spoke again.

"If you see Dean, I want you to call me right away," Loy told me.

"But what if he had nothing to do with it?" I asked.

"Hun, the shot was dead-on. The ME in Billings said that Joe's heart was cut in half. He was killed by someone who is really, really good with a bow."

"And Dean is the best shot in the valley. So you automatically assume it's him," I said. I didn't like it, but I had to admit the fact that Dean had disappeared the day after Joe's murder was not doing him any favors.

"Who else can you think of who is that precise?" he asked.

"Okay, why in the world would Dean kill Joseph Flies Low? Little Joe was the sweetest, most gentle kid in Killdeer. What could he have possibly done to make Dean want to hurt him?"

"He could have caught Dean poaching," Loy said without hesitation.

I felt my stomach clench. That same thought had occurred to me too. I just didn't want to acknowledge it.

"Loy, Dean saved my life. Remember? You really think he could kill a teenage kid? I can't see him as the type of man who would be that vicious."

"The way you couldn't see someone being that vicious last fall," he said.

I must have gone pale because Loy covered my hand with his big paw.

"I'm sorry," he said. "But you can't seem to see the evil in people. Sure, sure, Dean helped you out once when you were a little girl. But that was a long time ago. People can change. You always try to think the best of them. But it's my job to see the evil."

I was determined not to be a stubborn know-it-all this time. I let my eyes fall. "If I see him, I'll call you."

It was the right thing to do.

I walked him to the door and waved when he pulled away in his truck. He glanced back twice as he drove down the long driveway.

For my own reasons, it was safe to say I was incapable of seeing Dean Tisdale as a bad person. In my experience, he was the exact opposite.

As I watched Loy's sheriff truck disappear through the thick trees, a nagging question started to gnaw at me. What in the world had Joseph Flies Low been doing out on our road in the middle of the night? I couldn't believe that Dean would ever be surprised by someone in the woods. Dean was, as Loy had pointed out, a ghost. But there was no denying that Joseph's body ending up on Wendy's deck was damn strange. Why would someone take the trouble to move the body onto the deck at the caretaker's house if Joseph had been killed in another part of the county? I didn't think that they had. More than likely, Little Joe had been killed somewhere very close to the caretaker's house, and someone had dumped him there because it was handy.

That still left the question: why was Little Joe out there at night in the first place? Was he meeting someone? Was he doing something he shouldn't have been doing?

Shaking my head, I went back into the kitchen and told myself to forget about it. There wasn't a thing I could do, in any case.

Besides, the last time I'd poked around in things that weren't any of my business, the results had been disastrous.

I poured my last cup of coffee and finished my meager task of cleaning the counters in the kitchen. My shoulder was nearly healed, and even though I could have spent my time in Leif's house cleaning it from top to bottom, there was no need for me to do so. Leif had two housekeepers who came regularly.

I couldn't actively look for a new job until the final two weeks of my medically recommended inactivity came to an end. So, in effect, I was useless for another fourteen days.

I'd go crazy before then, never having been any good at sitting still.

I showered, made the bed, and flipped the switch that turned on the fireplace in the living room. All of the fireplaces in the house were gas. No ashes to dump, no wood to haul.

There wasn't a pile of dishes in the sink to wash. Leif had a silent dishwasher that did the task for me. I'd already finished what little laundry had accumulated. The windows were all washed. Apparently, Leif's housekeepers were quite thorough.

I couldn't even find any dog hair to sweep up. When Leif's soon-to-be ex-wife had fled, she had taken her Welsh corgi with her. The housekeepers had efficiently removed every speck of dog hair from the house. The place was practically sterilized.

I sat in front of the cozy fireplace, trying to enjoy the moment but feeling as jumpy as a spring foal. My mind kept churning over the things Loy had said about Dean. They couldn't be true. Not Dean. He was harmless. Well, in my mind, Dean was harmless. That wasn't necessarily the common consent around Killdeer, however.

I tried to amuse myself with a magazine, but I couldn't concentrate.

Dean Tisdale suddenly going missing the same day that Little

Joe had been killed and dumped on our land was a very disturbing coincidence. Throw in the burglary at Julian's sporting goods store, and the pieces were starting to fit together to form a pretty ugly picture. It got me thinking about what could really have happened that night. Was it possible that Dean had been on our land the same night Little Joe died?

It was possible, as much as I hated to admit it. I could think of one very good reason why he would be on our land. And that reason was probably still out there.

That settled it. I had to get up and do something.

I slipped out of my sheepskin slippers, pulled on my hiking boots, bundled up in my heavy coat, and pulled a hat over my tousled hair. Rummaging for my car keys, I went outside to my little black Honda. It started when I turned the key, but it wasn't happy about it. A cloud of white smoke blew out the back. That was new. Usually it was black smoke. I wondered how much longer I could count on the little car to keep running.

I drove down the dirt road until I reached the southern edge of my father's ranch, parked off to the side, cut the engine and climbed out.

The sky was winter blue, clear of clouds but still not as cheerful as it was in summer. I shut the door of my car, and the sound reverberated off the trees with an eerie echo. Lodge pole pine trees stood sentry on the south edge of our ranch. Beyond the pines the low hills rose abruptly to seven thousand feet and crested into the razorback slope of the mountain. Below the mountain our ranch meandered through the valley, a thousand acres of prime farmland dotted with aspens and duck ponds. It was a hunter's paradise. Mule deer grazed our pastures throughout the year, and it was not unusual to see the occasional moose pillaging one of the ponds. Each spring a pair of Sandhill cranes would take up residence to nest in the elbow of the alfalfa field. My father always left that six-acre patch of the field alone when it came time to cut the alfalfa, giving the cranes a safe place to raise their single chick in peace.

I looked to the west, letting my eyes adjust to the grey shadows of the chilly afternoon light.

There was my caretaker's cottage. Well, Wendy's caretaker's cottage now. I could see the deck from where I stood. I knew the ranch house lay hidden in the trees north of the cottage. The ranch house wasn't visible from the alfalfa field. But at night, if the front porch light was switched on, I knew from experience that the deck of the cottage could be seen even from the furthest edge of the field.

I scanned the tree line, mulling the situation over in my mind.

The only reason Dean would be out in our pasture in the middle of the night was if he had been laying a trap. There was only one thing in season to trap in the winter on our property.

Bobcats. If he had been here that night, that was probably what he had been doing.

I tried to imagine that I was Dean Tisdale and that I was out laying a bobcat trap. Where would I put it? By the pond? No. Too obvious. I kept searching.

There. I spotted a seldom-used deer trail that cut through the trees, halfway between the pond and the crane nesting area. If Dean were going to lay a trap, he would put it someplace that wasn't well traveled by humans. That was the spot I needed to look first.

I pushed away from my car and was starting to cross the road when I heard truck tires.

A brown sheriff's truck came around the tight bend in the road. But it wasn't Loy. Nick Wilcox was behind the wheel.

"Oh, no," I said.

He gunned his engine when he saw me, then pulled up beside my Honda on the road, and rolled down his window. He stared at me, waiting.

When I didn't say anything, he put his truck in park and killed the engine.

"What are you doin' out here, Dearcorn?" he asked.

"I just got out of church," I said.

He laughed. "And I just got a raise."

I kicked a few pebbles with my boot, debating what to say. The deputy was the last person I wanted to see. Nick and I had never gotten along, and admitting to him that I was out looking for evidence Dean Tisdale had been in the area recently seemed like a supremely bad idea. Not that I wanted to hide what I was doing, but I didn't exactly want to broadcast it either.

"I didn't see you over at Wendy's place yesterday morning," I said.

His jaw clenched. "I was in Billings. I'm taking a night course in forensic anthropology."

I searched his face. "I thought you already had your degree in criminal justice?"

"Can't a guy take steps to improve himself without everyone having issues with it?" he asked defensively.

Nick was qualified to teach a course in advanced whining.

"So, if your career in law enforcement goes south, you have a plan B," I said. It came out a bit more snarky than I had intended.

The deputy made a move to start his truck, but his eyes flashed at my comment, and instead of turning the key, he rolled up his window, climbed out and locked the doors.

He sauntered over to my side. "Why don't you show me what it is you are looking for out here?"

My heart sank. Damn, stupid sarcastic sense of humor seldom

got me anything but trouble. "What makes you think I am looking for something?"

Nick grunted. "When are you not poking into things that are none of your business? I got all the time in the world. Loy and I already searched the road, but if there's something out here you think you need to see, I'll just tag along."

Nick was not going to win any personality contests, but he had me dead-to-rights and there wasn't a thing I could do about it.

"Fine." I started walking.

We climbed through the barbwire fence, and I noticed with a great deal of personal satisfaction that I could snake between the wires a lot faster than he could. I'd had years of practice, after all.

We walked across the field ignoring each other. The fact that I was cooperating with Nick Wilcox automatically meant I got a gold star on my behavior report card for the week.

When we reached the tree line, I stopped and looked along the edge of the field until I saw what I was looking for. A ponderosa pine tree had managed to squeeze itself between the lodge pole pines, shouldering them aside with its greater bulk. It sat a short distance from the deer trail, its thick trunk looking like a thoroughbred mingling with a heard of yearling ponies.

"Just try to keep quiet," I said.

He looked around us. "Why? Who's out here to complain about the noise?"

"Can you just try to keep your voice down?" I asked. I knew the possibility that he could was remote.

I edged my way around the ponderosa, wishing the deputy hadn't decided to tag along.

"I don't see why—" he started to say.

We stepped around the tree and stopped. Nick shuffled to a halt, staring.

A bobcat, trapped inside a cage, stared back at him.

It was big, an adult, and probably weighed at least thirty pounds. Its grey spotted coat was thick, and the black-tipped ears swiveled backwards and forwards rapidly. When it saw us it crouched down, watching.

It growled.

Nick drew in a sharp breath. "Holy sh—"

"Will you shut up?" I said, glaring at the deputy.

He closed his mouth. Finally.

I kept still as I studied the cage.

A half a rabbit carcass was tied to a pressure plate inside the cage. The cage itself was wire mesh. It had a release mechanism on the top. The wire mesh looked like it was too small for the bobcat to get his claws through, but if I was going to be putting my hands there, I wanted to be sure.

I saw a branch on the ground, about the size of my arm, and I reached for it.

"What are you doing?" Nick asked. "Just let me shoot the thing."

"We don't need to do that, all right? Give me a second. Dean wouldn't want us to kill it, or just leave it here, so I'm going to turn it loose."

"Dean Tisdale?" Nick asked suddenly. "This is his trap?"

Oops.

Grimacing, I eased towards the cage, hoping that the trapdoor on the front end was secure. The bobcat snarled, its ears plastered flat with anger. It hissed as I stepped closer.

"Easy now," I said.

It growled a low warning.

I took another step closer. The cat lunged and hit the side of the cage with both paws. The cage jumped from the impact.

I swallowed. This wasn't as simple as I had thought it would be.

"Easy there," I said.

The bobcat lowered its head, watching my every move.

I lifted the branch and let it fall on the top of the cage. The bobcat turned and tried to claw it through the wire, but as I had hoped, the mesh was too small. The branch was about the same size as my arm, and the cat wasn't able to reach it. If I was careful, really careful, I could release the mechanism on the top of the cage and not lose a hand in the process.

I tossed the branch away and started to move in closer.

"Easy, fella. I'm on your side," I said in a soft voice.

The bobcat hissed.

I kept my legs well away from the sides of the cage, just in case, and I leaned over it awkwardly, trying to work the release mechanism and not lose my balance in the process.

The bobcat froze, some instinct or other telling it to stay still until it knew what was happening.

I pulled on the wire latch. It resisted. I tugged harder, and it sprang free with more force than I expected. I lost my balance and had to put a hand on top of the cage to keep from falling over.

The door to the cage fell open.

I scrambled back, ready to bolt for cover. The bobcat sat inside the cage and didn't move an inch. It's head swiveled back and forth rapidly.

Nick stood cringing two paces behind me. "What the hell? Why is it just sitting there?"

I watched it for a moment. Then I waved my arms.

"Go on, shoo!"

The deputy moved up beside me. "Shoo? You think that will work?"

I crossed my arms. "You have any better ideas?"

He pulled out his pistol. "Sure do."

"You don't have to shoot it!"

Nick waved me off. "I know. I'm just going to scare it."

"Why don't we walk away and let it leave on its own time?" I asked. But it was too late.

Nick cocked his pistol and aimed it at a random tree. I slapped my hands over my ears as he pulled the trigger. The shot cracked through the air.

The bobcat flinched, its eyes darting wildly. It backed up, frantic to escape and bolted from the cage—and started running straight for us.

Nick jumped aside, his skinny legs pumping like a stork on a bed of coals. "Oh god, oh god!"

I leapt away from Nick, and the cat raced between us. It was running blind from panic.

I lost my balance and fell to my knees as the bobcat scrambled past. It sprinted across the field, leaving us staring after it.

I looked at Nick, my expression sour. "That was a *great* idea."

"It worked, didn't it?"

"And we were almost a couple of pincushions," I said. I got to my feet, dusting off my knees.

The deputy holstered his pistol. "Stupid animal."

"Don't you have to fill out a bunch of paperwork if you discharge your weapon?" I asked.

"No. I'm technically not on the clock right now."

I wanted to get back in my car and warm up my feet, and get away from the pushy deputy. The bobcat had disappeared, so I started across the pasture, stomping my way over the hard-packed ground.

"You know that Loy is looking for Tisdale?" Nick asked, too casually.

"I know Loy thinks he might have had something to do with Little Joe's death, but that doesn't mean he did," I said.

"Right. He was out in your field hunting rabbits," Nick said facetiously.

"You don't have any idea who killed Little Joe, Nick. You don't even know where it actually happened."

"It's only a matter of time before we locate the place he died," the deputy told me, walking beside me and matching my pace.

My eyes were locked to the ground so that I wouldn't have to look at Nick. That was the only reason I saw it in time to stop.

I halted mid-step and put up my hand. My palm hit the deputy's chest.

"What?"

"I think I can help you with that," I said.

The deputy looked at the ground where I was staring.

A pool of dried blood was at our feet. It was dark brown, frozen, and had seeped into the powdery soil like spilled paint. There was far too much blood for it to have come from a rabbit.

Nick grabbed my arm. "Jesus! Step back, Marley."

The deputy pulled us away. Then he glanced behind us and swore. "We are contaminating the hell out of this crime scene."

I stopped where I was and looked carefully at the ground. "I don't see any tracks. The ground is too dry, and it's frozen. There hasn't been any snow, and the chances of finding a track are next to nothing."

The deputy studied the ground, squatting on his heels so he could peer at the dirt. Remnants of alfalfa plants jutted out from the hard-packed soil.

"I hate to agree with you," he said. "But I think you might be right."

Nick stood up, and we both stared at the blood pool. It only spanned a couple of feet across, but it was obvious that Little Joe had died here. We could see the outline where the blood had seeped underneath the body. It was human shaped. One shoulder and the torso were clearly outlined in dried red.

The deputy turned to look back at the bobcat trap. It was less than a hundred feet from where we stood. He rotated slowly until he was facing the opposite direction, and he stared at the caretaker's house that was a straight walk from where we stood. A strong man, a healthy man, would be able to carry someone as small as Little Joe from here over to the deck of the caretaker's cottage.

Dean Tisdale was remarkably strong.

I felt my heart tighten up with regret. I knew exactly what the deputy was thinking.

He fixed me with a hard look. "You still think Tisdale had nothing to do with killing Little Joe?"

A streak of black and white darted through the trees in the distance, catching my eye. A pair of magpies flew down from the branches of the ponderosa to investigate the remains of the rabbit carcass inside the bobcat cage. The pair of them disappeared behind the ponderosa, and I could hear them squabbling over the scraps.

I had to turn away, feeling sick.

I didn't want to believe that Dean could have been responsible. In all the years I had known him, I had never taken him for anything but a kind, if eccentric, man.

But as Loy had told me only this morning, I had been wrong about people before.

CHAPTER 4

Lil's was packed.

It was a busy, late-afternoon lunch crowd, and Irene stood behind her café counter with both fists propped on her bony hips like a ranch foreman on branding day, directing traffic and haranguing her waitresses.

And her waiter.

Stephen, the only man brave enough to apply for a job at Lil's working the floor, breezed past the counter loaded down with an armload of pancakes and French toast, and hurried to a table filled with a group of women from the bank. He placed the plates before them with a flourish, greeted by giggles from the ladies.

"Shameless hussies," Irene said. She took a long drink from a cup of coffee so black it looked like she was drinking motor oil.

The bank ladies cooed over Stephen, and he played to them like he was on the world's biggest stage. They couldn't seem to take their eyes off him.

"So, Stephen is working out?" I asked. I was sitting in my usual center stool at the counter.

I watched the young man, who had just turned twenty, tease and banter with the women. He looked very much like a young

Nick Nolte. His blond hair was swept back; his blue eyes sparkled. His biceps rippled.

"He's making a killing off me," Irene said. But she said it with grudging respect.

"There does seem to be a large female crowd here today," I said, looking at the booths and tables.

The waitresses shot Stephen nasty looks. Irene had told me Stephen had been cutting into their tips since his arrival.

"I'm making a killing off of him, too. It's one of those parasitic, symbiotic relationships that occur in nature sometimes," Irene said, setting her empty coffee cup on the counter.

"Like dairy cows and blackbirds," I said. I slid my empty plate away. Irene's cook was trying something new with chipotle sauce and pulled pork sandwiches. I had given it a thumbs-up.

"So, am I the cow or the blackbird?" she asked.

"Oh, the cow. Definitely the cow," I said.

She chuckled. "Cows are worth more."

The events from earlier that morning hovered on the tip of my tongue, but instead of spilling the news that Joseph had definitely been killed on my father's ranch, I decided that there were some things that could be kept secret for a little while longer. It would eventually come out anyway, so I made up my mind not to mention it to Irene just yet.

The doorbell chimed and the Chan twins came into the café. They were not their usual cheerful selves.

They took a seat by the window at a table with four chairs, sitting as far away as they could from the other customers. The high school final bell must have rung for the day, and the two of them had moped into the café burdened by book bags and looking cold in their letter jackets. They both looked miserable and unhappy.

"Poor kids. I think they knew Little Joe," Irene said.

"They went to school together," I told her.

The Chan twins were a little bit older than Joseph, but Killdeer's school was so small the kids often made friends with someone outside of their grade. I had seen Meg talking to Joe from time to time at the high school basketball games.

"It's got to be a shock for them having a classmate die like that," Irene said. She shook her head in sympathy.

Matthew was saying something harsh. Meg, her straight black hair and dark eyes looking stark against her pale skin, was nodding and trying not to cry. She looked miserable. Matthew looked intent.

They were twins, but fraternal and not identical. Matthew was slightly taller than Meg, though his short hair was as straight and his eyes were as dark as his sister's. Where Meg was dainty and willowy, Matthew was lean and hard with muscle. He was on the Killdeer wrestling team. With only four members on the team, it was not difficult for Matthew to distinguish himself.

"What do you suppose has got Matthew so worked up?" Irene asked.

I was embarrassed to realize that both of us were staring at the twins.

"He probably got a B- on a test at school," I said.

"I can't believe he hasn't thrown himself on his sword," she said.

I should have scolded her, but it was common knowledge that Matthew was going places. He never let a day go by without mentioning to someone that he was getting out of Killdeer and would make a name for himself in the world. He was the brightest kid at Killdeer High, and he made sure that everyone around him knew it.

"The world needs rocket scientists too," I said.

"You've got that right," Irene told me. "We've got plenty of ditch diggers."

Irene paused and shifted her gaze to me.

I could feel her staring at me, but I ignored her, hoping she wouldn't ask me what she was so clearly about to ask me.

"So, how's it going with Finn?"

"You just can't leave it alone, can you?" I said.

"You too have been dating for two months..."

"Six weeks," I said. "More or less."

"And I would have thought you'd have a pretty good idea where things are headed by now."

I stared at my empty plate. Irene snatched it away, so I would be forced to look at her instead.

"Who knows? He is the most frustrating, distant man I have ever met. I can't tell from one day to the next how he feels."

"Of course you can," she said.

"Irene, I don't even know his full name."

She laughed. "So? Maybe he doesn't like his first name. Lots of people use their middle names because they don't like their first names."

"But you would think he would have at least told me what it is by now," I said.

"Look," she said, refilling my iced tea, "he really likes you. If he didn't, he wouldn't spend so much time trying to be evasive. He's had a rough past, from what you said, and it can't be easy for him to be vulnerable."

I pasted a sarcastic expression on my face. "Thank you, Doctor Baker."

"Talk to him, Marley. He gets shot at for a living. I think he can handle a grown-up conversation about how he feels."

I had my doubts, but I didn't say anything. For some men, getting shot at was easier than and preferable to having an adult conversation with a woman about feelings.

Stephen skipped by, juggling an armload of omelets, on the way to a table loaded up with four gals who worked at the Big R hardware store.

It must have been breakfast day at Lil's.

Irene noticed me watching.

"I wanted to see how well the kid could sell, so I told him to push breakfast items for lunch. He's doing great."

Irene turned her attention to a waitress who was chatting up a couple of coal bed methane workers a little too much.

While Irene was distracted with shooting a blistering glare at her chatty waitress, I noticed Meg Chan get to her feet and go to the women's restroom, practically in tears. It was rude and pushy, but I stood up and followed her. Kids sometimes knew things about classmates that adults were not privy to. Maybe Meg knew what Little Joe had been doing out in the middle of our pasture the night he died?

When I went inside the restroom I could hear Meg in one of the stalls. For one horrible moment I thought she was being sick, but then I realized she was sobbing uncontrollably.

I knocked on the stall door, and then pushed it open slowly.

Meg was sitting on the stool with the lid down. A wad of toilet paper was smashed to her face, and she cried like it was the end of the world. At seventeen, a great many things could seem like the end of the world.

"Meg, are you all right?" I asked, feeling stupid for saying it. She was anything but all right.

She looked up, startled. She hadn't heard me knock.

She tried to pull herself together, but the sobs kept coming. I squeezed inside the stall with her and unrolled a long loop of paper from the dispenser. I knelt down and handed her a fresh wad of toilet paper. She had soaked the first one.

"Does this have something to do with Joseph?" I asked.

She really looked at me then. Her eyes were bloodshot. She accepted the fresh paper and wiped her face. "I just can't believe it."

Her voice sounded so small. Her hands were dainty, like a porcelain doll. I didn't have the heart to start prodding her with questions. She was obviously devastated.

"Were you and Joseph close?" I asked carefully.

Her eyes welled with a river of new tears. "He was my best friend."

Her best friend? That was a surprise. The high school kids tended to clump into groups, and I knew Meg was friends with Joe, but I hadn't realized they were so close.

"Meg, do you have anyone you can talk to? Maybe your parents?" I asked.

Her face froze. "Oh, god no. I can't tell my parents."

"Is there anyone else then?" I asked.

She thought for a moment, and then she nodded. "The school counselor has been okay."

"Meg, I'm so sorry. I didn't know that you were his best friend," I said.

"It's all my fault," she blurted out. Her lips and her hands trembled. "He never should have been out there. The other kids never liked Joe, and he just shouldn't have been out there."

"Meg, what do you mean, it's your fault?" I asked, stunned. "Did you know that Joseph was in our pasture Tuesday night?"

She looked up at me, stricken. "I was supposed to—"

Someone knocked on the door of the restroom.

"Meg?"

It was her brother, Matthew.

A panicked look crossed her face.

"I've gotta go," she said.

I didn't want to make any trouble for her. Reluctantly, I stood up and moved aside so she could dash to the sink and wash her face. She had already forgotten all about me as she darted out the bathroom door and back to her brother's side. The Chan twins had always gone everywhere together, and today was no exception.

I washed my hands, only to give myself time to think.

Teenage girls sometimes blew things out of proportion. That was wisdom I had gained from personal experience. Thinking that Joe's death had been her fault somehow was probably a huge over-reaction on her part. But, she had said that he wasn't supposed to be there. Wasn't supposed to be where? It was not making that much sense to me.

More than likely, I would never know what she had meant.

As I left the restroom I saw Meg sitting quietly at the table with Matthew, her sobs contained. I walked past them, hoping to catch a word or two of their conversation, but they weren't talking.

As I passed the twins and headed back to my seat, I walked by the table with the two coal bed methane workers, not meaning to eavesdrop, but catching their conversation accidentally.

A scruffy blond with thick glasses was leaning in towards his bearded, well-manicured companion. They were both talking fast. It sounded like an argument.

"I'm telling you, there are only two variations of tessellation. There are regular, and there are semi-regular versions," said the scruffy blond. His hair stuck out at odd angles, making him look like a washed-out rock star.

The man with the neatly trimmed beard shook his head. "What? You're crazy. There are four, Seth."

The scruffy blond, Seth, erupted. "Four? There are the congruent regular polygons, and there are self-replicating sets of polygons, *Will*."

"And what about the self-dual tessellations? Did you think about those?" asked Will.

There was a pause.

Seth, the lanky blond, waved his arms. "Of course I thought of those! They are irregular, tessellations. Dork."

I took my seat at the bar, transfixed by the conversation.

I gave the two men a good long look.

They wore the usual garb of field workers and roustabouts everywhere. Stained shirts, jeans, heavy boots. Usually a field worker's boots were caked with mud. But these two looked like they had just taken their boots out of the box. They looked brand new.

Seth, the blond, was lean like a marathon runner but lacked an ounce of muscle. The other, Will, was clean cut with a trim beard and sharp, green eyes. Seth wore his clothes comfortably. But the other man looked like he was in costume. His hands were perfect. Not a scar or a scratch that I could see. Neither one of them looked like they had seen the sun for six months. They were both pale as a sliced potato.

These men were *not* coal bed methane workers.

They continued the argument, laying a meager tip on the table and rising to leave.

I gave Irene a nod, stood up tossed a fat tip on the counter. I headed for the door, and Irene jerked her chin at me with a smile. It was her way of saying, "See you later."

I followed the two men out to the parking lot, and as they headed for the battered field truck, they noticed I was behind them. They made a feeble attempt to beat me to the truck and escape, but I was hot on their heels.

Seth climbed into the driver's seat quickly and shut the door.

His companion followed suit, and they were rummaging for the truck keys when I knocked on the driver's side window. I smiled.

Seth stared at me, not looking like he knew what to do next. His eyes were wide with surprise, and he blinked at me like a stunned owl.

Finally he rolled down his window.

"You work with Finn, don't you," I said. "Up at the weather station?"

They looked at each other. Then back at me, silent and uncomfortable.

"It's all right," I said. "I'm his girlfriend."

"No way," Seth said.

I smiled again. "I was hoping you might be able to tell me something about him."

They looked at each other again. They looked back at me. It was like watching two people watching a tennis match.

"Everyone here calls it Area 49," I told them, trying to loosen them up.

"We know," Seth said with a groan. "Because it doesn't rise to the level of Area 51."

Will growled a warning. "Shut up. What are you doing?"

"So, will you help me out?" I asked, trying to draw their attention back to me.

"Only if you tell us something about him," said Seth, his eyes suspicious.

Will slugged his slim companion on the shoulder. "What are you doing, man?"

"We're in the middle of nowhere. Like anybody here cares?" said Seth.

I leaned my arm on the window of the truck. "I know it's not really a weather station," I said.

Will, sitting in the passenger seat and looking uncomfortable, grumbled something about lousy cover stories, but he was starting to thaw.

I held up a hand. "Don't worry. I don't need to know what you really do up there all day. I was only hoping you could tell me something."

Seth shrugged. "Sure. Whatever. What do you want to know?"

I took a breath and plunged in before I lost my nerve. "What is Finn's real first name?"

They both gaped at me.

"You are kidding, right?" Will asked.

I shook my head. "I'm not."

Will laughed outright. Seth leaned forward in the seat. "Ignore him," he said.

I watched them, my most earnest and pitiful expression painted on my face.

"Do either of you know what it is?" I asked.

Seth shook his head. "We don't know a thing about him."

"I told you he was the guy we saw in strobe alley back in '09," Will said.

I must have looked confused. Will stared at me like it was impossible I had never heard of the place. "You know, strobe alley? At MIT? Never mind."

Seth shook it off, looking at Will with irritation. "You don't know it was him."

"I *saw* him, man."

They were very close to another argument. I knew it could go on for hours like this.

"What was it you wanted me to tell you?" I asked, breaking up the fight before it could begin.

They turned their attention deficit back to me.

Will leaned forward so he could see me around Seth. "We want to know if it's true that he was bitten by a great white shark."

"Totally. I mean, does he have any scars?" Seth asked.

I felt my eyebrows pop. "A great white shark?" I said.

They nodded.

"Yeah. Does he have like a huge bite mark someplace?" Will asked.

I thought it over. Finn did have a lot of scars, but I didn't recall anything resembling a bite mark. "Well. Not that I've seen."

They looked crushed.

"Come on," Will said. "It's got to be a lie. Who lives through that? I mean, what's the probability that someone can survive that and not lose at least one appendage?"

Seth waved his hands. "If you calculate the percentage of shark attacks and divide the number of fatalities—"

"Let it go Seth," Will said. It flowed off his tongue so easily it was pretty clear he said it often.

I turned my head to the side, thoughtful. "I can find out if it's true. And I'll get back to you. If you find out his name for me."

They watched me, considering.

"Deal," Seth said.

Will slugged him on the arm. "Dude! We don't even know her."

"You really are in the middle of nowhere," I said. "Who am I going to tell?"

They both nodded, mumbling about me having a good point.

"I come here all the time," I said, nodding towards the café.

"Next time we see you, we'll have your information," Seth told me.

He started the truck, and they lurched out of the parking lot in a display of bad driving skills that rivaled Irene's. I could tell by watching Seth as he struggled with the truck that a stick shift had not been his first language.

I watched them go, conscious of the strangeness of the situation.

I still didn't have Finn's phone number. He was always the one who called me. I remembered thinking it was odd that the first night I had gone to stay at Leif's house, Finn had called to see how I was doing. I hadn't remembered giving him the phone number out there, and Leif had told me it was unlisted.

This was a fun game for the moment, but I had a sad feeling when I thought about a future with Finn. It was very likely that I would never really know who he was. I got butterflies in my stomach every time I saw him, but I wasn't entirely certain I could be happy with a man who couldn't be bothered to tell me his first name.

CHAPTER 5

Thursday morning I ventured into the kitchen, noticing that the coffee was made, the lights were turned on low, and I could hear soft, acoustic guitar music coming from the office downstairs.

When I heard the door swing open behind me, I was a little surprised to see Leif Gable standing there.

He gave me a warm smile. "I'm sorry if I startled you, Marley. I tried to call to let you know I was back in town but you must have been out."

I was more surprised by the fact that he was so quiet I hadn't heard him come in at all. I'd slept right through it.

"I got in a little after midnight, and I didn't want to wake you so I tried to keep the noise down," he told me, taking a sip of coffee.

It was barely six and already Leif was up, had been for a while, and was hard at work. I tried not to let my curiosity get the better of me. What did he actually *do* for a living? I had no idea. Something in business, but he never spoke of it, and no one in Killdeer ever gossiped about Leif. Not because they weren't intrigued by him, but simply because they didn't have anything to gossip about. Leif spent absolutely no time talking about himself.

I returned his smile, my surprise at seeing him wearing off. I tried to remember if I had left any dirty clothes lying around the house anywhere. "It's no problem, Leif. It's good to see you again. How was your trip back?"

He gave a thin smile. "The usual. Too much to do, and not enough time to do it."

I poured a cup of coffee, spot cleaned the kitchen, and tied my hair up in a high ponytail.

"It's good to be back," he said, taking a seat on one of the tall barstools and letting out a relieved sigh. "But I understand that Killdeer has seen more than its fair share of trouble recently."

"It has," I said, sitting down beside him.

"I heard about what happened to Joseph. Terrible thing."

"Yes. Everyone thinks that it was Dean Tisdale."

Leif studied me. "What do you mean when you say *everyone*?"

"Sheriff Shucraft and Deputy Wilcox seem to be pretty convinced of it."

"And you don't share that view," he said. He took a long, thoughtful drink of coffee and set his cup aside.

"No. Dean isn't like that. He is…not like other people. But he isn't a killer."

"I imagine it will all get sorted out in time," Leif said. "Listen, Marley. I've taken the bedroom downstairs, and I want you to keep the master bedroom."

I started to protest, but he cut me off.

"No, you keep it. I don't mind. It's closer to my office downstairs anyway. I want you to feel comfortable staying here as long as you need to. I know you have at least a few more weeks before you can work again, and I think it would be easier on you if you stay in one place until you are ready."

Leif had a gently persuasive way about him. He also had a way of making a person feel at ease while at the same time managing to get them to acquiesce to his wishes. He seemed like the type of man who could inspire a person to want to follow him up a hill, charging into certain death with bayonets fixed. I'd seen him wheedle a $10,000 donation out of a wealthy tightwad at a barbeque fundraiser when our tiny local museum was on the verge of closing. The museum was still open now, thanks to that donation.

He smiled his blue-eyed smile, and I caved in. "Sure, I'll stay. But I will be able to work again in two weeks. As soon as I find a job I will be out of your hair."

We both laughed at my comment. Leif was totally bald. I always thought it made him look distinguished, very much like the actor Yul Brynner, but with an easy disposition and a degree in accounting.

We sipped our brew and talked about Washington D.C. in the wintertime. I was careful not to bring up Virginia and his recent divorce. I knew the divorce must be final now that Leif was back in Killdeer. For someone who had just suffered a separation, Leif was remarkably chipper.

He noticed me tiptoeing around the subject, and he chuckled.

"I'm fine, Marley. Virginia and I haven't been in love for months. Possibly years. She loved who I was back when I lived in D.C., and I suppose I was guilty of feeling responsible for her."

"But you always seemed so dedicated to her," I said.

He sighed. "I was. Completely dedicated. When I make a decision, I follow it through, and I had decided to be a good husband to her. I knew about her affair. That wasn't what forced my hand. It was the drugs. When I found out Virginia hated it here in Killdeer so much that she was taking pain killers just to get through the day, I knew I had to let her go back to Washington. She never was cut out to live in the wilderness."

I recalled that Virginia had developed a dependence on pain

pills right before she and Leif had split up. If she was that unhappy, I could understand why he had finally ended the marriage.

"Some women love Killdeer, some hate it," I said, trying to be sympathetic without sounding sappy.

"She had some very fine qualities. Virginia donated vast sums to her animal welfare charities, and she always found time to volunteer at the animal shelter over in Parkman. She had a good side that other people rarely got to see," Leif told me, a bit wistfully.

"I didn't know she volunteered at the animal shelter," I said, truly surprised. That didn't sound at all like the Virginia that I had known. But when it came to people, it was a safe statement that you always knew less about them than you imagined. Our conversation shifted away from divorce, and we chatted for close to two hours about goings on around Killdeer. When we'd exhausted every topic, Leif stood up and explained that he would be in his downstairs office for most of the time, but that if I ever needed anything, to feel comfortable knocking on his office door and asking.

Before he descended the stairs that led to the door that was always locked, he turned and gave me a serious look.

"Marley, I mean it when I say that you are more than welcome to stay here as long as you like. Honestly, it is good to have your company. It always has been."

With that he disappeared inside his office and quietly shut the door behind him.

His remark made me feel more at ease. Maybe I wouldn't need to rush out and find a new place to live after all.

I spent the morning gazing out the picture window that faced the driveway and the road that led back towards town. I wished that Finn's black Jeep would roll around the corner, but it didn't. Finn kept his own, bizarre schedule. I never knew when he would appear, but it always seemed to be when I wasn't expecting it.

By late morning I couldn't take it any longer, and I shrugged off my sweatpants and pulled on a pair of jeans. I had to get out and do something before I ended up lying around the house all day watching the History channel.

There wasn't much of a chance that I would be able to talk to Meg Chan any time soon. She was distraught and the last thing I wanted to do was upset her even more. But her admission that she had been Little Joe's best friend was a true surprise. If it really was the case, maybe Joseph's grandmother, Wilma, would have some insight into what had really happened the night her grandson died?

Talking to Wilma about that night was not something I wanted to do, but I didn't see any other way of finding out what had really happened in our pasture Tuesday night.

As I drove into Killdeer I veered off Main Street and drove down Buckthorn Lane, out towards the trailer court we called the Burbs.

Wilma Flies Low was all alone in the world now, as far as I knew, and in addition to finding out if she knew about Joe's friendship with Meg Chan, I could also take the opportunity to see if there was anything she needed.

I turned off Buckthorn Lane and into the trailer park where she lived, struggling to remember which trailer belonged to her, when I saw the wooden roadrunner screwed to the top of a mailbox that marked the driveway to her place.

I parked and got out of the car, not paying attention to the black Dodge Charger parked on the street. I walked down the long sidewalk, climbed the three steps up, and knocked.

The door flew open.

"What do you want?"

I blinked and took a step back. I had expected Wilma to answer the door, but the man staring at me was hardly an eighty-something widow.

I stammered. "Ah, I wanted to check on Wilma and see if she needed anything?"

The man glared. He was perhaps forty-five, lean and fierce and definitely a Crow Indian man. He shared Joseph's same narrow features and dark eyes. Or, more correctly, Joseph had this man's features.

I tried to smile. "Are you Joseph's father?"

"Wilma is fine. You don't need to be here."

He radiated open distain. Maybe this had been a bad idea. A cloud of burning sage smoke wafted through the door. It wasn't unusual for people in Killdeer to burn sage bundles. The tribes in Montana had been doing it for centuries, and it was not uncommon to this day. But the smoke inside Wilma's house was so thick it turned the air grey.

A voice came from inside the house. "Who's that? Who's there, Martin?"

Wilma shuffled into view at her son's elbow. She squinted at me, leaning against the door frame. She wore a turquoise colored skirt and a loose black shirt. I noticed she wore sheepskin slippers around the house. Her silver-black hair was coiled in a tight bun. It wasn't easy for her to walk. Wilma had suffered from arthritis for as long as I had known her.

"Some woman," Martin tried to shut the door, but Wilma held up her hand.

She peered at me, her milky eyes doing what they could to identify who was standing in the doorway.

"Dearcorn? Nathan's daughter?"

"Yes, ma'am. I'm Marley. I came by to see if there was anything you needed."

"Huh," she said, surprised.

Martin crossed his arms, clearly angry that his mother was preventing him from sending me on my way. He wore a pair of pristine beige cowboy boots, buffed to a glossy sheen. His black jeans were spotless and his white dress shirt was pressed. His hair looked exactly like his mother's, minus the streaks of silver. He wore it long and loose.

Wilma wasn't about to invite me in, but she did shuffle closer to the door. "Lady came by from the church, too. Brought me a tuna casserole."

"That would be Mrs. Gunderson," I said. She was the town's official ambassador of public relations, as Irene liked to call her. Mrs. Gunderson was retired and suffered from the predicament of having too much energy to be retired. She was a member of the local Episcopal Church and made it her personal responsibility to take care of the entire town of Killdeer.

"You the one who found my Joseph?" Wilma asked suddenly.

I lowered my head. "No, ma'am. My father's tenant did."

Wilma's eyes were already so cloudy and watery I couldn't tell if she was crying or not. But I assumed she had been. It was common knowledge that Wilma had suffered from glaucoma for years. It made the loss of her grandson all the more difficult, I thought, knowing that the one person she had relied on for help was gone forever.

"He was a good boy," she said softly.

"Everyone liked Joe, very much," I told her.

Martin Flies Low—I assumed his last name was the same—watched me with open hostility. He was allowing me to stand on his mother's porch simply for her benefit. Certainly not for mine.

"What I want to know is what Joe was doing in your pasture?" Martin asked, pointing at me.

"You must have talked to Loy," I replied, trying to keep my

tone neutral. I was having a difficult time with Martin, but his son had just died so he was well within his rights to be angry.

"He came by to tell us his deputy found the place Joe was murdered," he said. "On your land."

Wilma waved a hand at her son, angry and disgusted. "Go get me soda."

Clearly not accustomed to taking orders, Martin was just stunned enough to obey. He spared me one final glare and vanished inside.

Wilma held onto the door frame, steadying herself.

She was looking past me when she spoke, her eyes staring in the distance at something I couldn't see. A memory.

"Joe loved the stars," she said.

"Stars, like, astronomy?" I asked. I didn't think Joe was the type to follow Hollywood buzz.

Wilma murmured, nodding. "He wanted to go to that school in Bozeman and study the stars. Joseph liked math. He loved school. His room is full of books with pictures of the solar system and things he says are galaxies." She seemed mystified by that, but maybe proud, too.

I knew I wouldn't have another chance to talk to her like this, not if Martin was going to be a presence in her life from now on, so I felt like I couldn't waste any time in being careful.

"Wilma, was Joseph friends with Meg Chan? Did they spend time together outside of school?"

She looked at me quickly, and then looked away, back over my shoulder. "That Chan girl."

She looked regretful and angry.

"Was Meg meeting Joseph Tuesday night? Did they have any plans to go someplace together? Maybe out with some other kids?" I asked, recalling what Meg had said in the bathroom at the café.

She had said it was her fault Joe had been there, that he shouldn't have gone because the other kids never had liked him very much.

Wilma's face flickered with shock. She shook her head so hard her coral earrings swung back and forth. She looked at the ground when she answered.

"No, he didn't like to go to any parties. Joseph liked to be by himself."

I put my hands inside my coat pockets. A gust of wind teased my hair, chilling me. I had no real business asking her any questions, but I felt like my father and I had a right to know what violence had occurred, literally, in our own backyard.

"Joseph didn't have his own car, did he?" I asked.

She sighed, and I could see the cold air was starting to take its toll. "We never owned a car," she said. "My neighbor takes us to the grocery store on Saturdays. Joseph wanted to buy one, but it's too expensive."

Walking all the way from the trailer court out to our pasture in the winter seemed unlikely to me, even for a teenage boy. Someone had to have come to the trailer park and given Little Joe a ride, but Wilma would not be able to tell me who it was. She obviously wouldn't have been able to see the car because of her bad eyesight. Whoever it was, they were probably the last person to see him alive.

"Did your grandson have a friend who owned a car?" I asked.

She looked disgusted. "He sometimes went to school with that Chan girl. Sometimes to the movies with her."

Maybe Meg had given him a ride to the pasture that night. It could explain why she blamed herself for his death.

"You didn't talk to Meg that night, did you?"

"I never talked to her," Wilma muttered. "She took Joseph to get my eye medicine sometimes, but she never came inside to even say hello to me."

Her body slumped suddenly. She looked past me, her mouth quivering as if she would speak, but she didn't.

She tucked a hand under her arm, warming it. All of the heat from her trailer house was spilling outside. It was clear I was starting to become a nuisance. The only polite thing to do now would be to leave.

"Thank you for talking to me, Wilma," I said, turning to leave.

"Who's gonna get me my eye medicine now?" She wasn't looking at me; she wasn't expecting an answer.

"I'm sure Martin can pick up your eye medicine," I said.

She did look at me then, but her expression was filled with doubt. "He won't do something like that. Martin is too worried about what people think."

If he was too proud to go into a pharmacy for his own mother, then Martin Flies Low was on a higher level of inconsiderate than I'd originally thought.

Wilma let out an agonized sound, like a soft gasp of helplessness. "Before he left, Joseph said—"

"Are you still here?"

I looked over Wilma's head and saw Martin glowering at me.

"It's cold. Shut the door," he said to his mother.

She bowed her head.

From somewhere inside the trailer house, a telephone rang, and Martin scowled when he was forced to walk away to answer it.

Wilma turned her head, making sure that Martin was out of earshot. I felt her grab my hand; her stiff fingers clutched at me like talons.

"He was always going out at night. I didn't want him to go out," Wilma said.

"Why?" I asked.

"Tell me the name of the man who killed my grandson," she whispered.

I stared at her, speechless. "I…I don't know," I said at last.

She shook my hand once, her knobby knuckles creaking. "You saw who killed that big man when nobody else did. Go and *see*, Dearcorn. See who killed my grandson."

She closed the door, leaving me standing there with my heart thudding, feeling the way I had felt when I had seen the owl watching me silently from the trees. Feeling like I was going someplace that I didn't belong, and knowing there wasn't a damn thing I could do to stop it.

The big man she had referred to was Paul Nesbit, my neighbor who had died so suddenly in October. Thanks to my snooping, I'd managed to stumble across the real reason behind Paul's death. Wilma probably thought that I was some sort of detective, but the truth was that I'd been incredibly lucky.

I drove to Lil's, feeling shaken from Wilma's desperate plea, and when I walked in Irene hastily cleared a spot at the counter. When I sat down she gave me a minute to compose myself. I must have looked haggard.

"What do you know about Martin Flies Low?" I asked. It was an explanation as well as a question. When I mentioned the name Irene knew at once why I looked pained.

"You must have gone over to Wilma's. I heard Martin was in town. He is good friends with the vice secretary of the tribal council over at the Crow Agency, and he drives semi-trailers for a trucking company out of Billings."

I rested my arms on the counter. "Why is it that he rubs me the wrong way?"

Irene pulled her stool out from under the counter and propped herself up on one hip. "Martin rubs everyone the wrong way. He and Joe were night and day. You know how sweet Little Joe was."

"Martin is sort of like sandpaper," I said.

"I'm not sure he and Little Joe got along so well," she said.

I nodded thanks when she passed me a steaming cup of coffee. "Why do you say that?"

She slid the coffeepot back on the warmer. "I think he's a capable parent. But the scuttlebutt concerning Martin Flies Low is that he hated the fact that his mother wanted to live in Killdeer instead of moving back to the Rez. When Joseph came to live with Wilma when he was a kid, Martin got really involved in local politics for the tribal council, and sort of threw himself into his work. He's not married, and I think Joseph and Wilma are the only family he has. I think he always resented the fact that the two of them stayed in Killdeer."

I knew better than to ask Irene how she knew all of this. But I was willing to bet she had her facts straight. Irene was more informed than the local newspaper reporter, and more accurate.

"Do you know anything about a party Tuesday night in town?" I asked, shifting gears.

Irene looked a little surprised. "No. I don't. But I can find out. What kind of party?"

"High school kids, I imagine. Will you let me know if you hear anything?" I asked. "It might have something to do with what happened to Little Joe, but I'm not sure what that is just yet."

She was about to say something when a commotion erupted from the parking lot. Four of the ranch hands from the Lazy Ox-Yoke came across the lot, jockeying for position at the door. They jostled each other, pushed open the door, excited and noisy. They paused when they came inside and searched the café, looking for someone in particular. Their apparent leader was a short man with small eyes and a determined expression. Willy Pittman.

I let out an involuntary groan. This could be trouble.

Willy caught sight of who they were looking for and led the pack through the café, hitching up his jeans as he walked.

Harvey Wilson, a local rancher who always sat on the same stool at the very end of the counter, watched as they headed towards him, an amused and curious expression on his face. They stopped and clustered around him like a pack of hungry dogs.

"Harvey, we want to go up on your place and look for Tisdale," Willy said. His boots sported tall heels, but the extra boost did little more than allow him to break even. What he lacked in height, he made up for in intensity. He vibrated like a coiled rattler.

The four of them surrounded Harvey, feverish with the promise of action. Young male energy radiated off them like cheap cologne. Cowboy hats were pushed back on their heads, and one of them had a pistol shoved in the back of his belt.

I glanced at Irene. She was already bristling with annoyance.

Harvey shifted the worn toothpick around his mouth, enjoying the attention. His worn coveralls strained at the belly. He gave them a slow, sweeping look.

"Why do you think Tisdale is up on my place?" he asked, amused.

Willy rocked from foot to foot. "Your place butts up against that public access point just outside the Custer wilderness area," he said, as if that explained everything.

"So?" said Harvey.

Willy threw out his arms. "So? It's the only place Tisdale could be. Nobody's seen him since he killed Joe. He don't drive. So, he walked someplace that's hard to get to and has public access. You think Loy is gonna go up there in that wilderness area and look for him this time of year? It's like, the perfect hiding place."

I felt my own anger starting to rise.

Irene was starting to simmer too. If this went on for much longer the posse would be getting a lot more than they had signed up for.

"You don't know that Dean killed Joe," I said, facing the mob.

The four ranch hands turned towards me. It was like being stared at by a pack of wolves.

The youngest member of the bunch sneered at me. "You don't know he didn't."

Irene had had enough.

She stood up off her stool and put her palms on the counter. Her glare chilled the room. "Out of my café. Now."

They looked at her with confusion.

"You comfortable with a killer just hiding up there in the wilderness area, Miss Baker?" asked Willy.

"I'm not comfortable with goons taking the law into their own hands," she told them, a scathing glare fixed firmly in place.

"Dean is a good man," I said with certainty.

Willy looked directly at me with disdain. "We all know how *you* feel about ol' Dean Tisdale."

I felt my cheeks grow hot. My history with Dean was common knowledge around town. He and I had crossed paths many years ago, when I was only a child. The experience had affected me so profoundly that it colored everything I knew about the man. In my eyes, Dean Tisdale was nothing short of a hero, and he always would be.

"What gives you the idea that Dean would ever hurt anyone?" Irene asked, incredulous.

The posse laughed in unison. Willy Pittman stopped laughing long enough to answer.

"Oh, sure. Dean wouldn't never hurt nobody. Any man who kills bears with nothing but a bow and arrows has to be the real timid, gentle sort."

"Just because he is a good shot doesn't mean he is dangerous," I said.

Willy strutted over to me and leaned in until his nose was inches from my face. His eyes were wild. "Sweetheart, that's the very definition of the word *dangerous*."

I jumped when a wide hand slapped the counter between me and Willy. Someone had muscled his way between us, and when I focused on who it was, I saw Lewis Pritchett standing beside me, his face red with anger.

Lewis stared the younger man down. "Go back to the Lazy Ox-Yoke, Willy. If you are a real good boy, maybe Santa Claus will bring you some brains for Christmas."

Willy was perfectly comfortable intimidating a 125-pound woman, but didn't have the fortitude to challenge a man who had spent his youth and adulthood bucking hay bales every day. Lewis Pritchett weighed close to two hundred pounds and loomed over most folks with his six-four frame. He was fifty years old if he was a day, but still plenty tough enough to handle at least two of the ruffians from the Lazy Ox-Yoke at once. It was safe to guess who was going to win this standoff.

After a few wayward brain cells kicked in long enough to tell him that he was outmatched, Willy turned to his comrades and jerked his head towards the door. They shuffled around him and started to leave.

Harvey Wilson watched them from his stool with a hint of disappointment. He had enjoyed the show and didn't necessarily want it to be over. He chuckled and called to the four ranch hands loud enough so that everyone in the café could hear. "Sure, Willy. Why not? You boys think he's up there. Then go on ahead and look for him. You got my permission."

Irene looked at him, aghast. "That is the single most stupid thing you have ever said, Harvey. And you said you once saw Bigfoot."

"I did see Bigfoot," Harvey said.

The ranch hands crackled with energy and let out whoops of delight.

"Thanks, Mr. Wilson. If we find him, we'll let you know right away," Willy said. He gave me a smug grin.

The posse scrambled for the parking lot. They clambered into two battered pickup trucks and tore into the street.

"There go the Pinkertons," Lewis said, disgusted. He grumbled and went back to his chicken-fried steak.

I watched the ranch hands until they were out of sight, a sick feeling in the pit of my stomach.

Irene patted my hand. "Don't worry, Honey. They couldn't find a well if Lassie herself was leading them right to it."

I couldn't help but feel a measure of dread. "But what if Dean is up in the wilderness area? He might be up there trapping."

"In the middle of December?" Irene asked.

"Otter and wolverine are still in season. They haven't reached the quota yet," I said.

"You know, Marley, you haven't worked for the Fish and Wildlife office for months. At some point you will have to find something else to focus on."

She was right, and I knew it. Sometimes it was hard to move on, even when life was moving on without you.

Irene started folding napkins around freshly washed silverware. She stood closer to me; her tone was cautious. "I know you and Dean are, well, sort of like friends. But do you really think it is just a coincidence that he disappeared on the same day that Little Joe was killed?"

I hesitated. But I had to tell Irene the truth, even if it was an ugly truth. "No. I don't."

Irene brushed an errant lock of her short blond hair behind one ear. "I don't agree with the Lazy Ox-Yoke boys running up into the hills to try to find Dean," she said. "But I don't think you should be looking too hard for him either."

"Of course I'm not going to go look for him," I said.

For a moment, Irene actually looked reassured.

I didn't have the heart to tell her I already knew where Dean Tisdale was hiding. I had a bad feeling I wasn't the only one.

CHAPTER 6

It was common for Finn to disappear for days at a time, leaving me wondering if he was even still in the country, much less in Killdeer. As I drove down the lonely dirt road that snaked past the deserted fields of our ranch, I wondered what Finn was up to today.

Instead of driving back to Leif's, I parked on the side of the road leading to the ranch, shut off the engine of my car, and I waited. It was almost a half an hour until I saw a familiar black Jeep drive down the road towards me, flip a U-turn, and park behind my Honda. I didn't know how, but Finn always knew when I was parked on the road leading to my father's ranch, and he always came. The weather station overlooked the valley, and even though there was no way that Finn could see the road from the station, he always seemed to know when someone was parked there. I didn't have his phone number, and I knew better than to try to drive up to the weather station to find him. When I wanted to see my boyfriend, the only way I could contact him was to practice this covert nonsense. The routine had been exciting in the beginning. Now it was tedious.

Finn shut off his engine and waited for me while I climbed inside his warm Jeep.

"Everything all right?" he asked.

I started to answer, but he smothered me with a kiss that would have made my knees wobble had I been standing up. The man had two speeds: full stop and full throttle.

He leaned back and tossed his arm over the seat, giving me his complete attention.

"The entire town thinks that Dean Tisdale killed Joseph," I said.

Finn's expression changed. He gave me a hard look. "And this applies to you how?"

"I don't think he did it," I said. He didn't respond.

I took off my gloves and stuffed them in my coat pocket. "My father has been friends with Dean for years. Doing little things, like helping him with his taxes once a year, making sure his electric bill gets paid. You know, paperwork. Dean has never been very good at doing things that required math."

"And because your father is friends with this man, you don't think he could have possibly had anything to do with Joe's murder," Finn said. His tone was so flat and caustic I could have cooked pancakes on it.

"I wouldn't hold him up as a suspect in any murder," I said.

"Haven't we had a conversation before about you doing the coppers' jobs for them?" he asked.

"Nick thinks that Dean is guilty, too," I said. I wasn't getting a very sympathetic ear.

"Nick might very well be right. He's a smart deputy. And you should bloody well stay out of it," Finn said. His accent always got a bit more pronounced when he was upset.

"Aren't you supposed to listen to me patiently and nod your head, or something? Isn't that what boyfriends are supposed to do?"

"Not when their girlfriends are acting stupid," he said.

I clamped my mouth shut. I waited for him to mutter that he was sorry, or at least pretend to look like he was.

Nothing. Finn stared back at me, his mirrored sunglasses hiding every trace of emotion.

I opened the door, got out, and slammed it shut. I went to my car, waiting for him to call out to me to come back, that he wanted to apologize.

But he simply watched me as I climbed into my car and drove away. I was more disappointed than I had any right to be that he didn't try to stop me.

I was so angry I had to force myself to drive slowly, knowing my little car didn't deserve to be beaten to death on the washboard road just because I was upset. I drove out to my father's house and parked in the driveway, staying in the seat until I could calm myself down.

The trouble with being in a relationship with a man who is willing to call you stupid is that once they start doing it, they never seem to stop.

When we had first started dating, I'd had my misgivings about Finn because of his distant nature. But I had never thought his emotional wall would be a problem, until now.

I took a few deep breaths, sitting in my father's driveway like a pouting six-year-old. When I had finally collected myself, I went up the steps to the front porch and tapped on the door. My father whisked it open and pulled me inside.

"Boyfriend troubles?" he said, leading me inside the warm kitchen. He pulled a chair away from the kitchen table and pushed me into it.

He set about puttering inside the refrigerator.

"How did you know?" I asked. I took off my heavy coat and draped it over the back of the chair.

"Dads just know. You look confused *and* mad. Your mother would get that exact look on her face when we'd had a fight about something."

I watched my father's back as he methodically built two sandwiches, side by side, the same way he had always done since I was old enough to eat sandwiches.

"Dad, I don't like liverwurst, remember?"

He made the sandwich for me anyway, laying the lettuce leaves carefully over his painstakingly crafted and perfectly sliced compressed meat slices. He plunked the plate down on the table in front of me.

I took the sandwich and ate it obediently. He dropped into the chair across from me, grabbed his own sandwich, and took a bite.

"So, what did you kids fight over?" my father asked around mouthfuls of wheat bread.

"Dean," I said, swallowing.

My father stopped chewing for a moment and slid his plate around on the table. "What about Dean?"

I put my half-eaten sandwich on my plate. "Quite a few folks around town say that he is some sort of a maniac running around killing people."

My father stopped eating and sat back in his chair. He looked worried. "Why do they say that?"

"Because apparently Dean is the only man in Killdeer who can shoot a bow with any accuracy," I said, laying the sarcasm on pretty thick. My father offered me a sympathetic look.

"Kiddo, you know Dean wouldn't ever hurt another human being, don't you?"

I folded my arms, feeling tired. "I know that. I just wish I could convince other people."

My father pushed his plate away and folded his hands on top

of the table, watching me. His fingers were scarred from years of stringing barbed wire and fixing broken-down tractors. He had scars on the inside too. We both did.

"Marley, how much of that night do you remember?" he asked.

I looked up, meeting my father's eyes. He propped his chin in his palm, waiting for me to reply.

"You mean, the night I ran away from home?" I asked.

He nodded. "I always took it for granted you knew everything that happened that night. But, do you?"

"Well, it had been a year since we had lost mom," I said. "Is that right?"

He gave a half shrug. "Ten months, give or take. You were about to turn nine."

I felt the tug of the memory pulling me back to the past. Losing my mother had been the catalyst for my starting to believe I was too much of a burden for my father. She had been killed by a drunk driver, and her death had nearly broken my father's will. He had struggled to be a good parent, but there were times, even as a child, when I could tell he was overwhelmed. I'd convinced myself that he would be better off if he didn't have me to look after all the time. I had decided to do him a favor.

I had convinced one of the girls at school who lived in Fable to let me ride the bus home with her. I told the bus driver that I was spending the night with her since it was a Friday and we didn't have school the next day. The driver had reluctantly let me. He'd been suspicious, but my plan worked, and I got off the bus in Fable like I belonged there.

When my friend and I got to the end of the driveway leading to her front door, I told her I had changed my mind and was going to walk home. Never mind that it was a ten-mile trek if I followed the road back down to my father's ranch. She waved goodbye, and I walked back towards the road until she was inside her house and out of sight. Then I turned west towards the thick trees that surrounded Fable, and I started walking. I had my school backpack and a windbreaker, and not much else.

My plan was to live in the woods, scrounging an existence off the land like Mowgli from *The Jungle Book*. It was spring and still warm during the day. I walked as far into the trees as I could, searching for a cartoon cave and waiting for the buffet of wild berries to appear. After the sun went down, I started to realize how much trouble I was really in. It was cold. Colder than I thought it would be. By the time I decided I'd made a mistake and turned around to walk back to Fable, I was so lost I didn't know which way to go.

"I remember getting off the bus," I said.

My father waited, silent and still.

"I remember thinking that if I just walked a little bit further I was sure I'd find the road again."

"Do you remember it getting dark?" he asked.

I had to look away from him. His voice was steady, but his eyes were shot through with the pain of the memory.

"Yes. And I remember the wind. It was freezing cold."

My father folded his hands in his lap. "What else?"

I shook my head once. "The rest of the night is sort of a blur. I get the feeling that there are bits and pieces of that night that are missing."

When I didn't say any more he put his scarred hands on the tabletop. His eyes lost their focus and he drifted away from the here and now, remembering. Then he leaned in and told me the rest of the story of what had happened that night.

"By the time we figured out you were missing it was close to six thirty. Still plenty of light. We thought it would be a piece of cake to find you before eight o'clock, when it would start to get dark. The sheriff at the time was a man named Larson, but I don't remember his first name. He organized a search and rescue party, and before I knew it there were twenty guys beating the bushes outside of Fable looking for you."

I felt ashamed all over again.

My father went on, letting the story spill out in a rush. "I was with them, the search and rescue team. We looked for hours. We couldn't find a trace. By ten that night I was starting to be afraid we wouldn't find you. It couldn't have been more than forty degrees. We had been getting a hard frost every night."

"You thought you'd find a little Marley popsicle," I said, laughing. My father's expression stopped me cold.

"I thought that if we didn't find you fast, we wouldn't find you alive," he said.

I started to say I was sorry, but he went on before I could apologize.

"Some of the best trackers in the valley were searching for you. Men who had fished and hunted the mountains around Killdeer for decades. But how much sign does an eight-year-old girl leave behind when she walks through the woods? Not much."

I was listening to his side of this story for the first time. I wasn't about to interrupt again with a smart comment. I gave him all the room he needed.

My father sighed and ran a hand over the back of his neck. "We had to call off the search at one a.m. Conditions were getting too bad to be out. I didn't want to stop, but the wind was nasty, the clouds were rolling in, and we couldn't see or hear each other enough to communicate. It was only a matter of time before the rain started to fall. If we hadn't called it off, it was likely that two or three of the search and rescue team would have gone missing too.

I was all set to let the others go back. I was planning on keeping up the search without them, and then, I broke my damn leg."

"What happened?" I asked, my stomach sinking. "I remember you wearing a cast around the house for a while, but I don't remember how you got hurt."

"The rain was nearly on us," he told me, his eyes glassy. "The wind was crazy. I was trying to get back to the truck for a second flashlight, and I couldn't see a foot in front of me. I started hearing things. It sounded like I could hear you calling out, yelling for help. When I ran towards your voice, I lost my footing and fell about twelve feet off a slope and into some dead timber. My buddy had chased after me, and he'd seen me fall. It took two guys over an hour to get me back to the truck. Dammit, they should have been looking for you, and here they were, carrying me out of the woods like a useless side of beef."

I watched him fighting with that memory. He was still pained by it, even now.

"What did you do?" I asked.

Prompted back to the here and now, my father sat up a little straighter. "We came back here, to the ranch house. Two guys carried me in, and someone was calling for the doc, because Killdeer had a physician back then. While the doctor was on the way, we pulled out maps and tried to round up more volunteers on the phone, and our idea was that we would start searching again as soon as it was dawn, regardless of the conditions. I was hurting pretty bad at that point, and I was not acting very grateful for the help I'd gotten so far. I was yelling at everyone that they needed to get back out there. I was calling every last one of them a bunch of cowards. Anything I could think of to get them to go back out to look for you. They said it was too dangerous."

He had taken on that thousand-mile stare, and his voice

dropped to almost a whisper. "But I had an ace in the hole."

"How do you mean?" I asked.

"One of us hadn't quit. One of us was still out there looking for you. That was Dean."

I was flashing back to that horrible night a piece at a time. I remembered the lightning, the wind. I had never been so cold before. It was like my fingers were made of wood. I recalled lying down at the base of a huge pine tree, shrugging off my backpack and trying to curl underneath it, wishing that the wind would stop. It felt like I was going to sleep, but I'd really been fading in and out of consciousness.

"So here is this seventeen-year-old kid," my father said, "and he's out there, by himself, with one old flashlight and no walkie-talkie. He didn't have any backup, no search buddy around who could help him. And what does he do?"

I felt my eyes well up watching my father tell the story.

"He saves my daughter's life, that's what he does."

My father forced himself to laugh, but I knew he didn't think it was funny. He thought it was miraculous.

"It started to rain not long after the doctor got to the house. I think I went a little crazy then, trying to make it to the door on a broken leg. The sheriff had a guy sit on me to keep me from hurting myself more. It couldn't have been more than a couple of hours, but it felt like years had gone by. I remember not being very happy about them not letting me go look for you, but I was working on my first shot of morphine and not thinking all that straight, gimping around with some kind of makeshift splint on my leg. Well, I was yelling to beat all, and the sheriff was yelling back, and then there was this knock at the door. We all got so quiet you could hear us breathing. Moe Johnson was standing closest to the door, and he pulled it open."

He swallowed hard, blinking back moisture from his eyes.

"And there's Dean. Standing there in the doorway, drenched through, handing you inside the door like he's returning a baseball some kids threw into the neighbors' yard. He never said one word. He just gave you over to Moe, and then he turned and walked away. Some of the guys, after they figured out what was going on, tried to go find him to give him a ride to his place. But he was already gone."

I felt my throat tighten. All I remembered of Dean that night was his face peering over me the moment he had found me. I certainly didn't remember the journey back to the ranch.

"He…he carried me?" I asked.

My father folded his arms tight across his chest. His eyes were unfocused as he stared back at the memory of the night he'd almost lost me for good.

"Some Forest Service guys found your backpack the next fall, and they couldn't believe how far you had walked up that mountain. Our search and rescue teams weren't even close. But Dean? He must have found you about the time we were calling off the search. Like he knew it was about to rain and he was running out of time."

I stared at my father's hands. They shook ever so slightly.

When he finally looked back up at me, his eyes were intent. "You've got to understand him, Marley. He doesn't think like other folks think. He didn't go looking for you because he expected people to be grateful or proud of him if he found you."

"Why did he, then?" I asked.

My father studied me with an expression I couldn't read. "He tracked you down because he could."

I felt a chill rush through my chest. A teenage boy had succeeded where a team of trained rescuers had failed.

"But how did he manage to carry me all the way from Fable?" I asked.

My father let himself smile when he answered. "He didn't bother with using the road. Dean cut straight through the trees, came out of the woods below Fable, and walked right down into the valley where that drainage comes out by the old culvert across the road from our pasture. He didn't even have a compass. But he walked straight to our front door in pitch dark, in the rain, and I'll be damned if I can figure out how he did it. Marley, he carried you for almost five miles. By himself."

I didn't know what to say, so I didn't say anything. I looked in my father's shining eyes.

"Now you know why it is that Dean Tisdale could never have hurt Little Joe," my father said. "God didn't build him that way."

CHAPTER 7

By Friday I was so sick of my physical therapy I was ready to throw my broom handle in the nearest fire pit. To help with the healing, my doctor from Parkman had instructed me to do very light lifting and resistance exercises to stimulate bone growth. It was so painful the first time I lifted the broom handle I had cried. But that had been two weeks ago, and now it was a pointless and tedious daily torture routine. Still, I had to admit that my shoulder was feeling better every day, and I would be able to start looking for a job soon.

I could faintly hear Leif talking on the phone for most of the morning behind the closed door of his office. A part of me wished he would come out and take a break so we could chat. I was surprised to realize I liked Leif's company, and he was pleasant to talk with.

After I was done torturing myself with my physical therapy I sat down on the sofa in the living room with a fresh cup of coffee, and had just gotten settled in when I heard the crunch of tires on gravel.

A black Jeep rolled into the driveway and parked.

I watched from the window as Finn got out of his vehicle and came up the steps. Normally, I sprinted for the door when I saw him, but I was still perturbed.

I let him stand there in the cold for a few moments before I went to the door.

"Finn," I said.

He examined my face. "You are angry."

I stood aside and held the door open. He came in and stood on the tiled entryway, watching me warily.

After I shut the door against the chill from outside, I let my manners override my irritation, and I offered him a seat on the couch.

He stayed where he was.

"Explain," he said.

I sat down on the couch slowly. "Finn, it's not nice to call your girlfriend stupid."

He pondered that before he spoke. "What would you call it? Being persistent?"

I sighed. This was going to be like plowing a frozen field. "Even if I am doing something that isn't very smart, it's a bad idea to call me stupid. It's going to make me feel even less like I should listen to what you have to say."

He paused and really thought about it. One point in his favor. "That makes sense, I suppose."

"Hasn't anyone ever told you this stuff before?" I asked.

He laughed. "Many, many times."

"Then, why would you say something harsh to me, when you know it's going to push me away?"

He shifted his feet. "It saves time to be direct. Why should I take twice as long to tell you something that happens to be the truth anyway, when I can say it straightforward?"

"Because it is better to be respectful," said Leif.

I jumped and looked at the stairs leading to the basement.

Leif was standing by the banister, watching us. He had spoken before I knew he was there, startling me.

Finn looked less surprised, but he did nod his head to Leif in greeting.

Leif smiled at me, and nodded back to Finn.

"Were we disturbing you?" I asked.

Leif shook his head and crossed over to the couch. He sat down beside me, leaned back comfortably and folded his arms behind his head. "No, no. I just like to know who is in my house," he said.

I'd never noticed before, but today Leif's ancient, threadbare t-shirt revealed a secret stash of muscles. As he threaded his fingers behind his head, biceps that had obviously been built up over the course of years popped up. Leif kept his eyes firmly fixed on Finn.

The room crackled with something that hadn't been there a moment ago. Tension?

I felt embarrassed I hadn't asked Leif's permission to have guests over.

Finn's eyes didn't leave Leif as he replied. "I'll call ahead next time."

"That's a good idea," Leif told him, his expression unreadable.

I wasn't exactly sure what was happening, but I could see that Leif and Finn were having a conversation with more than words. Whatever communication was going on between the two of them, it was above my head.

"Marley," Finn said, still looking at Leif. "I was going into town to have lunch at Lil's. Why don't you come with me?"

"Sorry, she can't make it," Leif said. He smiled when he said it. "We already took out a couple of steaks to put on the grill."

I wouldn't have been as surprised if I had just seen a trout swimming in my coffee cup. "We did?"

Leif's blue eyes shifted in my direction. He winked at me.

I almost fell off the end of the sofa.

Finn's teeth ground together so loudly I could hear them from across the room. He zipped up his coat and bolted out the front door.

"I'll walk you out," I said, jumping to my feet.

Finn was already halfway to his Jeep when I finally caught him.

"Wait," I said, putting a hand on his arm.

He spun around. "When were you going to cop to the info that you are doing spade work with Gable?"

"What?" I said. "What the hell did you just say?"

"My accent isn't that bad," he said.

"Finn. I am not sleeping with Leif. That's ridiculous."

"Is it? I don't know, Marley. Doesn't seem that ridiculous to me."

He was flaming mad.

"I cannot stress this enough, Finn. I am not sleeping with Leif Gable. Okay?"

He put on his sunglasses, but at least he wasn't climbing inside his Jeep. Yet.

"Then what was all that about just now?" he asked, waving a hand at the house.

"Finn. I think Leif was teasing you. I think he was trying to get a rise out of you."

"The way you Yanks play around with people is just bloody damn weird."

"We are weird?" I asked. "I'll tell you what's weird. Throwing your girlfriend to the ground when someone shoots off a string of firecrackers. Or, how about the fact that you have been bitten by a shark and never told me?"

He looked directly at me. "How did you find out about that?"

"Seth and Will told me."

His face flushed red. "You should not be talking to those two."

"Why not? I don't care that you work for some secret government organization. I don't even care that you can't talk about your job. What I do care about is the fact that I know absolutely nothing about you as a person. Are your parents even still alive? Do you have any brothers and sisters? I don't even know your first name!"

I let my arms drop to my sides, feeling helpless.

He pulled his keys out of his pocket. "Those things are not important. The less you know about me as a person the better it will be for you."

"Not important?" I said. "How can you say that? You seem so determined to protect me and watch over me, but you can't even tell me who you really are."

"But you see who I am, Beth! You see who I am whenever we spend time together. Why isn't that enough?"

I stood very still, pausing to make sure I had heard him right. "My name isn't Beth," I said quietly.

He rocked back on his heels, stunned at what he had just said. "Marley, I...I..."

"It's fine," I was lying to him but I couldn't see any other way to let him save what was left of his pride.

Finn rubbed the back of his hand over his mouth, unsteady.

I tried to reassure him. "I know you are under a lot of pressure. Don't worry about it. It's just a silly mistake."

He seemed to be searching for something to say, but he was lost. I never thought I would see Finn close to panic, but I could see that he was on the verge.

I pasted an easy smile on my face, willing my expression to look understanding. But all I wanted at that moment was to pry him apart with a can opener and see what was really going on inside his head.

"You know that Leif and I are only friends. I wouldn't go behind your back like that," I said, my voice even.

He nodded, his eyes downcast. "I know. Marley, there are things about me…" His voice trailed off and he closed his mouth quickly.

I felt him slipping away. He had inadvertently told me something about his past that he hadn't wanted to share. He'd accidentally let himself be vulnerable, and I had a feeling that was something Finn never, ever did.

I knew it was only a matter of time before he sat me down to explain why this relationship wasn't working. I dreaded it, but there wasn't any other way this could go. It was obvious to me now that Finn had never gotten over the woman who had been killed back in South Africa. Back when he had been a bodyguard and she had presumably been someone he was supposed to protect.

So. Her name had been Beth.

"Maybe we should try to do lunch some other time?" Finn suggested.

More than anything, I wanted to sit down with him and have a normal, easy-going meal. I wanted to show him that his blunder hadn't shaken me up at all. But I could see that he was not up to it.

"I'll be around," I said.

He nodded, leaned in, and gave me a half-hearted, one-arm hug. I patted his shoulder, feeling my heart wrench. I wasn't ready to have the conversation yet, but we both knew how this was going to end.

Finn wouldn't ever be able to let me into his world.

Maybe he was right. Maybe I was stupid. I had let myself fall for a man who couldn't ever love me back. How smart was that?

Finn climbed into his Jeep and shut the door, his face blank.

He drove away, and I stood in the driveway for a few minutes feeling sorry for myself. When I finally went back inside the house, Leif was still sitting on the couch, thumbing through the latest edition of *The Economist*.

I sat down in a plush leather chair across from him. He had propped one foot on the mahogany coffee table.

"What just happened?" I asked.

Leif looked at me over the top of his reading glasses. "I wanted to show you something about him, that's all. Now you know something that you didn't know before. You know that he doesn't trust you."

I pressed my lips together. Dammit, he was right. "I'm not even sure how you managed to do it."

He set the magazine aside and carefully folded his glasses and set them on the table. "Marley, I like you. I can see you have had it a lot harder than most people, and I don't like to see you in a position where you can get hurt again."

I was a little puzzled. "Do you know something about Finn that I don't?"

"No. But I know his type."

I leaned in. "His type?"

"He's a carbon-copy military man. Takes orders. Does his job. Doesn't ask too many questions and spends his time avoiding situations that could, God forbid, ever let him feel something for another human being."

"That's a bit harsh, don't you think?" I said. Actually, it sounded exactly like Finn.

"Listen," Leif said. His tone was genuine, and his expression was open, honest. "You are a grown-up, and you can make your own decisions. If you want to be in a relationship with a man like him, that's your choice. I just want you to know that there are other options out there. It's a big world, and not every man you come across is going to shut you out."

He got up, stood beside my chair, and lifted my hand. He kissed the back of my fingers, a bright smile playing across his face. "You have been through a lot of heartache. I think that you understand the world can be a scary place. Your boy Finn might seem like he is solid, tough, and capable. But he is like a piece of glass. A man who isn't strong enough to let himself love another person isn't really strong; he is fragile."

His hand was warm, and I felt a surprised flutter in the pit of my stomach.

He let my hand go, the gentle smile still in place. "There is a very real difference between a boy, like him, and a man."

"And I suppose you know the difference between the two," I said.

"A boy hopes that everything will be all right in the end. A man makes things all right."

"How does he do that?" I asked, trying to see if he had an angle.

"By taking action when it is crucial. A boy will hesitate; a man won't. It's that simple."

It occurred to me Leif had probably been born without the hesitation gene. I couldn't imagine him ever letting uncertainty rule his life.

"I really do have a couple of steaks thawing," he said.

He headed for the kitchen, leaving me on the couch to mull over what he had just said.

Was he offering himself to me as more than a friend?

The absurdity of that question practically made me laugh. Why in the world would a man like Leif Gable be interested in a girl like me? He was older, distinguished, and poised. I was, well, a mess for the most part. At least, that is how I imagined I must look to the outside world.

Had I imagined the confrontation he'd had with Finn? Finn certainly seemed to think there was a reason for him to be riled.

But the idea was ridiculous. A man as accomplished as Leif would never see me as anything other than a nice girl who needed a little charity from time to time.

I shoved the whole notion out of my head and went into the kitchen to help him make lunch. I was determined not to let my imagination get carried away. More than likely Leif's only motivation was to be a nice man. In my mind, that was the end of it.

We divided cooking duties, me taking over the salad and Leif grilling the steaks. It occurred to me while we prepared lunch that spending time with Leif was about the easiest thing I had ever done. Why was everything with Finn such a battle?

Lunch was slow and pleasant. We bantered back and forth about little things, speculating on the likelihood of another drought, and whether or not global warming was genuine. Our conversation flowed so easily I felt like I could ask him just about anything. Even if I wanted to ask a question that seemed morbid, or strange, I got the impression that Leif would give it consideration and answer as best he could. The situation with Little Joe had never really left the back of my mind. As the afternoon slipped by, I started to really wonder about some of the facts surrounding the incident.

When we were mopping up the last of the steak juices with thick slices of French bread, I opened my mouth and blurted out a question that had been rattling around my skull since the first time I'd seen Little Joe's body.

"Why would a man kill someone with a bow?" I asked.

Leif looked over at me, curious.

I pressed on. "I mean, why not use a gun instead? Why use a bow? We are in Montana, after all. It's not exactly as if a gun is hard to get here."

He pushed his plate aside, tossing his cloth napkin on top of it. "That's a good question. Why do you want to know?"

"I suppose if I can figure out why someone would do that, it would point me to who would do it."

"It might," he said. "Are you sure this is something you want to get into?"

I felt my shoulders slump. The last time I had asked questions about someone's death it had ended pretty badly for me. But asking questions wasn't the same thing as snooping, was it?

"It doesn't make any sense to me, that's all. A gun is more effective. With a bow there is a much greater chance you could miss. It's messy. I can think of all sorts of reasons why you wouldn't want to kill someone with a bow."

"I can think of one very good reason why you would want to use a bow," Leif said.

I gathered up the plates and put them in the sink. "What's that?"

He let the corner of his mouth play up a bit. "Because it doesn't make a sound."

I stopped and stared at him. "If there were other people around and you wanted to kill someone quietly, you could do it with a bow. But a gun…"

"Would draw attention," he said. "A bow is silent."

He was right. Whoever had killed Little Joe had wanted to do it quietly. But why? Was it because there were other people close by when he had died?

I recalled what Meg had said about it being her fault that Joseph was dead. I squeezed my eyes closed, trying to remember her exact words. She'd said that it was her fault and that he shouldn't have been there because the other kids hadn't liked Joe very much.

But Little Joe had been killed in our pasture with nobody else around. If he was going to meet up with other kids someplace close to where he had died, where could that have been?

The only place I could think of that a group of kids would go to mingle that was close to my father's pasture was the old culvert.

Back in the late nineties, a flood had torn through Killdeer and had wiped out a huge galvanized culvert that had been installed under a dirt overpass a few miles from our ranch. The culvert had acted as a bridge, but it was partially smashed in the flood, and it was so large that the highway department had dumped it across the road from my father's pasture temporarily until they could find a trailer big enough to haul it off. That had been almost fifteen years ago. The culvert was still there, gathering moss and growing an avid following of high school kids who wanted someplace safe to build a fire and drink beer. It was difficult to see from the road, but it was only a stone's throw away from our alfalfa field.

I nearly smacked myself on the forehead. "I think I know where Little Joe was going the night he died."

Leif gave me a puzzled look. "Really?"

"I think he was going to a bonfire party. And I think that someone killed him with a bow because there were other kids around and they didn't want to make any noise."

I had to get to the high school before the last bell.

I put my hand on Leif's forearm. "I'll do the dishes when I get back."

He chuckled and waved a hand. "Go. I run entire companies for a living. I think I can handle doing a few dishes without supervision."

I went to the door and snagged my coat, rummaged in the pocket for my car keys, and jogged down the front steps to my

Honda. I turned the key and the tired engine cranked to life, sputtering and sending out a cloud of black smoke.

"Come on baby, hold together," I said to the car.

As I drove towards the high school, my teeth rattling as I raced down the washboard road, I knew I needed to find Meg Chan and pin her down about what had happened Tuesday night. She probably didn't know it, but I was fairly sure she knew who had killed Joseph. I just had to ask the right questions until I knew who it was too.

CHAPTER 8

I drove down Main Street until I crossed the short bridge spanning Killdeer Creek. I turned left to head up the low hill towards the high school in a hurry and ended up cutting a little too closely in front of a truck. A brown truck with emergency lights on top. I swore under my breath. I'd just cut off Deputy Nick Wilcox. Hoping he would let it slide, I pulled into the parking lot at the high school, but when I looked back I saw him coming up the hill after me.

I checked my watch. It was ten minutes to the final bell, and I knew it would be impossible to talk to Meg Chan with the deputy standing around looking federally curious. I had to get rid of him as quickly as I could. The only way I knew how to do that was to be nice and cooperate.

I stood by my car until he parked beside me. I forced myself to look friendly.

"Hi, Nick," I said with as much pleasantness as I could muster.

"Dearcorn, you just about ran me off the road back there." He pulled a citation booklet from inside his truck and slammed the door.

"I'm so sorry, Deputy. I don't suppose you could overlook it just this one time?" I asked sweetly.

He looked at me like I had just asked him to perform an appendectomy on himself. "Sure, I could overlook it. And maybe monkeys will fly out of my ass, too."

This wasn't going well. Maybe it would help if I told him the truth?

"I don't guess you would be at all interested in what I am doing up here at the high school?" I asked.

"Maybe you would like to guess the location of Dean Tisdale for me," he replied.

I had to force myself to keep my smile. "I couldn't even begin to do that."

"Yes, that's exactly what your father said, too." He stopped two paces away from me and started printing in neat script on the citation.

My smile faltered. "When were you talking to my father about Dean?"

He didn't bother to look at me. "Tisdale has six cans of chili, a Coleman stove with enough propane to last another four days at the most, and the winters here in Killdeer can be murder. If you would excuse the expression. If you and your stubborn father would tell us where his is, we could bring him in before the weather kills him."

It was Dean who had burglarized Julian's sporting goods store?

"I told you, I don't know where he is."

"You just don't want to tell me because you think you are doing him a favor."

"Dean did not kill Joseph Flies Low," I said. My smile was long gone.

Nick was searching my face, pondering my motives. I was getting disgusted with the whole process.

"Give me one good reason why Dean would have done such a thing," I said.

"Just one? I can do that," he said. "Dean is a known poacher. The local game warden has been trying to pin him down for years, but nothing has ever panned out. Joseph caught him in the middle of taking a game animal out of season and threatened to report it."

"Dean wasn't poaching. Bobcats are still in season," I said.

"You got to have a license to trap, you know," Nick said, ripping a ticket off of his citation book. He handed it to me with a grin like a shark.

"Disturbing the peace and dignity of the State of Montana by driving recklessly?" I said, reading the ticket. "Are you kidding me?"

"I could get you for speeding, too. What in hell were you racing up here so damn fast for?" he asked.

"Maybe you ought to spend a little less time bothering me and find out who was at the bonfire party Tuesday night down at the culvert. The bonfire party that happened to be going on at the same time that Little Joe should have been at home in bed. But as it turns out he wasn't at home in bed. He was in our alfalfa field. You might want to look into that."

Nick was taken totally off guard. "What bonfire party? What culvert?"

It came out before I could stop myself. "Stick around, because that is what I am about to do, because obviously you don't know what's going on."

Nick scanned me like a lie detector. I'd just said something that was way across the line, and I knew it.

Sometimes my mouth had a mind of its own. "Look, I shouldn't have said that. I know you are only trying to do your job. But I know Dean. This isn't who he is. I think that Little Joe was killed by somebody he knew. Somebody a little closer to his own age."

"I will ask you again, Dearcorn," he said, pointing at my face with the tip of his pen. "What bonfire party?"

The final bell rang. An instant later the parking lot was filling up with bouncing teenagers, eager to escape from class.

I started searching the parking lot for Meg Chan. I knew she and her brother drove an older silver-colored Volvo to school together every day. They were seldom seen apart, and Matthew was always in the driver's seat. I glanced at Nick.

"Maybe we can both find out," I said. "Meg and Matthew Chan will be coming out here any minute now. I think that Meg knows who was at the bonfire party, but her brother will try to keep her from talking to me."

"What has this damn party got to do with Joseph Flies Low?" he asked.

Nick had moved to Killdeer from Billings to take the deputy position. He wasn't a local, and sometimes his lack of experience concerning Killdeer history put him in a bad position.

"The culvert is on the other side of the road from our alfalfa field," I told him. "Didn't Loy ever tell you about the place all the kids go to drink beer?"

"Loy only tells me what he thinks I need to know. I've never even heard of the culvert."

"Meg Chan told me that it was her fault Little Joe was killed. She said something about the other kids not liking him very much. So, if there was a bonfire party at the culvert across from our pasture, what if somebody got hurt feelings and there was a fight?"

"And you raced up here to ask her about who was there?" he asked.

"If she knows who was there, maybe she would be willing to share that information,"

"Fine. You talk to her. One condition," he said.

I nodded. "Sure."

"You stand close enough to me that I can hear what she tells you."

"So you don't want to ask any questions?"

"She is a minor, and I'm not technically allowed to question her without a parent or an advocate."

I shifted my feet, thinking. The kids were starting to thin out, and I caught sight of the twins coming straight for us.

"Agreed?" he asked.

"Fine."

I saw Matthew heading towards the Volvo, Meg at his heels. I nodded my head in their direction and started walking towards them. We didn't have time to negotiate now. We had to catch them before they got in the car.

"Hi," I said. She had been staring at the sidewalk, but when I spoke Meg jerked her head in my direction, her straight black hair falling across her eyes. She cast a frightened glance at her brother.

"We need to get home," Matthew told me, putting a shoulder between me and his sister.

"I wanted to make sure you were all right," I told Meg.

Matthew stepped forward, trying to disengage us. "My mom doesn't like it if we come home late."

I pulled Meg to the side but kept her close enough that whatever she said would be within earshot of the deputy. Nick stood far enough away that he wasn't crowding us, but I could see from Matthew's puzzled expression that he was trying to work out why the deputy was there.

"Meg," I said, trying to tune out the noise of the other kids in the parking lot. "What can you tell me about the bonfire party?"

She paled noticeably. "I'm...I'm not supposed to talk about it."

"Were you supposed to be at that party Tuesday?" I asked.

She folded her arms across her chest. She was shivering, but not from the cold. "No."

I frowned. "Who was there?"

She glanced at her brother. He was standing with his back to her, looking sullen.

"I don't know who was at the party. I didn't go," she told me. She seemed to be delivering rehearsed lines. "I got in trouble, and Mom grounded me."

That was a bit of a surprise. I searched her worried face. "Meg, I know that Joe wasn't going to the party. I know he didn't like to socialize like that. What was he doing that night? Why was he in my father's field?"

Matthew darted a glace my way, his brow creased. Just as quickly, he regained his sullen expression and looked at the ground.

Meg's eyes swiveled back and forth between me and her brother. Whether she was looking to him for reassurance or trying to determine if he was upset about her responses, I couldn't tell. But whatever hold Matthew had on his sister was well and firmly in place.

I would have to appeal to her friendship with Joe if I was going to get her to open up. "Joseph was planning to go to school in Bozeman after he graduated. Where are you planning to go to college, Meg?"

Her brother spun around and looked directly at me. "She's going to Vassar."

Meg swallowed, staring at her shoes. "I wanted to go to Bozeman, too. We both did. Joe and me. But Mom wants me to go to school at Vassar. She says that Bozeman is too provincial."

"Is that what you want to do?" I asked.

She shrugged with one shoulder. "I guess. It's a good school."

"But you and Joe planned something different?" I asked.

110

She stifled a response. She looked up at me, her face drained. "Joe was a lot smarter than anybody gave him credit for."

"So, what was a smart kid like Joe doing out in the middle of a field alone at night?" I asked. "Was he meeting someone?"

Her faced twisted with sudden pain. "Mom and Dad grounded me for a month because I was friends with Joe, and I couldn't leave the house after dark. They said it was wrong to hang out with someone from the Reservation. They said I was better than that."

"That's not the only reason why you were grounded," Matthew said sharply.

I was dismayed by her admission, but not too surprised. Sadly, it wasn't unusual for kids from the Reservation to receive hostile treatment from classmates.

I had to tamp down my frustration. I wasn't asking the right questions, and Nick was watching me like I was an exhausted swimmer too far from shore.

"Look," Matthew said, loud enough for all of us to hear. "Little Joe was a nice enough guy. I'm sorry he's dead, but he wasn't the most popular kid here at school. Mom and Dad wanted Meg to stop wasting time on her friends and concentrate on homework, that's all."

"That's not fair," Meg said, her voice strained. "You never even tried to get along with Joseph."

A ruckus behind our little group made us all turn. Noisy banter from across the parking lot halted our conversation.

Two boys about Matthew's age appeared at his elbow and shoved him playfully. They both wore identical letter jackets.

The bulkier of the two spoke first, shoving Matthew with his shoulder. "Hey, Chan. Who's he? Your parole officer?"

Matthew gave them both the alpha male stare. "Cool it, Hooper."

Both boys ceased their teasing and stared openly at Nick.

Hooper's face twisted into a mask of worry. "They're not doing another drug search of the school, are they?"

They wore the same letter jacket that Matthew was wearing. Red and black. The school colors. Since Matthew was the captain of the high school wrestling team, I assumed these were two of his teammates. I knew one of them. The larger of the two, Hooper Bukowski, had a reputation as a bully. The kid had a brow ridge like a Neanderthal—but not necessarily as high an I.Q.

I leaned around Meg and looked at Hooper and his companion. "Did you two know Joseph Flies Low?"

Hooper looked around him wildly. "Who?"

Matthew sighed. "Little Joe."

The wild stare graduated to a nervous laugh. Hooper nudged his buddy. "Oh, yeah. We knew Little Joe."

Meg was staring at Hooper with naked disgust.

Nick was looking at Hooper with mild curiosity. "When was the last time you saw Joseph?" he asked.

Hooper's eyes rolled towards the sky. He turned to his buddy. "I don't know, ah, when did we last see him, Connor?"

Connor, suddenly in the spotlight, balked and looked at Matthew. "Um, I don't know."

Matthew kept his mouth shut. His teammates searched his face, hoping for backup. They didn't get any. Matthew continued to stare at them wordlessly.

Finally, Hooper looked at the deputy with a slack-jawed expression. "We don't know."

Both boys were suddenly very nervous. They obviously didn't want to talk about Little Joe, so I dove right in. "So, Hooper. You and Joe must have been friends."

Hooper laughed. His cheeks flushed. "Joe and me? Friends?

You got to be kidding, right?"

I turned a slight smile. "You hang out with him after school?"

Hooper's eyes darted around the parking lot. He obviously didn't want anyone to hear that.

"No. Little Joe was freak, okay?"

Nick's expression didn't change, but he was suddenly watching Hooper with narrow eyes.

"That must have been hard," I said. "Hanging out with a kid from the Rez. Did anyone give you grief about your friendship with Joe?"

"Little Joe was *not* my friend," Hooper said. His jaw muscle was working so hard I could see his entire neck spasm.

"He was my friend," Meg said.

Hooper jabbed a finger at her. "Everybody knows what good buddies you were with Joe. How did your folks feel about you being a squaw?"

For a split second, Matthew's expression flashed to anger. "That's enough," he said, staring Hooper down.

Hooper cowed at once and took a step back.

I recalled from my high school days that brothers normally took it hard when their sisters were harassed. Matthew was no exception. He openly glared at his teammate.

Meg looked instantly ashamed. Her neck was starting to take on a red, blotchy color from embarrassment.

Nick was ignoring the exchanges around him. He was focused on Hooper with unusual zeal. "Do you ever go to bonfire parties, Hooper?"

The big teenager froze. He looked at the deputy like he hadn't heard the question. "What?"

"Answer the question," Nick said, his tone harsh.

Hooper swallowed. Sweat was beading on his upper lip. "Sure.

We've been to lots of 'em."

"You go to one Tuesday night?" Nick asked.

Hooper laughed. His eyes darted from side to side. "No. It's December, man."

Connor was looking like he wanted to make a run for it. He pulled out his car keys, rattling them loudly. "Hey, we've got homework and stuff to do. Can we go, or what?"

Nick let his gaze slide over to Connor. "Sure. You boys can go."

The two boys nodded and headed off to their cars, casting multiple glances back at the deputy as they walked across the parking lot.

Matthew took his sister by the arm and tugged her in the direction of their Volvo. "Let's get out of here."

His sister looked crushed. She didn't respond but simply let herself be pointed towards the car.

Matthew was talking to her as they got inside the Volvo. "He can be a real jerk sometimes. Don't worry about Hooper, Meg."

She pulled on her seat belt and turned her head towards her window. She couldn't look at her brother as they drove away from the school.

Nick Wilcox watched the dirty white pickup truck carrying Hooper Bukowski drive out of the lot and down the hill towards Killdeer. He didn't blink until the truck was out of sight.

"I think you found out who was at the bonfire party," he said.

I tried to clear my head. "I thought you couldn't question a minor without an advocate present?" I asked.

Nick headed for his sheriff truck. "You were the one asking questions, remember?" he said.

He slid into the driver's seat, and I called out to him before he closed his door.

"Hey, Deputy. Do you still think Dean killed Joe?"

Nick crammed his keys into the ignition. "Not anymore."
He slammed his door and sped out of the parking lot.

CHAPTER 9

Christmas was only seven days away. I hadn't done a lick of shopping, and I was feeling guilty. It had always been my habit to do holiday shopping at the last minute, so why change now? There would be time next week.

I drove past the caretaker's house and saw Loy's sheriff truck parked in the driveway. I'd been feeling like I had been remiss in not checking on Wendy. It was time to make up for it and stop by to see how she was doing. When I climbed out of my Honda, Loy was coming down the steps on his way to his truck. He paused when he saw me. Then he glanced behind him, looking like he wasn't sure what to do. Looking guilty.

I closed the door of my car and leaned against it, grinning. "Howdy, Sheriff."

Loy actually blushed.

Wendy waved at me from the living room window. She was smiling. It was the first time I had seen her look happy since her divorce.

The sheriff crammed his hat on his head. "Marley. How are you?"

I kept grinning. "Not as good as you are, apparently."

He ignored me and headed for his truck.

"Listen," I said, standing by his shoulder. "Something happened today and I think you need to know about it."

He fumbled his keys, dropping them to the ground. He bent to retrieve them and let out a groan. I could see his belt was notched as tight as it would go.

"Maybe you ought to let out your corset first," I said.

He stood up and held up his finger. "Marley…" He let out his breath and dropped his head. "Dammit."

I averted my eyes as he let his belt out several notches.

"Can you breathe now?" I asked.

"Can we just discuss what it was you wanted to tell me? Please?" he said.

I patted his arm. "Hey. Don't worry about it, Loy. Wendy is a sweetheart, and she's adorable. I don't blame you a bit."

Loy fumbled with his keys again. "She *is* adorable. I think she is too adorable."

"And when's your date?" I asked.

His face fell. "I haven't even asked her out yet."

I shook my head. "What is it with you men? You carry a gun, for crying out loud."

"But I can't carry it on a date."

I stifled a laugh. "That's not what I meant. Loy, you are a very brave man. You have been shot at. Why is asking someone out for coffee more frightening than that?"

He let his arms droop to his sides. "What if she says no?"

"What if she says yes?"

He gave me a hopeful look. "That would be…nice."

"Nice. Uh-huh. Listen. Your deputy thinks that Hooper Bukowski had something to do with Little Joe getting killed."

Loy blinked and leaned against his truck. "Nick thinks Hooper…

what? Say that again?"

"I would guess that Nick thinks Hooper had more than just something to do with it."

"Since when are you and Wilcox speaking to one another?"

"Are you listening to me?" I asked.

He propped a hand on his truck. "I'm listening to you, Hun. I just keep waiting for you to make sense."

It was not as warm today as it had been, and the weather report for the next week was not looking good. We were due for heavy snow. I crammed my hands inside my coat pockets.

"There was a bonfire party Tuesday night at the culvert," I said. "Meg Chan told me about it, accidentally. She was either invited to go, or she planned to sneak out of the house. But it seems her parents were not crazy about the idea of her spending time with Little Joe, and she was under house arrest."

Loy rubbed his chin. "What in God's name are the kids doing having a bonfire party in the middle of the week? Okay, never mind. One thing at a time. Explain Hooper to me."

"I went to the school to talk to Meg, and I ran into Nick, in a manner of speaking. While I was talking to Meg, Hooper and one of his buddies came by to harass us. That kid was so nervous when I starting asking about Little Joe I thought his head would explode."

Loy didn't look happy to hear that. He pressed his lips together until they turned white. "Marley, I really want you to stop talking to folks about my case. This is damn close to tampering. I know how you feel about Dean, but you can't go laying bread crumbs around for us to follow just because you don't want your buddy Tisdale to go to jail."

"It's not like that," I said.

"It is like that. Now my deputy is going to be chasing his tail around instead of looking for Dean."

"You and I both know that if Dean doesn't want to be found, nobody can find him," I said.

Loy couldn't argue with that. He let his eyes drift over the pasture across the road, his expression hard.

"So let the facts come out, and when they do, I think you will owe Dean an apology," I said.

"Like he cares what anyone thinks," Loy said.

"I care."

He searched my face, sympathetic. "Tisdale has a lot of personal credit because he saved your life. But he is about to run out. What happened to Little Joe erases any brownie points the guy has accumulated. I'm going to have to keep looking for him. And I'm not going to stop until I find him. So far, Dean is looking good for this murder."

"It doesn't make any sense," I said.

"Because you don't want it to," he told me.

"There's something else you need to know about," I said, toeing the dirt driveway.

"I can't wait," he said, holding out one hand. "Now what?"

"Willy Pittman and his buddies from the Lazy Ox-Yoke have it in their heads that they are card-carrying members of the Pinkerton Detective Agency. They are looking for Dean, too."

"Son of a—"

"They got permission from Harvey Wilson to go up on his place and use his land to access the jumping off point into the wilderness area. They think Dean is hiding up in Custer National Forest."

"This time of year, that's like committing suicide," Loy said. He shook his head. "Is there anything else you want to tell me?"

"That's all," I said.

Loy jammed his key in his door and unlocked his truck. "Marley, I'm telling you once and for all. You stay out of this, you hear me?"

"It's not like I got involved intentionally. It's just sort of worked out that way."

He climbed inside his truck, his hand on the door, and gave me a sour look. "Before too long we will have to bring your dad in for questioning."

"What? What for?" I asked.

Loy stuck his keys in the ignition. "I know that your dad was the one who warned Dean to get out of Fable before we could bring him in. He has always watched out for Dean. I need to question him about what he knows because if there is anyone in Killdeer who knows where Tisdale is hiding, it's your dad. Don't be surprised when it happens."

"My dad doesn't know where Dean is," I said.

Loy started his truck. "I don't want to do it, but if I have to, I will make your dad help us find him."

He shut his door and backed out of the driveway, leaving me standing there feeling helpless. I have never been very good at helpless. I wasn't about to start now.

The situation was deteriorating so fast I was starting to feel desperate. It was more than likely true that my father did know where Dean was hiding. But December in Killdeer was not a good time of year to be away from civilization. The sun was close to setting, the air growing colder with each passing minute. In my heart I knew that my friend Dean was innocent. But the people involved with Little Joe's life were too scared, or too stubborn, to talk about him. Well, I would just have to make them talk about Joe.

I got in my car and drove towards town, turning on Buckthorn and taking a sharp left through the Burbs trailer park until I was pulling up in front of Wilma's trailer. I parked behind a small moving van and saw to my dismay that Martin Flies Low was standing on the porch directing two movers who were carrying an old sofa through the front door.

When Martin saw me he glared like a startled wolverine. Any other day I would have been intimidated, but not today.

I got out of my car and walked straight for him. "I need to talk to Wilma. It's important."

He looked me up and down, weighing and measuring me with disdain. "What about?"

I lifted my chin. The only way I was going to get past him was if I spoke a language he understood. "There's been some talk around town about Joe. People asking questions about him and a girl from school."

Martin's eyes widened as I spoke. "What girl?"

"A girl his classmates thought he shouldn't be friends with. Now, if someone in Joseph's class was angry about him and this girl, don't you think that is something that might be pretty important to know?"

Martin's eyes darted from the movers back to me. "Who are these classmates?"

"I might be able to straighten this all out if I just ask Wilma a couple of questions. In private."

He looked over at the movers again. They had halted in the doorway and were staring at us. "What are you waiting for? Put it in the truck," he told them.

He looked over his shoulder into the house, considering. "You think she knows about this girl?"

"It would be better if I talked to her alone."

He struggled with it for a lot longer than I had expected, but finally he stepped out of the doorway and waved me towards the door. "Do not upset her. Ask her what you want to know. And then leave." He went to the back of the moving van to bully the movers at close range.

I didn't have time to be polite. The door stood ajar, and I walked into the house without knocking, pulling the door closed behind me.

"Mrs. Flies Low?"

The house reeked of sage smoke. It was like walking into a seedy bar.

I went through the living room and stepped around the corner of the small kitchen. She was sitting at the old Formica table folding a stack of dish towels into a box. She turned her head when I came in, and her face looked shocked.

She squinted, trying to make out who I was.

"It's Marley Dearcorn, Mrs. Flies Low."

"How did you get in here?" she asked.

"I told Martin I needed to talk to you," I said.

She grunted a laugh. "Nobody tells Martin anything."

I sat across from her without waiting for her to offer me a seat. It was horribly rude, but I needed her to see how serious I was.

"Wilma, I need to know what Joseph told you that night before he left the house. It's important."

She clicked her tongue a few times, unwilling to answer. She kept looking back at the living room.

"Martin is in the moving van," I said. "He can't hear a word we are saying."

She folded the last dish towel into the box and put her hands in her lap. She looked defeated.

"Martin is moving me back to the Reservation," she said.

"I thought he might be," I said, feeling bleak.

"I like it here. I don't want to go. But without Joseph around…"

"Wilma. I think your grandson told you something Tuesday night before he left the house. What did he tell you? It might be very important."

She rocked back and forth in her chair. Whatever it was she wasn't saying, it was paining her greatly.

"If Joseph was still here, I could stay in Killdeer."

I forced myself to sit back in the chair. I wasn't going to get her to tell me what Joe had said by wheedling her. I had to convince her that telling me what her grandson said before he left the house that night was the right thing to do.

"The sheriff here in Killdeer believes that Dean Tisdale is to blame," I said. "But I don't think he is. I think he is innocent. You know who Dean is, don't you?"

Wilma stopped rocking and put a gnarled hand on the table. "Tisdale didn't have nothing to do with it."

I kept my face passive. "They want to arrest Dean and put him in jail."

Wilma shifted in her seat. "You know that Dean? He lets the females go. The bobcats he traps? He don't trap the females."

"I didn't know that," I said.

Wilma nodded. "He lets the females go in case they got kittens."

"Kittens need someone to take care of them," I said.

Wilma glanced over her shoulder again. We could both hear Martin in the van, arguing with the movers.

"Joe took care of me," she said. "He always made sure I had my medicine."

"Joe had someone who needed him," I said, agreeing.

"But my Joseph is gone now."

"I can't change that," I said. I kept my eyes averted, giving her respect. "But, I would like to be able to tell you the name of the man who killed him. And I know it's not Dean."

She put both of her hands in her lap and leaned towards me, staring at the table. She couldn't look at me when she spoke. Her face was red with shame.

"Joe said…" she began. She sat back.

I stayed still when I spoke. "Nobody else needs to know what he said."

She breathed out, hardly able to speak the words.

"Joe said he was going out."

"Do you know where he was going?" I asked quietly.

"Thought he was going to get my eye medicine from the heart man in Fable. But he told me he wasn't."

Eye medicine in the middle of the night? And what did she mean by the "heart man"? Could she be talking about a doctor? I certainly couldn't think of any twenty-four-hour pharmacies or cardiac physicians that were up in Fable. Probably Wilma was confused. But I needed to be patient if I was going to get the whole story.

I nodded, staying quiet.

Her lower lip trembled, and then it all came out in a rush. She spoke the words so softly I had to strain to hear them. "Joe said he was going to go watch the twins take a shower."

She sat back like a mountain had been lifted from her shoulders. I didn't dare say a word.

She rocked again, but then she stopped and she wiped a tear from her face. "I told him that sounded bad to me. But he laughed and said, 'Grandma, you don't understand.'"

"Did you tell this to Loy?" I asked.

She looked at me, mortified. "No. I didn't tell this to nobody. I won't ever."

Martin came around the corner and stood in the doorway to the kitchen. "Are you finished bothering us now?"

Wilma jumped in her seat, startled into a panic. Her eyes pleaded with me to keep her secret.

"Yes," I said. I stood up, thinking that the Martins of the world made things unnecessarily difficult sometimes.

"Yes, I'm done bothering you."

"Good. Next time you come back, we won't be here."

I made sure to speak clearly so Wilma could hear me. "Thank you, Wilma. I don't think I will need to ask you anything more."

I walked past Martin to my car, feeling his eyes targeting my back.

The trailer house door slammed shut behind me. I stood by the road for a moment, thinking about what Wilma had said. Something still bothered me, and before I left, my feet seemed to carry me of their own accord across the street to the trailer house directly opposite from Wilma's.

A woman answered the door, and I recognized her, but I couldn't quite remember her name. She smiled when she saw me, her white hair brushed back from her deeply wrinkled face and her voice soft but clear. "Can I help you?"

"Are you the neighbor Wilma rides to the grocery store with on Saturdays?" I asked. It was a long shot, but maybe she could help me with something.

"Yes, I am. It's such a sad thing," she told me. "What a kind child he was."

"You didn't happen to notice any cars outside Wilma's house that night, did you?" I asked.

"Only the same cars that are always here," she said, shaking her head slowly.

"Did you see a silver Volvo?"

"Oh, the Chinese girl," she said at once. "Pretty little thing. She was here all the time. I think the girl was Joseph's sweetheart."

"You don't remember any other cars parked in front of Wilma's place?"

She thought for a moment, but shook her head. "Not really. Only that black sports car, but it's her son's, and he only comes about two or three times a year to visit."

Her tone suggested that she disapproved of that.

"But you don't recall if Meg came to the house on the night Joseph died?" I asked.

"I can't say for certain. But if the Chinese girl was here I wouldn't have thought anything of it. She was always coming and going."

I thanked her and went back to my Honda.

As I drove away, I struggled with what Wilma had said. The sun was setting, glowing a pale orange and casting thin rays of light through the winter clouds on the horizon. I slowed down so that I could think and drive at the same time.

What could it have possibly meant? I was sure Joe hadn't meant that he was going over to watch the Chan twins take a shower. That didn't make any sense at all. She had to have misunderstood him. But, on the other hand, I remembered what I was like at sixteen. The last thing in the world I ever wanted to do was say things my dad wanted to hear. Maybe Joe had said he was going over to watch one of the Chan twins take a shower just to get under his grandmother's skin. That was something I could imagine a sixteen-year-old boy doing deliberately just to be difficult.

Maybe she had misunderstood him completely. Or, more likely, Joe had been saying it deliberately with heavy sarcasm to spite his grandmother. It was obvious that the friendship between Joseph and Meg was not well received. I doubted very much that Wilma Flies Low would understand teenage sarcasm.

It didn't answer all of my questions, but I believed I was a lot closer to understanding why Joe had been out in the alfalfa field that night. More than likely he had hoped to find Meg at the bonfire party and have a chance to spend time with her. Meg getting grounded by her angry parents had effectively put an end to her sneaking out of the house. If Hooper had been at the party drinking and mugging for his friends, and Joe had shown up there alone, it was a short walk for me to imagine the situation turning ugly.

Maybe I was grasping for anything that would explain what had happened, no matter how unlikely, just to prove that my friend Dean was not to blame. Even I had to admit that when it came to Dean, I didn't see things clearly at all.

I could think of lots of reasons why Hooper Bukowski would taunt Joseph, but did he hate Little Joe so much that he would be willing to murder him? Hooper was a big dumb jock, but was he dumb enough to kill someone simply because he disliked them? There had to be more to it than that.

I needed to talk to someone who was close to Hooper, someone who could tell me if there was a much more personal reason why the kid would harbor such open hatred for another person. The only problem was that I had no idea who that person could possibly be.

CHAPTER 10

Saturday morning the weather stations eagerly blared the news everyone had been dreading. By Sunday night Killdeer and the surrounding areas would be socked in with heavy snowfall. The forecast called for ten inches. That would be bad enough, but high winds would make travel impossible, and weather advisories flashed across televisions and squawked over radios throughout the valley. Our mild December was at an end. Winter had officially arrived in southern Montana.

Leif and I sat together at the tall counter in the kitchen, watching the weather station and munching hot oatmeal doused with brown sugar and blueberries. Since Leif had come back to Killdeer, I had certainly improved my diet. Supper for me normally consisted of something out of a box, and I typically ate standing up with my butt propped against the counter while I wolfed down whatever it was I'd just taken out of the microwave. Lately I'd actually sat at the table using a knife and a fork like a civilized human being. I hadn't eaten anything out of a box all week.

"It's always the end of the world when weather forecasters talk about a snowstorm," Leif said. He picked up the remote and switched off the television that hung discreetly on the wall over the low bookcase. When it was turned off, the television looked like it could have been a framed picture because of its low profile. Televisions were simply newspapers and stock ticker tapes to Leif. Not one of his televisions sat in a prominent place. He had better things to do than sit around all day watching reruns.

"Have you ever been snowed in for three days?" I asked.

He finished the last of his oatmeal. "No. Have you?"

"A few times," I said. "It's a good idea to have provisions handy."

He thought it over while he washed his dish in the sink. "I've only spent five winters in Killdeer. Does it really get that bad?"

"It can," I said.

"Maybe we should go to the store and buy a few things."

His tone was so light I almost missed the gleam in his eye. Going shopping was positively the most domestic task two people could do together. Aside from sex, nothing demonstrated couple-hood more effectively than wandering around a grocery store with someone, tossing pasta and French bread in a cart. Going shopping with Leif would feel like cheating on Finn. At least, it would to me.

I hadn't seen Finn for nearly twenty-four hours, and his absence was painfully telling. He'd been so distant the day before I was surprised he hadn't come by today to let me down easy and tell me it was over between us. Since I could sense I was on the verge of being dumped, I doubted going shopping with another man constituted a breach of epic proportions.

I put my dish in the sink, and Leif washed it without a word. I gave him a smile. "Shopping isn't a bad idea. Would you like to take my car?"

He chuckled. "Sure. I'll get a coat."

We climbed into my Honda, and I started the engine. Black smoke exploded from the tailpipe. The engine sputtered, gurgled, and eventually coughed to life.

"What have you been feeding this thing?" he asked.

"It's got 247,000 miles on it. You should be grateful it still runs."

"If you can call this running," he said.

I ground the stick shift into reverse, and the car bucked backwards. I spun around, stopped, and put it into first gear. When I let out the clutch, the engine died.

I turned the key, listening with growing concern as the car whimpered. I turned the key again. A grinding noise came from the engine. I started to turn the key, feeling a sense of panic.

Leif put a hand on my forearm. "Stop. Let it die in peace."

I rested my forehead on the steering wheel, my eyes squeezed shut. "This is just great."

"It's fine," Leif said. "And, really. I'm not pretentious. But even I wouldn't be caught dead in this pile of junk. We'll take my car."

I couldn't argue. Even I had to admit my Honda was officially a pile of junk at this point. We left my little black car where it had breathed its last breath and walked behind the house to the garage.

I purposefully kept my eyes down. I didn't want to see the spot where I had stood when I'd been shot. Thankfully I was through the garage door quickly, and the moment passed. Someday I would get over the horrible feeling of panic that I got when I revisited this spot. But not today.

Leif pulled a set of keys from his jeans pocket and clicked a button. A car alarm deactivated, and the headlights on an SUV flashed once.

I stopped with my mouth hanging open. A silver, sleek shark of a vehicle sat before me. "This is what you drive? It looks like it should be in a car commercial."

He smiled and handed me the keys. "Why don't you drive?"

"Are you sure? I don't think I have ever had enough car insurance in my life to afford to drive something like this."

He wordlessly hopped into the passenger seat.

Another SUV sat beside the silver car, but all I noticed about it was that it was black. I was having a hard time with the sudden responsibility of being behind the wheel of a vehicle that obviously cost more than my first house.

I climbed in, and he shut the door. Before I got into the driver's seat, the engine started.

Leif waggled his eyebrows, a mischievous grin on his face. "Remote start. Nice, huh?"

"Nice? That's amazing," I said. "What is this thing?"

"This is a Mercedes GL 450," he said. The garage door opened when he clicked a button on the steering wheel.

I backed out slowly, carefully. The engine was almost silent.

"I'm afraid to ask how much you paid for this," I said. I looked at him, covering my mouth. "Oops. That was rude, wasn't it?"

He smiled. "You know, I don't remember. Fifty or sixty thousand, I think."

I tried to calculate what the monthly payment would be on a $60,000 car loan and gave up almost at once.

"It's only got three thousand miles on it," I said.

Leif glanced at the dashboard. "I use it to drive into town once a week to pick up groceries."

"You are joking, right? If I owned this car, I'd sleep in it every night."

I buckled my seat belt when the SUV started to chime a warning.

We drove into town, chatting about the advantages and disadvantages of studded snow tires. I felt almost normal sitting next to Leif as we drove.

He seemed at ease and relaxed. Something occurred to me, sitting beside him. Maybe I could gain insight into the psychology of a teenage boy if I asked someone who had once been a teenage boy.

"Hey, who would you talk to if you were a big dumb jock with a personal problem?" I asked suddenly.

Leif looked puzzled by my spontaneous shift in topic, but he turned to focus on me. "I'm not sure. How old am I?" he asked, jumping into my game without missing a beat.

"Seventeen. And you are on a team with three or four other boys, all your age, give or take a year."

Leif mulled it over. "Am I a leader or a follower?"

"I would say a follower. Not the team captain."

"Am I respected?" he asked.

"Not really. I would say, maybe feared."

He considered that. "So I am a bully."

"Yes. Without a doubt," I replied.

"Does this personal problem have something to do with grades? A girl?" he asked.

"Maybe a girl, definitely not grades. I don't think you care about that very much."

He rubbed his chin. "Well, I probably wouldn't talk to my teammates. More than likely I wouldn't want them to know I had a problem."

"Usually the last person a teenager will talk to is their parents, right? Who does that leave?"

He shrugged. "My coach. I would probably talk to him. But, let's be clear about it. I certainly wouldn't do it unless I was sure my teammates didn't know about it."

"Your coach," I said. "Why didn't I think of that?"

We pulled into the parking lot of the Stock Market, Killdeer's own cleverly named grocery store. It was called the Stock Market—short for "livestock." Each of the shopping carts had a pair of horns that stuck out from the handles. The horns were supposed to mimic the head of a steer. All of the parking spaces were painted with lines that resembled lassos, and a corral doubled for the shopping cart rack in the parking lot. On more than one occasion I'd come to the market in the summertime and watched a group of tourists posing in front of the store for a family photo, their teenage kids dying of embarrassment.

This was the main store. There was a second store owned by the same family on the other end of town that sold gas and a few groceries. It was called the Stockyard.

No wonder Meg and Matthew Chan wanted to get out of Killdeer. It was amazing that any young person would willingly endure living in a town possessing so much shameless kitsch.

Leif shut off the engine, and we went inside, bracing against the cold wind whipping in spirals by the front door. He grabbed a shopping cart, and we set about filling it with impulse items.

The grocery store was decorated for the holidays, with Christmas lights and ancient paper reindeer tacked to the walls. Luckily the speaker system had conked out years ago, so we were not subjected to irritating, repetitive Christmas carols.

We wandered through the magazine aisle, making fun of the tabloids, and as I was setting a canister of hot chocolate mix into the cart I had the feeling someone was watching me. I turned around slowly and saw two coal bed methane workers standing at the end of the aisle. They were trying not to look like they were loitering, and doing a horrible job of it.

I blinked, recognizing them. Will and Seth.

A flutter of excitement shot through me. If they had managed to find out what I had asked them, I was about to discover Finn's real first name.

I put a hand on Leif's arm and gave him a wink. "Act natural. I need to talk to those two guys over there, but I'm not supposed to look like I'm talking to them. I know it's strange. But, well, they are sort of strange anyway."

His eyebrow quirked up. "Okay."

We strolled around the end of the aisle, and I stopped with my back to Seth, pretending I was fascinated by a display of Gatorade products.

Seth, the scruffy blond, kept his back to me but edged closer until he was only a few inches away. Leif was leaning on the cart, watching the performance with amusement.

"Did you get the information?" Seth asked in a whisper.

"Yes. Did you?" I asked, keeping my voice low.

"Yes."

We both waited. Nobody spoke. I looked over my shoulder. "Well?"

Finally, I saw Will nudge Seth impatiently. He was holding a gallon of milk with one hand, and it must have been chilling his fingers. "Just tell her. *DS9* is on in twenty minutes, and I don't think I set it to record."

"I own the box set, man."

Will groaned. "Can we just get out of here, please?"

Seth threw back his head. "Fine."

He leaned back closer to me. "It's Angus."

I laughed out loud, all pretense of keeping the conversation clandestine forgotten. "Angus? Really? No wonder Finn never told me his first name."

Seth held up both hands. "I know, right?"

Will stood a few feet away, watching the ceiling and looking uncomfortable. "We shouldn't be talking to her where all these people can see us."

The chubby girl standing at the checkout register was chewing her gum and watching us. She looked at Will holding the gallon of milk. "You got a coupon for that? It's two-for-one day."

Seth tilted his head towards me conspiratorially. "Is it true? About the great white shark, I mean. Finn really did get bit by one, didn't he?"

"It's true. I don't know when, but it did happen."

Will let out a groan of exasperation. "Aw, man. I can't believe it."

Seth jumped away from me. He jabbed a finger at Will's arm. "You owe me twenty smackers, loser."

"Knock it off. Is twenty bucks worth making an ass out of yourself for?"

Seth thought about it for a moment. "You bet your sweet bippy it is."

Without a single word of thanks or an attempt to be polite, they both simply walked away, forgetting me almost at once. They were squabbling their way through the checkout line before Leif and I were ten steps away.

I heard them arguing at the cash register. "Dude, you owe me money."

"And?"

"And I forgot my wallet. So buy me some Doritos."

Leif was looking at me with a puzzled expression. I didn't even know how to explain it to him.

"They work up at the weather station," I said. "You know, the place everyone calls Area 49."

"Area 49?"

"Because it doesn't quite rate an Area 51 label," I explained.

"Oh. The monitoring facility. Sure. They must be the guys who came here from Maryland."

It was my turn to gape.

He saw me staring at him and chuckled. "You really didn't think it was a weather station, did you?"

"No, but how do you know it's not a weather station?"

He was scanning the ingredients on a box of granola. "I asked some people."

He put the granola in the cart. "Hey, let's watch a movie tonight."

I folded my arms and stood in front of the cart. "Some people?"

He waggled his eyebrows. "Stick with me, kid."

I couldn't help myself and smiled. "So, what did these people tell you really goes on up there?"

He spoke in a low voice so anyone close to us wouldn't be able to hear what he said. "It's a SETI project. Those two jokers you were talking to are from the Goddard Institute. You wouldn't know it to look at them, but they are probably astrophysicists."

"So, they are pretty good at math," I said.

He gave a half smile. "You could say that, yes."

I frowned, trying to recall facts from my Discovery Channel education. "SETI. Is that the organization that—?"

"Searches for little green men? You got it," he said, pushing the cart further down the aisle. "More correctly, they are searching for signals from space."

"What is SETI doing in Killdeer?" I asked, hustling to catch up.

"Well, back in 1977 a researcher at Ohio State University was working for SETI on a new project. The only purpose of the project was to listen for signals from space that could possibly come from other intelligent civilizations."

"You must be kidding me," I said.

"Totally serious. The interesting thing is that some time that summer the researcher working on the project actually got a signal. It came in on a narrowband radio frequency, and it lasted for more than a minute."

"Wow."

"Funny you should say that," he said, setting a box of pancake

137

mix into the cart. "The researcher who was in charge of the project looked at the printout showing the location and the strength of the signal, and he wrote one word in the margin beside the graph. He wrote the word *wow*, with an exclamation point. If you ever ask anyone interested in astrophysics about the Wow Signal, they will know exactly what you are talking about."

"So, the weather station is really a SETI research project?"

"And the only job it has is to monitor the exact location the Wow Signal originated from. All of the satellite dishes in the compound up at the station are pointed at that position. Once a day they move off the location, then they rotate back to it. That's all they do up there, keep tabs on that position in case anything exciting happens. It's logical. Since a signal was once heard coming from that area of space, why not listen to that area continuously and see if you hear it again?"

"Why don't they want anyone to know about it? Finn never talks about work, but it doesn't seem like that big a deal to me."

Leif gave me a wry look. "It could be a big deal if someone thought you were on the verge of proving there is intelligent life, other than us, somewhere in the universe. Although I certainly think it is somewhat a waste of time to look, there are people who would be unhappy if their current paradigm was blown apart."

"You assume there is intelligent life in *this* part of the universe," I said.

He chuckled and stopped at the section dedicated to movies. He started scanning the titles.

I wanted to ask him how it was he knew this. The "someone" that Leif knew probably had serious government connections to have that kind of information.

"What do you want to watch?" he asked.

"How about *Lonesome Dove*?"

We negotiated movie titles for another few minutes before settling on one neither of us had seen. Stocked up with enough food to feed us both for a week, we carried our heavy bags out to the SUV and packed them in the back.

Leif said that he would drive us back, and as we pulled out of the parking lot of the grocery store, Loy's sheriff truck passed us on the left with lights flashing. He was driving with lights, but no siren. A moment later I saw Deputy Wilcox follow Loy down the street in his truck, and someone was sitting beside him. I caught a glimpse of who it was in my rearview mirror.

Hooper Bukowski, head down and face distraught, was sitting beside Nick in the deputy's truck.

"Oh my gosh, they just arrested Hooper," I said.

Leif pulled to the side of the road as Nick's truck, lights flashing, came up on our rear bumper and chirped its siren. Nick gunned the engine and whizzed past us, heading for the sheriff station.

"I know this is a terrible idea," I said, "but can we stop at the station?"

Leif pulled back onto the road and followed Nick's truck. "Sure. They probably won't be able to tell you much."

"I don't need to know much," I said.

We stopped in the parking lot behind Nick's truck, and I jumped out of the SUV just as he was leading Hooper inside. Hooper was sobbing uncontrollably and looked like he could barely stand up. Loy was talking to him sternly, his expression grim. He held the door and ushered the distraught teenager inside.

"Loy, what's going on?" I asked, stopping at the foot of the stairs.

"This is not a good time for you to be here," Loy said. He was in no mood to explain anything.

"Are you arresting him?" I asked.

Loy turned his back to me and walked straight into the station without another word. I knew better than to follow him.

As I was headed back to the SUV, Nick came out of the station and headed for his truck, obviously in a hurry.

I tried to match his pace and had to skip to keep up. "You arrested him, didn't you?"

He stopped and looked at me like I was a bug that had just hit his windshield. "You can't arrest someone for being stupid."

"I don't understand," I said.

"He isn't under arrest for murder because he didn't kill Joseph Flies Low intentionally."

"That's impossible," I said, stopping beside the deputy. Nick pulled open the door of his truck and started rummaging inside.

"How can you accidentally shoot someone with a bow?" I asked with disbelief.

"By accidentally having too much beer and betting your buddy you can shoot an arrow farther than he can into a dark pasture. Joseph ended up being in the wrong place at the wrong time."

I was stunned. "So, it was a competition?"

"That's what Hooper said, in between crying and getting snot all over my truck," Nick told me.

How was I going to tell Wilma that her grandson had been killed as the result of an accident? I decided that I couldn't worry about that now.

Nick found his notebook and shoved it in his shirt pocket. He looked disgusted. "We have him for impeding an investigation, reckless endangerment, and lying to law enforcement. Too bad it isn't a crime to be a moron."

I was relieved for Dean, and angry at Hooper. How could someone be so damn careless? "Thanks, Nick. I know you didn't have to tell me all this."

The deputy gave me a thoughtful stare. "I thought we had

our guy when the kid about had a seizure in the parking lot of the high school. Jesus, when I asked him about Joseph at the school, I thought he was going to soil himself. Five minutes alone with Loy, and Hooper was spilling his guts."

"I can't believe it. Do you really think he is telling the truth about it being an accident?" I asked.

"The arrow Loy and I recovered from your father's pasture backs it up. It was identical to the one that killed Joseph."

"Can you tell me that Dean Tisdale is officially no longer a suspect?" I asked.

It pained him to say it, but Nick said the words with a disappointed expression. "Tisdale isn't a suspect any longer. I'll tell you one thing. I am particularly happy I didn't have to go crawling around in the bushes looking for him. He's the last guy I would want to go hunting for in the mountains."

"I think you might have been listening to local gossip a little too much," I said. "Dean is mostly harmless."

Nick laughed outright. It was not a pleasant laugh. "I haven't been listening to gossip. I just read the police file."

I heard a car door open behind me. Leif stuck one leg outside the SUV and stood up high enough to see me over the window.

"We've got ice cream in the car, Marley," he said.

Nick was already walking away, taking the steps up to the station two at a time, and it was clear I wouldn't be getting any more information.

I climbed back inside the SUV and buckled my seat belt. "They did arrest Hooper. Sort of. He said it was an accident. They were trying to see who could shoot an arrow farther into my father's alfalfa field in the dark, and they didn't check to see if anyone was out there. Little Joe was in the wrong place at the wrong time."

"That's too bad. Poor kid."

I couldn't help but think that it was incredibly ironic that the first time I had come up against a killing, it was a murder that had been made to look like an accident. This was an accident that ended up looking like a murder.

Leif squeezed my shoulder once. "I'm sorry, Marley. I know you said you liked Little Joe."

"Everyone liked him. He was a great kid. I just wish I knew why he was out in our alfalfa field while all the other kids were at the bonfire party. I guess it's not important now."

CHAPTER 11

I dreamed that I was lost on the mountain. Instead of rain, snow pelted me, freezing to my eyelashes and coating my hair. I was curled at the base of a huge tree, waiting for Dean to come and find me. It was night, but the snowy landscape around me reflected enough light to show me the lonely trees surrounding the clearing I'd found. Even in the dream I could feel the cold snow falling down on my hands, my face. It stung like needles. I kept searching the tree line, knowing that any moment Dean would step out of the forest and lean over me, his earnest face not showing any relief that he'd found me, simply satisfaction that his task was complete. Something rustled above my head and I looked up, expecting to see Dean looking down. But when I focused my eyes, I saw the owl staring back at me. It watched me, accusing and unsympathetic. I was just another animal in the forest, and it had no energy to spare to help me. It blinked once, then fluffed its feathers and flew into the trees, leaving me alone to die in the snow.

I sat up in bed, gasping for air. I flipped off the covers and stood up to shake off the aura of the dream. I'd slept fitfully all night, my thoughts drifting to the coming snowstorm and the knowledge that Dean was still hiding in the woods. When the snowstorm hit us that evening it would be almost impossible for anyone to get off the mountain.

It was impossible to shake off the feeling of responsibility I had for Dean.

Hooper had confessed to killing Little Joe, and now that Dean was no longer being hunted by Loy, someone had to go find him and tell him it was safe to come back.

A cordless phone rested on an end table beside the bedroom door. I picked it up and dialed, not knowing and not caring what time it was.

"Dearcorn's."

"Hey, Dad. It's Marley."

I could hear in his voice that I'd woken him.

"You all right?"

I could still feel my hands shaking. "Yes. I'm all right. But there is something we need to do."

He stretched, and I could hear him roll out of bed. "If you are about to tell me to stop jumping on those Silicon Valley IPOs, I'm all over that."

"I'm not even sure I know what that means, Dad."

He was making his way to the kitchen. I could hear water running and clattering silverware. It was never too early for coffee.

"Loy arrested Hooper Bukowski yesterday," I said.

The water stopped. "Did he, now?"

"And we are getting a blizzard tonight," I told him.

"I know it," my father said. He sounded perturbed.

"We need to go get him, Dad. We need to go get Dean."

My father let out his breath. "Yup. We do. Well, I do anyway."

"I'm coming with you," I said.

"And how do you know where we are going?" he asked.

"He's at the tie flume base camp, isn't he?"

The line was quiet.

"Dad?"

"Yes. He's at the tie flume base camp. I'd like to know how you figured that out."

"Because Loy hasn't been able to find him, so I knew he was someplace hard to get to. Willy Pittman and the boys who work over at the Lazy Ox-Yoke would have found him if he was camped in the wilderness area over by Harvey Wilson's ranch because they have apparently been searching up there, and they would have crowed about it to anyone and everyone if they'd managed to stumble on his hideout." I said.

My father and I had developed a strange bond with Dean after he'd saved my life. Whenever things went wrong for him, he would end up on my father's doorstep, asking for advice or simply seeking reassurance. He never asked for help unless he really needed it. Dean was the most self-sufficient man I'd ever met in my life. But when he was faced with a problem he didn't understand, it was my father he went to. In an odd way, he sometimes acted as if we were his surrogate family.

"It would make me feel better if he was home before this blizzard hits," my father said.

"So, you did warn him to get out of Fable before Loy started to look for him?"

"I did. First person they would blame when someone gets killed with a bow would be Dean. Thought it might not be a bad idea if he got a head start before the villagers got out the torches and the pitchforks."

I paced the floor. "And that's exactly what happened. Why do they hate him so much?"

"What time do you want to leave?" he asked.

I pulled the curtain aside and looked out the window. It was still dark. "A half hour?"

"I'll be ready."

He hung up the phone, and I replaced the handset in the base on the table. I climbed in the shower and made the water as hot as I could stand. When I dressed, I packed on the layers and made sure I had a spare set of gloves in case the first pair got too wet to wear. I stuffed a wool hat in my coat pocket. Wool insulates even when it is wet.

I went down the stairs, automatically reaching for my car keys when I remembered with a jolt that my Honda was dead in the driveway.

"Maybe I should get a dogsled team," I said to myself. I'd have to call my father back and ask him to come pick me up.

I was reaching for the phone when Leif came up the stairs, looking sleepy.

"Did I wake you?" I asked.

"No. I'm usually up by now. You don't need to shovel the sidewalk, you know. It won't snow until tonight."

I looked down at my winter wear. "There is something I need to go do."

"It must be important."

I set the phone back in the cradle. "I don't suppose I could borrow your car to drive over to my father's house?"

He took his car keys from a glass dish that sat by the front door and handed them to me. "You start it by pressing this button."

I studied the toggle switch attached to the keys and nodded. "You aren't going to ask me what I am doing?"

"No. Do you need my help?" he asked.

I thought about it. "I think we can do this, just my father and me. But thank you."

It occurred to me that Finn would have pitched a fit had I

tried to leave so early in the morning without an explanation. I would have probably found myself locked in the closet while he set booby traps around the house. But Leif seemed to have confidence in me.

"Where are you going, and what time will you be back?" he asked. He wasn't prying, he was simply asking.

"We are going to the tie flume base camp to look for Dean. He isn't a suspect anymore, but he doesn't know that. I would sure like it if we could get him off the mountain before the snow flies. Hopefully we will be back here by supper."

"Okay," he said. "If you're not back by dark, I'll call out the helicopters. Have fun."

He must have been half asleep, because he leaned over and kissed me on the forehead before roaming into the kitchen to start his day.

I shook myself back into the moment, wondering what to make of the gesture, but knowing I needed to stay focused on the task in front of me.

I headed for the garage and fumbled with the toggle switch, finally managing to start Leif's car and get the garage door open. As I drove to my father's house, I was thankful, not for the first time, that my last name was Dearcorn. Having a last name with so much history associated with it sometimes made life a lot easier in the valley.

Normally, anyone wanting to hike to the tie flume site would start the trek on the west side of the mountain. That meant they would start the hike with a full day's walk ahead of them. But my father and I had special dispensation. On the east side of the mountain, a private ranch sprawled across the foothills leading to the trailhead, and we had a close relationship with the woman who owned the ranch. She had been very close friends with my mother.

Their friendship extended to me and my father, and whenever we wanted to use the access to the eastern trailhead, we could. Our standing invitation allowed us to walk to the tie flume in four hours, rather than the ten it would take from the west side access point. I couldn't imagine living in a place where nobody knew who I was.

When I pulled up in front of the ranch house, it took me a moment to figure out how to shut off the engine. The ignition didn't require a key, just the proximity of the key, to activate. Pushing a button to start the engine was a slick trick, but it wasn't until I realized you had to push an ignition button a second time that I managed to shut it off. I suddenly missed my ancient Honda with its simple technology.

I climbed out of the SUV, remembering to lock it—although it probably wouldn't matter whether I did or not. If someone stole it, the doors would probably automatically lock, and it would drive itself to the nearest police station.

"Are you cooking crack cocaine in your garage, Kiddo?" my father asked as he came down the stairs. He was ogling the SUV.

"It's Leif's. He let me borrow it. The Honda finally gave up the ghost."

He let out an appreciative whistle. "You think he'd let me borrow this if my old truck dies?"

We went around to the back of the house, and I pulled open the garage door while my father climbed into his pickup and started it. The sun was peeking up over the horizon. It would be daylight by the time we reached the trailhead.

We bounced down the gravel road, our headlights nosing through the twilight.

As we drove past the alfalfa field my father almost drove off the road as he twisted his neck back to scan the pasture. Like all ranchers, the property was far more important to him than the road he was actually driving on at the moment. A two-ton truck could have been barreling towards us, and my father would still want to check for downed fence line.

"Maybe I'll mow that six acres this year," he said.

"The place those cranes nest in the spring?" I asked, struggling to snap my seat belt on as we weaved across the centerline. I nearly had to grab the wheel to steer him back to our side of the road.

"I haven't seen those cranes for two years now," he said. "I don't think they are coming back."

"It's a mess over there. Maybe you should mow it," I replied. The alfalfa had been taken over by tall weeds and one stubborn chokecherry bush. The elbow of the field looked more like river bottom than pasture land because of the mass of vegetation that had sprung up. It was a perfect place for foxes to hunt, so it didn't surprise me that the cranes had moved on. They preferred open ground, so they could see what was coming.

We passed through Killdeer, the streets deserted aside from one other battered ranch truck with only one headlight. We drove on the frontage road until we came to the turnoff, and we headed east for the mountain pass that would take us to our destination.

Deep Creek Ranch was owned and operated by Tatiana Phelps. She was as far away from the dainty Slavic maiden that the name Tatiana implied as it was possible to get. She was stooped from years spent in the saddle. She walked with a limp. Her face was worn and lined like buckskin that had been left in the sun too long. She laughed loud and swore softly. I had never seen her without her brown hair braided in a tight rope trailing down her back. I'd never seen her wear a dress.

Tatiana was rich. She was so rich she could afford to piss people off. She never said anything that she didn't mean. She had committed the ultimate sin living in cattle country. She raised sheep.

Once, when my mother and I were visiting her at the ranch, two of the stock dogs got into a scrap on the front porch. Tatiana bent down and pulled them apart with her bare hands, cowing them back into line with nothing but a look and a firm shake. When I was a child, I always imagined that one day she would be the president of the United States. Well, I still imagined it.

The pass over the mountain was clear and dry. For the moment. It took a little over an hour to drive to the trailhead. We stopped the truck, and I looked out the windshield at the grey sky. The clouds had us trapped.

"How long do you figure before the storm hits?" I asked.

My father rubbed his chin. "About the time we are walking back down, if we hurry."

I knew from experience that when the snow started to fall this close to the tree line, the ground would turn to mush. The soil around the base of the mountain here was full of clay, and when it got wet it was virtually impossible to navigate.

"Tell you what," I said. "I'll start walking, and you drop by Tatiana's to let her know we are here."

"Are you sure?" he asked.

"I'm slower than you are. By the time I get to the top you should be right behind me. I'll roust Dean, and we should be ready to start down when you get there."

He considered my plan. "I could do that. You want some bacon?"

I laughed. "What?"

"You know when I stop by to see Tatiana, she is going to try to force bacon on me."

"Nobody ever had to try to *force* bacon on you, Dad."

And nobody ever will," he said. He put the truck in reverse, and I climbed out, waving him off as he bounced back down the steep road.

Truck tires cut the soil at the base of the trail. I couldn't see a vehicle anywhere, but Tatiana's ranch was huge, and she had at least four hired hands working for her. Any one of them could have come up to the trailhead checking for stray sheep. I knew that any vehicles on the ranch wouldn't belong to Dean. He didn't drive. Once again I marveled at Dean's fortitude. I was already tired just thinking about the hike up, but Dean had come this way from the other side of the mountain, on foot.

I faced the mountain and dug in, hoping that we would be able to find Dean quickly. It would be a long hike up, and I couldn't waste any time. As I cut through the trees and set my foot on the horse trail leading up, I caught a glimpse of a vehicle parked off in the distance, back in the scrub brush. I stared at it for a moment, but I didn't recognize it. Shrugging, I resumed the climb. I had a long way to go and not very much time to get there.

I felt my boots dig into the powder-dry dirt as I started the climb. Not long after the snow started, this part of the trail would be little more than soupy mud. I put my head down and found a good pace. The sky was dark, but there was no wind. Had it been summer, these clouds would be shooting lightning. But in the cold dawn of December they did nothing more than warn of the coming blizzard. The air had a bite to it, but it was eerily calm.

I was grateful the wind was still. Hopefully, if I set a good pace, I'd reach the tie flume before the wind kicked up. If I was coming down before it got breezy, the wind would be at my back, and it wouldn't be nearly as cold.

A gang of ravens startled me. They were jostling each other from the branches of a tall ponderosa pine, squabbling and pecking each other. One of them turned its black eye towards me to see if I was worth investigating. It rotated its head to and fro, appraising my usefulness. I apparently wasn't worth further inspection. It turned back to its companions, and the troop continued to disturb the peace until they grew bored and as a group flew from the tree down towards the river below.

I could see the river from where I stood. It had been used long ago by loggers to ferry the felled trees down the mountain to the sawmill located at the bottom of the valley. A wooden tie flume had been constructed to hasten the process, allowing the logs to shoot down the mountain and ultimately land in the river far below. The trees were used to make railroad ties, and the flume had taken its name from that utilitarian mission. There wasn't much left of the old base camp at the head of the tie flume. There was even less remaining of the flume itself. But one little-known fact about the site was that perched above the skeleton of the flume was an old miner's shaft. It wasn't very deep. It penetrated the mountain perhaps sixty feet at the most. But it was sheltered from the wind, and snow didn't accumulate in the mouth of the shaft. It was the perfect place to be if you didn't want to be found. What made it so appealing was that it was almost impossible to reach. When it had been blasted out of the mountainside a generation before I was even born, the shaft had been easy to reach because of a carved trail leading to its mouth. Today, that trail was gone. It had collapsed years before, leaving the entrance of the mine shaft suspended above the ground, high atop a rock wall. To get inside the shaft required fearless climbing skills. Unless you were a bird, or Dean Tisdale, it was impossible to reach.

As I walked up the trail, I knew that if Dean wanted to hide, this was the place he would go.

I heard my stomach rumble, and I suddenly hoped my father would remember he'd promised me bacon from Tatiana. I'd forgotten to eat breakfast in my haste. This day already promised to be full of inconveniences.

I trudged on, my head down, for close to two hours. The trail narrowed, and I could hear the river rising up to meet the worn path. I was getting close to the top.

As I put one foot before the other I felt a growing smile play across my lips. This time, I was the one who was saving Dean. It was high time I repaid this debt. Not that I worried he wouldn't be able to survive a bad snowstorm. It would take a lot more than that to kill someone like him. But, at the very least, I could save him the worry of wondering if the sheriff was coming up the trial after him. And he could sleep in his own bed tonight.

I felt cheerful, and my pace picked up.

The steep trail jogged to the right as it hugged the mountain, and as I rounded the corner, my head was down, and I didn't see them until it was too late. Voices made me look up, and I came face to face with Willy Pittman and the Pinkertons. The four of them stopped in the middle of the trail when they saw me. Then Willy shouldered his rifle and propped a hand on his knee. He licked his dry lips.

The three ranch hands with him stood stock still, watching me with interest. Willy paused to catch his breath and stared at me with a growing grin.

Then he cocked his head to the side and spat a wad of chewing tobacco on the ground. "I guess the day ain't a total loss after all, boys."

CHAPTER 12

It was too late to make a run for it.

If I sprinted back down the trail, they would catch me. I was too tired from the climb, and they would be faster. Where was my father? He had to be at least a half an hour behind me. Even if I screamed and he heard me, it would still take him twenty minutes to get here at a dead run. And then he would be walking into an ambush. All four of them had guns.

I didn't know beyond a shadow of a doubt that I was about to be gang raped, but I didn't know I wasn't, either. Instead of hoping these were just wayward, misunderstood boys with pent up energy to burn, I'd assume the worst and sort it out later. I couldn't hope for charity.

I held my ground, and I did the one thing that none of them expected me to do. I smiled.

"Tatiana said you wouldn't find him," I said. I somehow managed to keep my voice from breaking.

Willy scrunched up his face. "What are you talking about? She don't know we're here."

"She said that it was too bad about Hooper, but that she wasn't surprised," I told them.

Willy shifted his rifle. "What about Hooper?"

"He got arrested yesterday for killing Little Joe."

One of Willy's companions nudged him. "I don't like Tatiana knowing we're up here."

"Shut up, Eric. She's lying."

I kept my smile in place. "I see that the four of you are still breathing, so you must not have run into Dean."

"Dean ain't here, or we would have seen him," Willy said.

I dropped the smile. "Only if he wanted you to."

Eric, the nervous one with a shock of red hair and boyish freckles, nudged Willy again. "I think we should get the hell out of here."

"Jesus, you whine worse than my mom," Willy said. He looked me up and down. "We ain't in a rush."

Willy was in charge. No doubt about it. Given the chance, Eric would walk away now and never look back because he looked about as nervous as a rabbit, but he would also do what he was told if it came down to it.

I glanced at the other two. One looked like he had all the intelligence of a cinder block and the physique to match, and the other was reed thin and kept darting glances around the tree line. But the way they stood with their shoulders pointed towards Willy told me they were malleable. One cue from Willy and they would jump to do his bidding. Unless I could give them a very good reason not to.

"Tatiana says for you boys to not park your truck down there next time you try to sneak onto her place," I said. "It leaves ruts in the ground."

Willy jerked his chin in my direction. "She's laying in on pretty thick. I'd guess you aren't very good at poker, are you Dearcorn?"

Willy stepped away from the other three and walked a slow circle around me.

I could see he was frustrated that they hadn't been able to find Dean, and I hoped I wasn't about to be the beneficiary of that frustration.

"Well, I am good at poker. And I know tells when I see 'em," Willy said.

He reached a hand for me, but I stepped back fast.

"If you lay one finger on me not even the coyotes will find your body," I said.

Willy paused, amused. "Oh? Who's gonna kill me, then. You?"

He laughed and reached for me again. I knocked his hand away and shoved him hard. This was no time to be timid.

"Don't be stupid. I'm trying to save your life, Willy."

"You don't even have a gun," he said.

I did my best to look exasperated instead of desperate. "I don't need one. And neither does Dean."

He broke my gaze and searched the trees with a quick glance. "Like I said. He ain't here."

I could see a sliver of doubt when he spoke.

"Because you are such a good tracker, of course you'd know it if he was," I said.

"He's not that good a tracker," Eric said.

Willy cast an angry glance back at his buddy. "Like you know the first thing about it."

"There's four of us," said the skinny ranch hand. He repositioned his rifle, taking security from the weight of it on his arm.

"So, maybe Dean can only get two of you before you shoot back," I said. "But if that's the case, then each one of you has got a fifty-fifty chance."

The four of them were quiet while they did the math. It seemed to take quite a bit of their mental capacity to add it all up.

"Merrell down at the Stockyard said that Dean can shoot a

sparrow off a telephone line," said the cinder block. He cringed when Willy shot him an angry glare.

"He'd have a hard time shooting me in the back if I was on top of you," Willy said, leering at me.

"Are you willing to bet your life on that?" I asked.

"It depends on how good you'd be," he said, fingering his rifle.

I turned my head slowly towards the trees, stopping my gaze briefly at a stand of thick pines. I looked back at Willy and shrugged.

"You know? What the hell. Go ahead. You think you can make if off of this mountain alive, then you go on ahead and grab me. Let's just see what happens next."

The other three, particularly Eric, were searching the trees now. A light breeze blew, masking the sounds around us.

Even Willy paused.

Bless his soul, Eric the freckled whiner stepped forward and grabbed Willy's arm. "It's freezing out. Can we just get the hell out of here now?"

Seeing a chance to save face, Willy poked my shoulder with two fingers and walked past me down the trail. "She's too scrawny anyway."

The others followed suit, and the four of them trudged around the bend and down the path, leaving me standing in the middle of the trail with my legs about to collapse underneath me.

The moment they were out of sight, I wasted no time and started running up the mountain. If they changed their minds I wanted to be as far ahead of them as I could get. If I was too much work to chase, maybe I wouldn't be worth their time. I feverishly hoped the Pinkertons wouldn't confront my father when they ran into him.

I had to stop running when I was almost at the top. I'd run myself out, and I was near collapse. I staggered more than walked up the path, and when I caught sight of the flat clearing that marked the old camp, I let out a sigh of relief.

The river rumbled a few yards from the clearing, and the remnants of the flume still clung to the rocks over the water. Opposite the river a rough cliff rose abruptly, and I knew somewhere above me was the mine shaft entrance.

I forced my feet to move, one in front of the other, until I found a crack in a huge boulder that would make a good place to hide and dropped to my knees inside it. Six feet of split stone sheltered me on either side. I could finally catch my breath. The crack was just deep enough to conceal me from anyone coming up the trail. Though it was open to the sky, if someone came up the trail they wouldn't see me right away.

I propped my back against the sidewall of the rough stone and sucked in air as deep as I could. My lungs burned. Several minutes passed by, and I didn't hear a sound, and I felt certain that I hadn't been followed, but I decided I would stay inside the rock crevice until my father got to the top. I hoped that the Pinkertons wouldn't harass my father. My gut told me that cowards seldom bothered grown men and saved their attention for those who were weaker. I had to shake my head over the dumb luck of finding the four troublemakers on the trail. Of all the times it would have been good to have Dean Tisdale at my side, that certainly had to be at the top of the list.

As I looked out through the crack to my left I could see the remains of the tiny cabins that had been built by the loggers at the top of the trail. Mostly, the cabins were piles of rotting timber now.

I pulled off my wool hat and wiped hair out of my eyes, noticing that my hands were still shaking.

As I slid my hat back on I heard a scraping sound from above, and I looked up.

A shadow blocked the meager light. The shadow of a man.

I opened my mouth to speak, but nothing came out.

The man stood on the edge of the crevice looking down at me. He balanced on the rock lip with the balls of his feet perfectly positioned, standing there as still as a stone.

He gripped an elegant wooden recurve bow with one hand, looking down at me with no expression.

I swallowed hard, trying to find my voice.

"Hey Dean," I said at last.

He crouched down, his face coming into view.

"Miss Marley. What are you doing up here?"

I wanted to laugh, but the sound that came out was more of a sob.

"I came to find you. The sheriff arrested Hooper for killing Little Joe. You can come home now."

Dean gave a small hop and dropped to the ground in front of the crevice. He looked at me, curled inside like a mouse.

"You can come out of there."

I nodded thanks and stumbled to my feet. I found a smooth stone in the clearing the height of my knees and dropped onto it. Dean squatted on his heels in front of me.

He cocked his head to the side, looking at me. "Hooper killed Little Joe?"

"Loy arrested him. My dad is coming up behind me, and we wanted to give you a lift back to your place. There is a storm coming."

His blue eyes were so pale they looked like river ice. He traced an imaginary line across the palm of his hand with one finger, thinking. His forearms looked permanently tanned. His face was clean, but his clothes were mostly dirty. He was propped on his heels, absolutely still, his lean frame perfectly balanced. It didn't seem to me that a week alone in the wilderness had done him any harm.

I noticed that he wasn't wearing a coat.

"Hooper. That doesn't seem right to me somehow," he said, still tracing his palm. He turned his head back towards the trail. "You said you wanted to drive me back to Fable?"

"We do. If you would like to come with us," I said. My hands had finally stopped trembling.

"That sounds fine," he said.

I had finally caught my breath, and I stood up to see if I could catch a glimpse of my father.

Dean shifted his bow to his left hand, and I noticed that it was strung. He carried a quiver of arrows at his waist, and it occurred to me I'd never seen anyone keep their arrows in such a way before. Usually, the quiver was strapped to the back, but Dean kept his quiver on his hip, like a quick-draw gunslinger.

He wasn't shivering in spite of not wearing a jacket.

"Where's your coat?" I asked.

He thought for a moment, as if trying to remember. "I took it off and left it on a tree."

He stood up and laced his bow beneath one leg smoothly to unstring it.

"Why did you do that?" I asked.

He crouched down again and held the bow across his knees. "I didn't want it to get in the way of my draw," he said.

"Were you out hunting?" I asked, frowning.

"No. I was watching you."

I felt my legs shake again, and I sat back down.

So when I'd told Willy I was saving his life, I hadn't been bluffing after all.

Dean looked above us, and I followed his gaze. I saw the mouth of the mine shaft high overhead, a maw of dark stone cut out of the smooth face of the cliff. It was at least thirty feet above the clearing, and the rock face leading up to the shaft entrance looked too smooth to climb.

"I guess I can leave everything there for next time," he said.

"I don't think we have time to get it down anyway," I told him.

He glanced down the trail. "No. Nathan's here now."

I stood up and felt relief flood my chest with warmth when I saw my father come up the path and walk into the clearing.

He came straight to my side and put a hand on my shoulder. "You all right? I saw the Lazy Ox-Yoke hands coming down. I know they gave you trouble because they were nice to me."

"They gave me trouble," I admitted.

His face changed from worry to anger in an instant. "Did you see it?" he asked, looking at Dean.

Dean nodded. "Yes, sir. I was watching her."

My father relaxed slightly, looking a bit relieved. "We better get moving. I've got a feeling the four of them might be waiting for us to come back down."

Dean tilted his head back and searched the sky. "It will snow before we can get to your truck."

"I hope it does. It might persuade those four bastards to leave."

My father put an arm over my shoulder and pulled me away from the clearing. We started down the trail, and I took the middle, with Dean bringing up the rear.

We walked fast. My toes were aching in my boots after only a few minutes. The descent was so steep my feet slid to the front of my boots with each step. I'd be an achy mess in the morning.

We came to the spot the Pinkertons had harassed me, and Dean vanished from view for a few moments. He reappeared wearing a heavy brown coat, shiny with oil and age. It was greased heavily so it would be waterproof. His quiver of arrows was carefully hung from one shoulder now instead of at his hip, and he carried his bow in his left hand.

My father didn't slow his pace to wait for Dean, and he caught us easily as we made our way down the trail anyway. But I was practically jogging to keep up.

Halfway down the mountain, it started to snow. The flakes came down in slow, lazy clumps. It was wet snow, heavy and soggy. That meant it would be twice as cold after I was soaked through.

"How much longer?" I asked. If I never saw this stretch of mountain again, I wouldn't miss it.

"Another forty minutes," my father said.

"Nathan, think I'll go ahead," Dean said.

We stopped, mercifully, and my father glanced up and down the trail with a worried expression. "Probably best," he said to Dean.

"Do you want to take my bow, Nathan?" Dean asked.

My father shook his head. "I'm no good with them. If those Lazy Ox-Yoke hands want to give us grief, there's not much we can do about it. I didn't bring a rifle today because I didn't think I would need it."

"You didn't need it," Dean said.

He turned away from us and moved down the trail, setting a pace I would never be able to keep. I pulled my hat tighter over my ears.

"I don't think we need to worry about running into them again," I said.

"Oh? Why's that?" my father asked.

"All four of them are afraid of Dean. They won't stick around. I think they have some other revenge in mind."

"Because it would be more fun for them to jump us some other time?" he asked.

"Because they are down there trashing your pickup truck right now," I said, walking again.

He blew out his breath. "I just got new windshield wipers put on that thing."

We reached the trailhead in just over two hours. Going down was a lot quicker than going up, but I would be paying for it for days.

When we broke through the trees at last, we saw Dean waiting for us beside the truck. "They were gone when I got here, Nathan."

My guess had been correct; the ranch hands had opted for the passive aggressive form of payback. All four tires of the truck had been slashed and were completely flat. We wouldn't be driving it out today.

My father sighed and leaned against the grill guard. "I'm worn out. Dean, why don't you go down to Tatiana's and ask to use her phone?"

"She doesn't like me, Nathan."

"Why not?"

"She thinks I eat her sheep."

My father stared at the ground for a moment.

I took off my soaked gloves and stuffed them in my coat pocket. I slipped my spare pair over my freezing fingers, turned towards the road, and headed down the foothills towards Tatiana's house without saying a word. Somebody had to go get help. I nominated myself.

I could feel them both staring at me.

"Go with her, would you?" my father asked. I heard as he climbed inside the cab of the truck and started the engine. He couldn't drive it anywhere, but that didn't stop him from using it to warm himself up.

I struggled to walk through the slick mud, falling down twice the closer we got to the base of the foothills. Dean caught up to me easily, helped me up, not saying anything, just pulling me to my feet with no expression. I noticed that his boots were smooth as tanned leather on the soles. How he had managed not to fall at all while I'd found myself on my butt twice was a mystery to me.

I was cold, wet from the snowfall, and angry. Dean patiently strolled beside me in complete silence. He never seemed like he was at the mercy of the elements, the way I always felt. He moved across the mud soaked ground with ease. My arms shot out to my sides as I slipped again, and I waved frantically as I tried to keep my footing.

Dean held out a hand to steady me and kept me from hitting the wet ground.

"Thanks," I said.

He had every right to be impatient, but he gave no sign of it. I was slowing him down. But he placidly eased back the pace, taking the time to get me to Tatiana's house in one piece.

Her old homestead was lit with two cheerful porch lights. The porch was so wide it was more like a deck attached to the full length of the house, and it wrapped around three sides of the structure. It was an old house, but she had sunk a fortune into it to refurbish the place to its original splendor. I walked up the steps of her wide porch and knocked on the door, noticing that Dean lingered several yards behind me.

Tatiana opened the door, and when she saw me she registered surprise, and then sympathy.

"Got car trouble?" she asked.

"You could say that," I said.

She waved me inside, and I was grateful beyond expression when she closed the door behind me. She went to retrieve her phone, and I leaned against the door while I waited.

Out of the corner of my eye I saw Dean through the window. He stood in the yard holding out his hand.

I leaned closer to the glass, so I could see more clearly.

He held out his right hand at eye level, palm facing the sky, his arm darting from side to side haphazardly. I squinted in the fading light, trying to see what he was doing.

As I watched him, understanding dawned.

He was catching snowflakes with his bare hand, watching as they melted on his fingers, and then catching more.

He was playing in the snow, his longbow held at his side at the ready.

In the blue twilight Dean looked like he was standing in a field of stars, catching them on his fingers.

CHAPTER 13

Tatiana handed me the phone, and for one horrible moment I had no idea who I should call.

Loy? He had better things to do than drive over the mountain in a snowstorm to rescue a woman who had recently caused him enormous trouble. Finn? I would have called Finn, but I didn't know how.

I stared at the phone. It hit me with sudden ferocity that being in a relationship with a man who wouldn't allow me to contact him when I needed him was not really a relationship. It was convenient for him. He had the excuse of his job to prevent him from being available. But in reality, it was simply a reason, not an excuse. There was no excuse for his behavior.

I punched the button on the phone and dialed a number with my thumb.

I held the phone to my ear and waited. It rang twice.

"Leif Gable."

"Hi, Leif. Are you busy?"

"I am never too busy for you," he said.

"We have a bit of a problem," I told him.

"Are you stuck someplace?"

"Good and stuck. If I give you directions, can you drive over the mountain?"

I heard the sounds of rummaging. He was searching for a pen. "I'm ready."

I explained carefully how to reach Deep Creek Ranch and hung up the phone with the assurance that Leif would be arriving in about an hour.

I handed Tatiana the phone when she left the glow of her cozy fireplace to check on me.

"Leif Gable is on his way to get us," I said.

"You know, you can tell your father he doesn't have to stand outside to wait," she told me.

I hesitated, but I decided the truth was the best course of action.

"That's not my father," I said, looking outside.

Tatiana glared through the glass. "Is that Dean Tisdale in my front yard?" she asked.

"Yes."

Tatiana crossed her arms and worked her lips like she was chewing a piece of wood. "Child, I cannot tell you how much I wish you and Nathan would stay away from him."

"I don't believe that Dean has ever eaten one of your sheep."

"Oh? And why would you say that?" she asked, obviously not convinced.

"Because they are too easy to kill," I said.

That made her pause. She unfolded her arms and leaned over to peer out the window. She watched Dean standing in the yard, his head cocked to the side like he was listening to the night.

"Well, maybe there is something to that," she said.

"Besides which, he saved my life you know," I told her.

I could see her arguing with herself in her mind. Whatever it was she knew about Dean seemed to be at war with my opinion of the man.

"I had a blue roan horse like him once," she said. "The darn thing was drawn to the mean."

I had heard the expression before, but I wasn't exactly sure what it meant. I knew it was a term horse trainers used.

She saw me looking puzzled and explained. "When a horse is drawn to the mean, they are wild. You can't train 'em. They usually end up a pasture pony or dog food. They won't be ridden, and they are more comfortable being free than they are in a stall. You can chase them all day and never catch them."

"What happened to your blue roan?" I asked.

Her lips twitched. "Should have shot him, but couldn't bring myself to do it. I let him go. He's out in the basin now, running a heard of mustangs around like he owns the place."

She looked back at me, her jaw rigid. "I know you and your dad are fond of Dean. But would you promise me one thing?"

I kept my expression open. "If I can."

She looked at me, her eyes intense. "Don't ever be alone with him, Marley. Dean can be a little...funny when it comes to women."

I shook my head. "Funny, how?"

"Funny like, crazy," she said.

I wasn't going to argue with her, but I know my face showed my reluctance to believe her.

She sighed and leaned a weathered hand against the wall. "He can be very protective. Beyond what's reasonable. Just don't ever be alone with him so that he can get attached to you, that's all."

"Sure. I don't think that will be a problem," I said, as reassuringly as possible.

She seemed satisfied.

I thanked her again for her hospitality, and after I had warmed up sufficiently I went back outside to tell Dean we had a ride coming. I noticed that Tatiana kept a watchful eye on the window while I stood beside him.

"Someone will be here to pick us up soon," I said.

He looked at me, expressionless and still.

It occurred to me that I really didn't know that much about the man. I knew that he had become an orphan at the age of fifteen. His father, a man even more eccentric than Dean, had died suddenly one night of a massive bleeding stomach ulcer, leaving his son alone in the world.

Dean hadn't known what to do when his father died. So, he wrapped the body in a plastic tarp and buried it in the backyard of their modest home in Fable and never bothered to tell a soul. It took a year for anyone to notice.

By the time the investigation wrapped up and his father's body had been examined and reburied in the tiny cemetery in Fable, Dean was on the verge of turning seventeen. A sympathetic and well-intentioned neighbor of Dean's, who was a retired paralegal secretary, helped him file papers making him an emancipated minor. He managed to dodge the foster care system. He continued to go to school, his grades sufficient to allow him to advance to his junior year, and then he dropped out, dropped through the cracks, and never set foot inside a school again. The house was paid for, so Dean was somewhat secure.

Some speculated that Dean's father had once operated a thriving marijuana business and had stashed a pile of money in a coffee can someplace. But up in Fable, everyone speculated that their neighbor was into some sort of illegal behavior and nobody was very friendly to each other. But by the time Dean turned seventeen, the Tisdale house had such a reputation he could have left the front door wide open, and not one person would have dared venture inside to search for hidden money. Any boy who had the

courage to deal with his own father's death without asking anyone for help was obviously someone not to be trifled with. Not
long after that, Dean had rescued me from the forest, securing his
reputation as a person more comfortable in the wild than he was
with people.

No one knew who Dean's mother was. She had never been
mentioned, seen, or discussed.

Trapping was the only way he knew to make a living. Since
his father had survived by trapping, that was how Dean survived.
Without knowing it, I had been staring at him while thinking.

He noticed me looking at him, and he cocked his head to the side.

"Do you have a man, Miss Marley?" he asked.

My eyebrows arched. "Yes. I do have a man."

He considered that. "Why are you out here looking for me,
and he's not here with you?"

That was a very good question. "His job keeps him busy."

He seemed perplexed by my answer. "It must be an important
job."

I wanted to talk about something else, anything other than my
miserable love life.

"Where were you Tuesday night?" I asked.

He shifted his bow to his right hand and slid his left hand
inside his coat. "What night was that?"

"When Little Joe was killed. Where were you?"

He watched a particularly fat clump of snowflakes drift to the
ground. "I was there."

That got my attention. "You were there? In our alfalfa field?"

He looked at the ground, remembering. "Yes. I had set my
trap, and I was walking home."

I waited for him to tell me more, but he said nothing.

"Did you see Hooper kill Little Joe?" If he had, this whole

mess could have been avoided from the start, if only people had asked the right questions instead of jumping to conclusions.

"I didn't see Hooper. I only saw Joe lying in the field."

So, he had arrived after Little Joe was already dead.

"What did you do?" I asked.

"I thought he shouldn't be left there alone. So I put him on your porch."

He probably still thought that I lived in the caretaker's cottage.

"Were you thinking that no one would find him if you left him in the pasture?" I asked.

"No. I was thinking that the bears would find him before you did."

I felt my stomach flip-flop at that thought. It hadn't snowed yet, the night that Joseph had been killed. The bears wouldn't go into hibernation until it started to snow, so the location of their den would be hidden when they finally went inside. This year the snow had come very late to Killdeer, and that meant the bears were still prowling for last minute meals. If Little Joe's body had been discovered by a bear, there might not have been much left for Loy to examine.

"That was a nice thing to do," I said. I didn't know what else to say. I could have lectured him about knocking on doors and actually talking to another person before he started to move bodies around, but I knew it would be pointless.

Dean heard something that I didn't hear, and his eyes darted to a distant point across the yard and stopped at the edge of the foothills.

He watched the place for a moment, then seemed satisfied that whatever it was wouldn't be a bother to us, and he went back to watching the snow.

"You said Hooper killed Little Joe," he said, sounding confused.

I hopped from foot to foot, getting my blood going so my feet wouldn't turn into icicles.

"That's what Loy told me. Hooper said he was shooting arrows into the field that night. It was a contest to see who could shoot the farthest. He accidentally hit Joseph and killed him."

Dean's eyes narrowed as he pondered what I'd said. He shook his head once. "That doesn't seem right."

I wondered what Dean meant when he said it wasn't right. His interpretation of the events was probably very different than most.

"What's not right about it?" I asked.

Dean looked at his boots. "If he was practicing, there must have been a lot of arrows in the field. But I didn't see a lot of them."

I had to think hard about what he was saying. Dean must have thought that Hooper had shot several arrows into the field, and then walked out to retrieve them one by one until he stumbled across Joe and realized he had accidentally killed the boy.

"I think Hooper only shot one arrow into the field," I said.

Dean looked at me, his face puzzled. "One arrow?"

"That's what I was told. And another boy shot one arrow, too. They wanted to see who could shoot farther."

He shifted his bow to his other hand. "That doesn't seem right," he said.

It was my turn to be confused.

"It was an accident, Dean. What doesn't seem right to you?"

His gaze wandered around the yard as if he were judging spaces and distances. "You know what the chances are that Hooper could hit Little Joe in a pasture that big with two arrows?"

I shook my head.

He looked at me, his eyes calculating. "About a million to one."

I suddenly had a very bad feeling.

"A million to one," I said.

"I don't know. More than that," he told me. He seemed certain.

173

"It was an accident," I said again, not feeling at all sure I was right.

"No. It wasn't," he said.

I didn't want to have this conversation. I didn't like where it was taking my imagination. Try as I might, I couldn't stop myself. I just had to ask.

"What makes you think it wasn't an accident?"

He shook the snowflakes off his bow. He held it up as if he would draw back an arrow, and he aimed it straight across the field.

"See how I'm holding this, Miss Marley?" he asked.

I took a step back, so I could see his stance. "Yes."

He pantomimed drawing his bow and aimed it straight towards the foothills. "Where's this arrow going?" he asked.

I followed the line. "Out there. Towards the grass."

He nodded. "But, how far is it going to go?"

I tried to guess. "I'm not sure. Maybe, a hundred yards?"

"It's going to go about seventy yards," he said.

I frowned. "That's not very far."

"The air slows them down," he said.

"So, you don't think Hooper could shoot an arrow that far?" I asked.

"I think he didn't shoot like that," Dean said, shifting his stance.

He lifted his bow at a sharp angle, about forty-five degrees, and aimed for the sky. He pantomimed drawing back.

"Where's this arrow going to go?" he asked.

I followed his line. "Out into the grass, like the other one."

He relaxed his arms. "Yes. But how far?"

I shook my head. "I'm not sure."

"About two hundred yards. When you shoot up, they go farther."

"So, why don't you think it was an accident?" I asked again. I had no idea what he was trying to show me.

He lowered his bow and slid his right hand back inside his coat. "Because a clout shot like that is not easy. At night it would be impossible."

"I'm not sure I understand," I said.

"He was standing outside the pasture shooting into it, is that what he said?" Dean asked.

I was trying to imagine how it might have gone. "I know some high school kids had a bonfire party over at the culvert that night," I told him.

Dean nodded. "I know where it is. It's fifty yards from the road. They would probably stand at the end of the culvert and shoot at the pasture."

"That sounds like something drunk kids would do."

"That field is forty acres. If Hooper shot straight across the road from the culverts, his arrow wouldn't make it. It would go across the fence and not much further."

"So, you think he shot it up in the air, in an arc, and they could see whose arrow would make it across the road into the field?"

He wiped a clump of snow off his soaked hair. "Yes. Up in the air. That's called a clout shot."

I tried to slow down and be patient. I still didn't understand what was bothering him.

"Dean, why don't you pretend for a moment that I don't know anything about archery?"

"Hooper took a clout shot," he said patiently.

I shrugged hard with both shoulders. "Yes. Okay, he shot it up in the air."

"So, why was the hit a wand shot?"

I looked at him, confused. "A wand shot? What does that mean?"

"That arrow was straight in Little Joe's chest. It wasn't at an angle. If Hooper shot his arrow up in the air there was only one way it would hit Joe straight in the heart like that."

I was beginning to see what he meant.

I could imagine it in my mind now, and I didn't like what my imagination was telling me. "He had to have been lying down."

Dean nodded. "Like I said. The chances of Hooper hitting Joe, lying down in the middle of your field using two arrows, is about a million to one."

I saw headlights come down the road towards us. I looked over at Dean quickly, and I touched his arm.

"Listen. Let's keep this between you and me for now. Okay?"

He shook snow from his shoulders. "Sure."

A gleaming black SUV pulled up beside us, and the passenger side door swung open. My father beamed at us from inside.

"Hop in. It's got heated seats."

We climbed in the backseat gratefully. "Thanks for coming to get us," I told Leif.

He looked us over carefully. "Everybody in?"

"We're soaked. These seats will be a mess," I said.

He gave me a smile. "It's fine. This used to be Virginia's car and the back seat is stained from wet dog anyway."

We headed down the road. I had to help Dean buckle his seat belt.

We argued about who would get dropped off first, finally settling on getting Dean back up to Fable for the first stop.

The snow was already piling up in the road by the time we reached his tiny house in Fable.

"Thank you for bringing me home," Dean said as he stepped out. Fat white flakes collected on him at once.

I leaned over and grabbed his arm before he could close the door. "Hey. I will come by to check on you when it stops snowing."

He looked at my hand. "Why?"

"In case you need anything. Loy might want to come by and ask you a few questions, and if you like, I can be there to help you out."

I really wanted to ask him for a favor, but I wasn't about to do it in front of my father.

Dean rested his hand on the open door. "That would be fine."

He closed the car door and went inside his dark little house, looking back at the three of us once to see if we were watching him.

We left when the lights came on.

"He's quiet," said Leif, nodding in Dean's direction.

My father laughed. "That's why I like him so much."

I sat back against the warm car seat, thinking.

"How long is it supposed to snow?" I asked.

My father glanced at me over his shoulder. "Until tomorrow sometime. We should see the wind start to pick up soon. Why?"

I looked out my window at the trees as they flashed by. "There is something I've got to do."

"What's that?" he asked.

"Just a math problem," I said.

I would need help with this math problem. I wasn't qualified to answer the questions rattling around in my head. This problem required recruiting the experts. Luckily, I knew where to find them.

CHAPTER 14

Three days later the snow finally stopped falling. It hadn't been easy to wait for conditions to improve, but I'd resisted the urge to go out in bad weather to begin my experiment.

Killdeer was transformed by the storm. The grey, depressing landscape was now a white paradise of snowdrifts and icicles; the dead and dormant trees groaned under the weight of heavy winter frosting. Occasionally, off in the distance, a tired branch broke and fell from a tree, sending a muffled thump through the forest.

Everyone, including the weatherman, had expected the snow to stop falling by Monday afternoon. But as I stood on Leif's porch watching the sky clear at last, I glanced at my watch and noted with irritation that it was now Thursday morning.

"Finally," I said, heading back inside the house to retrieve my coat.

Leif was in his office. I could hear the crack and thunk, crack and thunk of an intense game of billiards going on behind the closed door. I'd caught a glimpse inside his office the day before and had seen a great hulking pool table in the center of the room. It looked less like it had been set up, and more like it had been constructed. Leif said when he had a nasty problem at work, playing pool while he thought things over helped him to concentrate.

We'd come to an uneasy agreement about the car.

I'd said there was absolutely no way, under any circumstances, that I would even consider driving Leif's BMW. I said it was too much to expect him to allow me to use the car and that it was impossible for me to see myself driving such an expensive vehicle that didn't belong to me, and I would collapse under the weight of guilt if I were responsible for it and anything happened. It was out of the question. I refused to drive it.

Leif had smiled and handed me the keys. He didn't argue; he just made things go the way he wanted them to go. He said it made him feel good to do something nice for me, and that had been the end of it.

I was driving the BMW.

At least it wasn't the Mercedes.

Leif had called a tow truck from Parkman to come and haul away my Honda. They said it would be two days before they could reach us. I still hadn't decided which repair shop I'd use, so it didn't bother me that they needed some time to catch up with all of the wrecks that had happened as a result of the snowstorm. I couldn't afford to replace my Honda, so I had decided on an engine repair. That would probably wipe out my savings account. But I had to be able to drive if I was going to get a job again in a week.

I had just hung up the telephone. Irene and I had been trying to coordinate this operation I had in mind since the day before yesterday, and at last she called with the news I had been waiting to hear. The two coal bed methane workers I had asked her to keep an eye out for had just come into the café.

I pulled on my heavy snow boots and went out the door, afraid of what I would find if I managed to pull this experiment off. I was also afraid of what I wouldn't find.

Lil's was packed, as usual, and I parked the BMW as far away from the other vehicles as possible while still technically in the parking lot. I was paranoid that something would happen to the car. Glancing through the window, I saw the two guys from the weather station—*monitoring facility*—sitting in a booth. They were arguing about something.

When I went inside, Irene was staring at the black SUV shamelessly. "Good God. Have you got a few hundred pot plants in your basement that I don't know about?"

I sat at the counter on my usual stool. "Why does everyone assume I am a drug dealer when I am seen in a nice car?"

She propped her elbows on the counter. "Because everyone knows a legitimate business person could never afford to drive something like that."

"I'll have you know a legitimate business person owns that car," I said.

She poured me a cup of coffee without asking if I wanted one. "I'm not sure you could call the Parkman car rental agency legitimate."

I should have kept my mouth shut, but I just didn't know how to do that. "I'll have you know that car belongs to Leif Gable. He's letting me borrow it."

Irene stared at me, her mouth partly open, holding the coffeepot inches away from the warmer. She seemed to have forgotten what she was doing while in the middle of doing it.

"That's Leif's car?" she asked.

I felt myself turn pink.

"It used to belong to Virginia. He's only letting me drive it until I can get my Honda fixed."

"Virginia. His ex-wife? Oh, Honey…"

"He's a nice man, and he's doing me a favor."

She finally managed to replace the coffeepot on the warmer.

"Doing you a favor."

"Come on, Irene. Leif is nothing more than a very nice man. You cannot accuse him of having an agenda."

"He is a very nice man," she said. "I can't argue with you about that."

I glared at her. "But…"

She held up her hands. "But it seems like it's not his responsibility to take care of you, that's all."

"He enjoys helping people," I explained.

She took the stool out from underneath her counter and propped herself up on one butt cheek. "Older man, distinguished, got lots of money…"

I rolled my eyes. "Oh, here we go."

"Vulnerable young woman, destitute, adorable…"

"He's not that much older than me," I said defensively.

"Marley. Which room are you sleeping in?"

"What do you mean, which room?"

"Which bedroom are you sleeping in while you are staying there?"

"The upstairs bedroom." I smelled a rat.

"The master bedroom?" she asked, a lilt in her voice.

I crossed my arms. "So?"

"Ah, poor Finn," she said. "He never stood a chance."

"I have no idea what you are talking about," I said.

She leaned down and nudged me quickly. "Hey. They are leaving."

I looked back and saw Will and Seth headed for the door.

I snatched a last sip of coffee and slid off my stool. "Gotta go. I'll be back later. Thanks for calling me."

I caught up with them in the parking lot and strolled along beside them.

"Hey, would you two have time today to do me a favor?"

They slowed down, glancing back and forth between each other and me.

Seth pushed up his glasses. "When? 'Cause, we have important stuff going on, and all."

I smiled. "Right now? It will only take a minute. I've got a math problem I need help with."

Seth looked around the parking lot for an escape.

"Are you still Finn's girlfriend?" Will was looking at me suspiciously. "He just ignores me when I ask him about you."

"If you come with me, you two can meet a guy who has roped a bear."

They swiveled their heads towards each other and back at me in unison.

Seth threw his hands out. "Well? Let's go!"

I led them to the BMW and pushed the toggle button that unlocked the car. It chirped and the headlights flashed once.

I cringed, waiting for a sarcastic comment about the opulent vehicle.

"My grandma has a car like this," Seth said as he bullied his way into the front seat.

Will reluctantly climbed into the back. "The one at Caltech?"

Seth nodded. "She likes it because it's easier to climb into than her Jag."

"Your grandma has a Jaguar?" I asked.

"Sure."

"Is she a professor there?" I asked.

Seth shoved his glasses back up on his nose. "Yeah, right. Like you can afford a Jag and be a professor. She's head of the Investment Office."

We drove down Main Street and headed towards Fable. The

roads were plowed but still slick, and I drove carefully. I pulled up in front of Dean's little house and put the BMW in park.

"You two wait here. I'll be right back," I said.

I knocked on Dean's door and put my hands back inside my pockets. The sky was clear but the air was frigid. Ice crystals drifted through the air.

Dean was home. I knew because I had called his next-door neighbor before I had talked to Irene. She said that she had seen his lights on all morning.

I knocked again.

The door opened. Dean smoothed his scruffy hair when he saw me.

"Miss Marley. How are you doing?"

"I'm doing fine. I hope I'm not bothering you, but I was wondering if you could come with me over to our alfalfa field and help me out with something?"

He looked inside the car. The two astrophysicists were wrestling over the radio.

"Sure. I could come with you."

"Could you bring your bow with you?" I asked.

He looked back over his shoulder. "Which one?"

"Ah. Well, how about you bring one that might be like Hooper's bow."

He scratched his forehead. "I can't do that. I don't own a compound bow."

"Do you have one that can shoot as far as a compound bow?" I asked.

"Yes."

"I'd bring that one, then."

He shut the front door, and I went back to the car.

"Now, Dean is a nice guy, but he is a little odd," I said when I climbed back in the car.

Will leaned forward in the seat. "Odd, like he raises box turtles for a hobby, or odd like he builds pipe bombs?"

"Just be nice to him. He might be a little shy, that's all."

Dean came out, dressed for the weather in heavy snow boots and toting a sleek recurve bow and a quiver.

He climbed into the backseat beside Will and set the bow across both of their laps.

I was so focused on the task at hand, I didn't introduce them to each other.

Seth had turned in his seat and was unabashedly staring at Dean over the top of his glasses.

"Dude. What happened when you roped that bear?"

Dean cocked his head. "Which one?"

Will and Seth looked at each other like they had just won the lottery.

"Oh, man! Seriously? You gotta tell us about it," Seth said.

"Guys, guys," I said, interrupting the interrogation. "Can we focus on the math problem, please?"

They looked deflated, but they settled down.

Will was trying to figure out what to do with his hands. He was afraid to rest them on top of the bow, so he held them out at his waist, looking like a praying mantis.

"Here is the problem," I said.

I slowed down, going around the tight turns as we headed out of Fable.

"I need to know the probability of something," I told them.

Seth stopped staring at Dean and looked at me. "Sure. What are the variables?"

"Our alfalfa field is about forty acres square. Well, it's not really square. It's longer than it is wide. But what I need to know is, what are the chances that an arrow, shot at random, would land in a certain place inside that forty acres?"

"An arrow?" asked Will.

"Yes. How likely is it that one arrow, shot at random, would hit a target roughly six inches square?"

"Why six square inches?" asked Will.

I glanced in the review mirror. "That's approximately the size of the human heart."

The inside of the car grew very quiet.

Dean shifted in his seat. "A human heart is a little bigger than that, Miss Marley."

I cleared my throat. "Let's use that number, just for the experiment."

Nobody argued, so I went on.

"If a person is standing outside the field and shoots an arrow at random into that field, can you two tell me what the chances are that they would kill someone? And to do that, they would need to hit that six-inch-square target."

Seth craned his head around to look at Will. "Buffon's needle. We can adapt that formula."

Will sat forward. "We need to know the length of the projectile."

Dean pulled an arrow out of his quiver and handed it to him.

"Ah…" Will said, holding it like it was a snake.

"Twenty-eight inches long," Dean said.

Will handed the arrow back to Dean, using two fingers to hold it like it was contaminated. "So, we have a grid size of forty acres. We need to have grid squares intersect every twenty-eight inches so the projectile and the lines are of equal value."

Seth craned his head back to look at Will. "Since the length of the projectile and the distance between the lines is equal, we can use two n for the probability."

"But our target area is only six square inches. So our probability will be smaller," Will said. He had lowered his hands. They were resting on Dean's bow. Apparently, math did break down barriers after all.

"Much smaller," Seth said.

"We need to adapt this to fit with the target size," Will told him.

"Okay, there are 6,272,640 square inches in one acre," Will said.

I turned to look at him. "How in the world…?"

"Simple. One acre has 43,560 square feet. One square foot has 144 square inches…"

"Yes, we know," said Seth. "What we need to know is the number of possible events."

"I *know* we need to know the number of possible events," Will said.

Seth drummed his fingers on the dashboard. "If we adapt Buffon's needle, we can use two n times one, divided by the number of events, and get our probability."

I kept driving and stopped trying to follow the conversation. If I listened to them too hard, there was a very real danger that my brain would start leaking out of my ears.

Will puckered his lips while he thought. "It doesn't need to be that complex. We can just divide the grid by the size of the possible event. So that would be 41,817,600 to 1."

"What if there are two arrows?" I asked.

"The chances that you could hit a person standing in a forty-acre field are…"

"A million to one?" asked Dean.

Will shook his head. "Not that good. Not even close. With two arrows, two chances, the probability that you could hit a target six inches square is more like 20,908,800 to 1."

"So, not very good?" I asked.

"Let me put it like this," Seth said. "You have a greater chance of getting struck by lightning while you are having sex with the pope after just winning the lottery."

"So, it's pretty unlikely," I said.

"More like, almost virtually impossible," Seth told me.

We had arrived at the field, and I stopped the car. I shut off the engine and looked out over the expanse of white.

"Dean, I think I'm going to owe you for the cost of a couple of arrows," I said.

"Why is that, Miss Marley?"

I noticed that the snow was about three feet deep across the pasture. "Because I don't think we will ever find them again after you shoot them out there."

We climbed out of the car, and the snow buried me almost up to my knees. Luckily it was powdery soft, or we would have gotten stuck, too.

The road had been plowed. We gathered in the center of the cleared roadway, and I shaded my eyes with one hand while I searched the pasture.

"Where was it that you found Little Joe?" I asked.

Dean let his eyes drift over the tree line until he saw what he was looking for. He lifted the end of his bow and used it to point.

"That big ponderosa? Come this way straight out from it and stop about a quarter of the way across the field. Close to 150 yards from here."

I turned and looked behind us towards the spot across the road where I thought the bonfire party had taken place.

The huge, twisted metal culvert lay beside the creek on the other side of the fence, directly across from our field. The culvert had been damaged beyond use, but it was still sound enough to

188

climb inside and was a perfect hideout.

"That happened in '98 when we had that horrible flood," I said, marveling that a small creek could become a raging river with only a couple of days' worth of rain fueling it.

"What is that thing?" asked Seth. He was looking at the remains of the culvert.

"Well, that used to be a galvanized culvert almost six feet tall. If you lay two of them side by side in a creek, you can cover them with dirt and use the top for a bridge. But this one was washed out and destroyed in the flood. It must have been too much trouble to haul it away."

The culvert was twisted beyond use but still maintained enough original shape so that, if you weren't too picky, you could sit inside. I knew from experience that the other side of the culvert had a clearing of sorts, home for a bonfire pit and probably the largest collection of cheap discarded beer cans in the county.

Mostly, the place was an eyesore.

"You think that a group of kids were over there, and they decided to shoot arrows into your field? And with two tries they killed another kid?" Will asked.

"One of them confessed," I said.

Seth and Will shared a skeptical look.

"Dean, could you show us?" I asked.

He straddled his bow and strung it with one smooth motion. He drew an arrow from his quiver and slid it into place.

"How do you want me to shoot first?" he asked.

"Straight across, like you are shooting for the trees," I said.

Will and Seth stepped back and watched with wide eyes as Dean pulled back the arrow and released the string with a practiced hand. As he had predicted earlier, the arrow flew about fifty yards and then plunged into the snow. The arrow hadn't even traveled half the distance necessary for it to reach the place Little Joe had died.

I studied the path the arrow had taken. If someone had fired an arrow like that, it was possible it could have hit Joe in the chest. Possible, but not very likely. But the person doing the shooting would have had to have been standing in the field with him.

"Now, shoot it up in the air like you showed me the other night," I said.

Dean nocked another arrow, lifted his bow towards the sky and released.

The arrow sailed up, slowed slightly, and arched towards the field. It headed for the ground, tip down, and disappeared in the snow. It looked like it landed close, give or take a few yards, to the place Joe had been standing when he had been killed. Once again, Dean had shown his prediction to be right.

"Dean, which way was Little Joe facing? I mean, where were his feet pointed?"

"South. His feet were that way, facing that stand of alfalfa Nathan never mows down."

"But, that's perpendicular to the bonfire party," Will said, looking from the field to the culverts.

"So, what, he was lying on his back with his feet facing south and an arrow comes out of the east and nails him?" Seth asked.

"That's why it didn't seem right to me," Dean said.

"Why?" I asked.

"Because it was a wand shot," he replied.

"Straight in, not angled," I said to Will and Seth. They mouthed *oh's* of understanding.

I tried to imagine what the pasture would have looked like the night of the party. I closed my eyes and concentrated.

"There hadn't been any snow," I said. "The ground was dry,

mostly. I remember that there wasn't any wind when we got to Wendy's house. It was warm for this time of year."

I let my mind recreate the field at night, and something occurred to me.

"Hey, Dean. Was there a moon up? Could you see the field at all?"

He shook his head. "No moon after midnight that night."

"But, was there a moon before midnight?" I asked.

He thought about it for a moment. "A quarter moon."

"It would have been pretty bright in the field, then," I said.

"Still was when I was here. There were lots and lots of stars," he said.

I opened my eyes, and they were resting on the crane nesting area. "You said his feet were pointed that way, towards the south. Why was he facing the south?"

"Something was drawing his attention," Will said, shrugging.

"Because *someone* was drawing his attention," I said. "He was talking to someone. Or he saw someone. But, what was he doing out there? Why was Joe in the pasture and not at the party?"

Nobody had an answer for that. It was the one piece of information that I didn't have.

I started to ask another question when I saw a black Jeep come down the road.

CHAPTER 15

"**A**h, crap," said Seth.

Both boys stood with their heads down like they had been caught sneaking out of the house by a strict parent.

Finn rolled to an abrupt stop beside us on the road and got out of his Jeep, slamming the door.

"Get your bloody carcasses back to the lab," he said to Will and Seth.

"Finn, it's my fault," I started to say.

"This is so beyond protocol," he told them, ignoring me completely.

"Hey, it's cool. She knows about the station, and she doesn't care," Seth said.

Will had clamped his mouth shut and had suddenly become wildly curious about his toes.

Finn lifted a rigid finger. "What she knows and what she is comfortable with isn't a factor in your procedures."

"Take it easy, man. We can't live like we don't exist. There is nothing to do here! We're in the middle of goddamn nowhere, so who's gonna care?" Seth said.

"Finn, I can explain," I said.

He shot me a withering glare and leaned towards me, inches from my face. "Stay out of this."

Dean took a step towards Finn. "Don't you talk to her like that."

Finn seemed to register Dean's presence for the first time. He scanned him briefly, and then dismissed him.

"You two get in the Jeep. I'm taking you back to your vehicle, and you are to report to the station immediately."

"No. Why are you being such a jerk?" Seth said.

Finn was astonished. "No? You cannot ignore a direct order from me. I can have your security clearance revoked."

"He's being such a jerk because he is mad at me," I said.

"We are not talking about this here," Finn said.

Dean was looking from Finn to me, and back to Finn. "This is your man?"

I crossed my arms, embarrassed and angry.

"Yes. At least, I think he still is," I said.

"I don't like him," Dean said.

"Neither do I," said Seth bitterly.

Finn looked around the circle of irritated faces. He looked at Dean again, his eyes locked on the strung longbow, and some animal instinct switched on. He took a step back. Dean was watching him like a snake watches a mouse.

Finn instantly changed from angry to intent. "Who are you?" he asked.

"He's with us," I said. "It's fine. We came out here to do an experiment. You don't need to be so upset."

Realizing that he had alienated the entire group, Finn managed to get himself under control, and he relaxed his stance. "You two know better than this. You can't associate with the locals. It's against policy."

"You seem to not have any trouble associating with the locals,"

Seth told him.

Finn's face turned crimson. "All right. I can understand want-ing to have some contact with other people from time to time. But would you please not make it a habit?"

"Make it a habit?" I said. "Is that what you are trying to avoid? Making me a habit?"

Will turned and walked to the other side of the road, keeping his back to us.

"Hey, Dean," Seth said, nudging him with a boot. "Show me and Will that culvert back there, would you?"

Dean stayed exactly where he was, watching Finn with slightly hooded eyes. He didn't say a word.

"Yo, dude. Come with me, why don't you?" Seth said, prodding Dean with two fingers.

Finally Dean glanced up at Seth and allowed himself to be led a few yards away.

Finn was looking more uncomfortable than I had ever seen him.

I tilted my head back and breathed out a sigh. "Is that why you don't show up for days and days at a time? Because it's against company policy to mingle?"

He didn't answer.

"That and it must be tough to let yourself feel something for another person. Because, who knows? I could get hurt and then you would be in the same spot you were in with Beth," I said.

His eyes flashed as he finally looked at me. "Please do not ever talk about that again."

"So, let me understand this," I said. I was doing the best I could to control my anger, and I was failing miserably. "You are not supposed to associate with the locals, and yet somehow you managed to do just that. On top of it, I remind you of the woman who got killed on your watch back in South Africa all those years ago. That's just great, Finn."

He was flexing his hands, his face sour. "It wasn't like that."

"Was I just a piece of ass?" I asked, beyond being under control.

"No. You were never…Marley my life is complicated."

"I was what, then? What am I to you?" I asked.

He rubbed his forehead, and his feet shifted. "I don't know."

"That's the first honest thing you have ever told me," I said.

He dropped his hands at his sides, looking defeated. "There is no way to communicate how impossible this situation is for me."

"So, what happens now?" I asked.

I wasn't about to make it easy for him. It was one thing to play at being a couple; it was another thing altogether to commit to someone.

Maybe it was selfish, but I wanted him to tell me he was committed, or at the very least tell me he wasn't.

"I don't know," he said again.

It was like a stone had settled in my stomach. I watched him standing in the road, swaying with indecision, unable to do the right thing.

"Finn, tell me what I need to hear," I said at last.

I was practically drawing him a picture. He opened his mouth, but no words came out. He watched me helplessly.

"All right," I said. "If that's the way it's got to be. I guess I will tell you what I need to hear."

A look of panic crossed his face. "Please think about this before you say anything. I never wanted to do anything to make your life difficult."

"But you did what was easy," I said. "Because it was too hard to do what was right."

"Can't we talk about this some more later?" he asked.

I considered asking Dean to shoot him, but it occurred to me that he probably would. I shook off the anger and realized that if someone was going to make a decision it would have to be me.

I pieced together what dignity I had left and tamped down my pain, my frustration, and did the best I could to let Finn off the hook with as much grace as I could muster.

"We don't need to talk about it anymore. I understand how important your work is to you. I know you wouldn't want to risk your job by doing something that was against the rules. It's okay. I think it would be better for us both if we were only friends."

I wanted him to argue with me. I wanted him to tell me that I was more important than his job, but I knew it was ridiculous to think such a thing.

His face washed over with obvious relief. "I can live with that. The last thing you need is for me to be stepping in it, mucking up your world for you."

I wanted to drop down in the snow and cry. I had given him an open window, and he had jumped through it like the whole house was on fire.

"Finn, if the timing was different, if you had been ready to want something more…"

"I know," he said quickly. "I know you would have. But believe me when I say I'm the last guy on the planet you want hanging round all the time."

We tried to smile at each other, and ended up both looking miserable and sad instead.

I stepped away from him. "I'll make sure the boys get back to their truck. Really, they never talk about work, and I think they cover their tracks pretty well."

He looked at Will and Seth, and he seemed to relax a little. "Maybe I am too hard on them. They have never had to live with security regulations before."

I didn't know what else to say. He was already shuffling towards his Jeep, and I could see he couldn't wait to end the conversation.

"So, I'll see you around," I said.

"Marley. If you ever need anything," he told me. "Anything. I can't be there the way you want, but..."

"I know how to find you," I said, although actually I didn't.

The cold air stung my eyes as they watered up. The last thing I was going to do was start sobbing in the middle of the road.

He got in his Jeep and flipped a U-turn, leaving me standing there watching him go. His Jeep's tires crunched through the snow as he drove away.

Dean had walked silently to stand beside me and was looking after Finn as he disappeared down the road.

"He's strange," Dean said.

I almost laughed. "Yes, he is. I told him I didn't want him to be my man anymore."

Dean stepped through his bow, bent the tip down and slipped the string off. "Good."

Will and Seth wandered over and stood beside Dean with eager expressions.

"So, would you want to come over now?" Seth asked.

"All right," Dean said.

"Are you sure this is such a good idea?" asked Will. "Finn might not like it."

I looked at the three of them, suspicious. "What are you up to?"

Seth bounced on the balls of his feet. "We can't use the lab computers for gaming. Some lame excuse about data contamination or something. So we rented a room at the Rock Stop Inn, and we set up a console there so we can play *Call of Duty: Black Ops*. Dean said he'd come with us and teach us how to shoot better."

"You are taking him to play video games?" I asked.

"Yeah, it'll be great," Seth said. He was already walking back to the car, Dean in tow.

I looked at Will, a skeptical expression on my face. "You know he is drawn to the mean," I said.

"That's all right then," Will told me.

I frowned. "You know what that is?"

"Sure. Dean is an outlier, an anomaly. An outlier is a phenomenon that exists outside the normal range of a pattern, and when it's drawn to the mean, the outlier exhibits a trend to become more like the others in the pattern. If Dean is drawn to the mean, it means he's strange, but that he is likely to become more normal if he's associated with other things that are normal."

I stared at Will, not having any idea how to respond to that. I guess we all had our own definition of "strange." Somehow, I felt sad at the thought of Dean becoming normal at all. I liked him the way he was. I decided I liked Tatiana's definition of the phrase a whole lot better than Will's.

Dean Tisdale playing video games with two of the brightest scientific minds of the age was an odd image in my head. I sighed and pulled out the car keys without a word.

Before we drove away I looked back across the pasture one more time and tried to piece together what I knew about the night Joe had been killed.

There was only one way that the arrow could have ended up killing Little Joe the way it had, if Hooper's story was true. Little Joe had to have been lying on the ground. Since that seemed practically impossible to me, the next best explanation was that someone had been standing in the field with him and had shot him at close range. Had Hooper done it and then concocted a story about it being an accident? Maybe. But I didn't think Hooper was smart enough to plan something so intricate.

The facts were not adding up. It all seemed too much to believe, that one of two randomly shot arrows could have accidentally killed Joseph. And I still didn't have a good explanation as to why he was in the pasture in the first place.

Unfortunately, the arrow experiment had only prompted more questions than it had answered.

I thought about Finn as I drove the boys back to their truck, and it was like being thrown from a horse and hitting the ground hard. I was surprised how much it hurt, considering I had only been dating him for a couple of months. But it did hurt.

I kept myself together long enough to leave my passengers in the parking lot at Lil's, thanking them for their help, and then I let myself fall apart while I drove to the ranch house.

Someday I would become a grown-up and stop running to my father whenever things got tough. But that wasn't going to happen today.

CHAPTER 16

My father set a cup of hot cocoa piled with marshmallows on the kitchen table in front of me.

"Thanks," I said. I wrapped my cold hands around the cup and savored the heat.

"Is this the part where we sit around and talk about what a creep your ex-boyfriend was?" he asked.

He dropped into the chair across from me and continued drinking his coffee.

"Finn's not a creep. He's just not the guy for me."

His face relaxed. "That's good. I mean, that you don't hate his guts now. I like Finn."

I smiled. "I like him too. But, it wasn't ever going to work out. He's already married to his job."

I glanced around the kitchen, noticing that things looked neater than usual. Maybe he had hired Leif's housekeepers? "Hey, Dad. Do you have yesterday's paper?"

He stood up and retrieved it from the counter behind him, setting it in front of me.

The headline shocked me.

"Hooper got released?" I said.

"Well, as far as they could determine, it was an accident," he said.

"Nick said something about reckless endangerment," I told him.

I scanned the headline briefly, then flipped to the fourth page and the help-wanted ads.

"You are not supposed to work yet," he said.

I started reading the jobs listing. "I have to do something. I can't sit around anymore and eat all of Leif's groceries and drive his car. I feel like a mooch."

"I'm sure he doesn't see it like that."

"Of course not," I said. "He's very generous. But I don't want to get used to it. I have to get back to work now, or I'll start to get soft."

The number of available jobs in Killdeer was pitiful. Unless I wanted to be a dishwasher or scrub toilets at the courthouse, I didn't have a lot of options.

"There's a librarian job coming open at that branch up in Fable," my father said.

I looked up from the paper. "I don't see it here."

"It's not going to be advertised. Not until next week. The manager told Irene that she is going to fire her assistant. You should put in for that. It's only a couple days a week, but it's something to get you going."

"When did Irene tell you about this?" I asked.

"Yesterday," he said, his face carefully neutral.

I watched him suspiciously. "Dad, are you and Irene...?"

"No."

I cleared my throat and went back to searching the ads. "Okay."

Sunset Veterinary Clinic over in Parkman was hiring a kennel cleaner. A local dairy farm needed a trained technician for artificial inseminations.

"I saw Dean today," I said, growing more depressed with each job title.

"Oh? How's he?"

"Fine. You know, Tatiana warned me to stay away from him. She really doesn't like Dean, does she?"

My father set his coffee cup down. "She has a pretty good reason. Dean sort of got attached to Tatiana's niece when the girl came out to spend the summer a couple of years ago. Pretty girl. Curly brown hair and big brown eyes. Anyway, one of the spring ranch hands who worked for Tatiana was hitting on the girl in the stable, and she got upset about it. Told someone about it when Dean was within earshot down at the tack and saddle shop. That was a mistake."

"What happened?"

"Dean nearly killed the guy. He probably would have, but the brand inspector happened to be there at the time and put a stop to it. The brand inspector used to be a farrier over at Lodgegrass, and the man has some meat on his bones. He knocked some sense into Dean, at least long enough to get him to quit choking the ranch hand with a halter rope."

"No wonder she doesn't like him. She said that I shouldn't be alone with Dean, so he wouldn't get attached to me."

My father leaned back in his chair. "You don't need to worry about that. When it comes to you, Dean won't ever go there."

"Because of what happened when he found me when I got lost?" I asked.

My father looked down at the table. "Well, not exactly."

He squirmed in his chair.

"Dad. What are you talking about?" I asked.

He rubbed his forearms. "Is it cold in here? Maybe I should throw another log on the fire."

"It's going to get a lot colder in a minute," I said, pinning him down.

He folded his hands in his lap, hesitating. After I crossed my arms firmly, he confessed.

"Dean thinks that you are his little sister."

I blinked and sat up. "He what?"

"He thinks that you are his sister. He won't ever get attached to you, so don't worry about it."

"And just how, exactly, did he get that idea?"

"I told him," he said, unapologetic.

"Why would you do that? He's not my brother. It's impossible, so why would you tell him that?"

Since he was already in it up to his neck, my father dropped his guilt routine and spilled the truth.

"I knew that if Dean thought you were his only living family member he would do whatever it took to find you the night you got lost in the forest."

It was a good thing I was sitting down already. "You lied to him so he would keep searching for me?"

"Yes I did."

"But that's a terrible thing to do," I said.

"Not from my perspective it wasn't."

"But it isn't true," I said, astonished.

"No. But it sure got the job done."

"But he never said anything to me," I pointed out.

"He won't ever say anything. Dean thinks that you were his father's illegitimate child. He thinks I married your mother because I felt sorry for her."

"Dad! I can't believe you—"

"It was dark, cold, and raining. It was the best I could come up with at the time."

"We have to tell him the truth," I said.

"Marley," he said, leaning forward and looking me directly in the eye. "I don't ever tell you what to do. I know you are a grown-up and capable of taking care of yourself without your father bossing you around. But in this case, I want you to do what I am telling you to do, because I know better than you. Do not ever, under any circumstances, tell him that you are not his sister. You understand me?"

He was dangerously serious. I could hear the tension in his voice, and all I could do was nod my head. "All right. If it's that important to you, I won't tell him."

"It's not that important to me; it's that important to you," he said. "Promise me."

I didn't like it, but to ease his concern I agreed. "I promise. I don't understand it, but if you think it's for the best I won't tell him."

I closed the newspaper and folded it face up on the table.

The conversation about Dean was officially closed, and I was eager to change the subject.

"I still can't believe that Hooper has been released," I said, staring at the paper's headline.

A photograph of Nick Wilcox and Loy Shucraft escorting Hooper to a car outside of the courthouse dominated the front page. I wondered why both of them were there, and then I saw in the background of the photo a contingent of protestors lined up on the sidewalk behind them. Martin Flies Low, his fist raised in rage, was leading the protestors, mostly Crow men, in an angry and vocal demonstration.

"Oh. I guess they wanted him to make it inside the courthouse in one piece," I said, scanning the photo.

"I don't blame Martin for being so angry," he said. "If it was my son who had been killed, even if it was only an accident, I'd be steamed too."

The protestors were holding sticks in their hands. "What are those? They have feathers attached to them." I turned the paper around so that my father could see the picture.

"Those are pipe tomahawk handles. It looks like the heads have been removed, but that's what they are."

"Pipe tomahawk?" I asked.

"You can smoke them, like a pipe. They are hollow. But usually they have a tomahawk head. I think even Martin knew better than to bring one of those to a public protest with the head still attached."

"But if they are used for smoking tobacco, why would that be such a bad idea? They are religious, aren't they?"

"They are also basically a really stout hatchet. When you weren't smoking one a hundred years ago, you were bashing someone over the head with it. They are a weapon, Kiddo. They were used in combat."

"So, Martin isn't waving one around because he is trying to invoke the Great Spirit," I said.

"He is invoking the Great Spirit, all right. Because he wants Hooper to hurry on to the afterlife."

I wouldn't want to be in Hooper Bukowski's shoes for the next forty or fifty years. Martin was holding a handwritten sign proclaiming that Hooper should be judged by the red man because the white man was blind to true justice.

I set the paper aside and sipped my cocoa. It was getting cold, like my mood.

"Dad, why is it that I never seem to end up with a good man?" I asked.

"Well, there's Allen," he said.

"He almost qualifies as one," I said.

Allen was my ex-husband, a game warden who worked in Missoula now. He had relocated there after the divorce. The divorce had been prompted by my catching him in bed with a cocktail waitress. Luckily I hadn't actually walked in on them together; otherwise I'd probably still be in prison. But I'd managed to gather enough information from Allen's credit card statements to put two and two together, so to speak.

I leaned my forehead on my palm and indulged in a healthy helping of self-pity. "I wish I could find someone who was more like you."

"Marley, I want you to find someone who is better than me. All fathers hope for that. But I'd settle for someone who made you happy."

"I think I am done with relationships, Dad. I don't seem to have very good luck with them, and it's too much trouble to try to sort through all the baggage to get to something like you and Mom had."

He smiled nostalgically. "We had it pretty good, your mother and me."

"How did you two do it?" I asked.

"How did we do what?"

"You always seemed so happy."

"We were happy. We had a great partnership," he said.

"But, how did you make it work?"

"Two things," he said. He held up his hand with two fingers extended. "One, we respected each other. And two, neither one of us needed the other to change."

"You liked each other the way you were? That's all there was to it?"

"And we treated each other with respect. When you have that going for you, it's pretty tough to fail at a marriage. That, and I made your mother laugh."

I traced my finger over the table, feeling depressed. "I don't think I have ever respected a man like that. Maybe that's why I have always bombed when it comes to relationships."

"That's not why," he told me.

I looked up, questioning. "Then why?"

"Because you haven't met the right person yet."

I pondered that. "It's not that Allen was a bad person, or Finn. But they didn't seem to be able to make tough choices. Neither one of them."

"Someday you will meet someone who knows the difference between control and strength," he said.

"I'm not sure I know what that means."

He folded his hands in his lap. "It's one thing to grope along and do the best you can to control your surroundings, trying to prepare for what's coming down the pipe and guess how things are going to go. But it's another thing altogether to live without worrying about what's coming, and instead of fretting over the future, deal with each situation as it happens. That's what a strong person does."

"You think there are strong men out there?" I asked, feeling doubtful.

"I know there are," he said. He stood up and scooped up my cocoa. It was cold now, and he dumped it in the sink.

"I'm not sure I will ever find a man who is like that," I said. I was depressing myself with my gloomy talk.

"Don't you worry about finding a man like that," he said, rinsing out the cup. "Just be yourself and live your life. You shouldn't have to go out there looking for a strong partner. It's the other way around. Any man who is qualified to apply for the job will find you."

He washed the cup and set it in the dish rack to dry.

I'd seen his old pickup truck parked behind the house, and I realized that he'd found someone to drive him over to Tatiana's to replace the tires. I wasn't sure what my father had planned by way of payback for the Pinkertons, but I judged from his silence on the subject that it was not going to be a pleasant experience for them.

The phone rang, and he leaned across the counter to lift the receiver. The original rotary phone still hung in the kitchen, and he tucked the mustard-yellow handset under his chin.

"Yel-lo," he said, grinning at his own joke.

He listened for a moment, glancing at me sideways. "Can I call you back later?"

His cheeks darkened when he took his seat again. I pounced instantly. "Was that a woman?"

"Marley, I don't know that I will ever understand where you got your curiosity."

"It was a woman, wasn't it?" I asked, my eyes twinkling.

He wordlessly stirred his coffee.

I stood up and grabbed my coat from the back of the chair, deciding that I would save the epic teasing for another day. "Thanks for listening to me complain, Dad. See you later?"

"What time are you coming over Christmas Eve?"

I felt awful suddenly. I'd been so wrapped up in the recent events I hadn't done a bit of Christmas shopping. "How about I drop by at four?"

"Perfect."

He gave me a fatherly hug and a kiss on the forehead.

I left and drove to Fable, heading straight for Julian's sporting goods store.

I had an errand to run and nothing better to do for the rest of the day. I certainly wasn't going to head back to Leif's and sit around the house moping.

Dean didn't have a lot of money, and though it wasn't a great expense for me, a two-dollar arrow was valuable to him. I needed to replace them as soon as possible. It was the least I could do for my own brother.

CHAPTER 17

"**D**ean shoots the ST Epic N-Fused Carbon 340s. Easton makes them. He likes them because they last. He says they handle vibration without losing accuracy, and by God, if Dean Tisdale says an arrow is accurate, you can bet on it."

I was leaning on the counter in the sporting goods store in what constituted downtown Fable, watching Julian show me a selection of arrows. The store was crammed with every imaginable hunting, fishing, and hiking tool or toy that a person could ask for. A long selection of guns hung in a locked rack behind the counter.

"I know he has them cut twenty-eight inches long," I said, trying to be helpful.

Julian slapped a package of arrowheads on the counter beside the arrows. They looked like triangle-shaped razorblades. "Then there are the broadheads."

"Ouch. What is that? It looks like something you'd see on a cooking show," I said.

"This isn't for chopping up rutabagas," Julian said. "This is the Tru-Fire 125-grain solid, machined broadhead."

"It's the pointy end, right?" I asked.

Julian laughed and reached under the counter for another

box. "You'll want two of them."

"How much is this going to cost?" I asked, feeling my check-book whimper.

"The broadheads are thirty-five bucks each. But I'll give you a deal on them since they are for Dean. So, how about sixty-five for two? And the arrows are usually sold in a dozen, and that's eighty bucks. But since you only want two, I have to charge you seven each."

"Seventy-nine dollars for two arrows?" I asked.

"These aren't just toys," Julian said, his face serious. "If Dean doesn't hit what he is aiming for, he won't eat that day."

I lifted one of the carbon arrows and ran my fingers down the shaft. It was cool and strong, but lighter than it looked. "I didn't know that."

"Dean won't shoot just any junk arrow that he can get his hands on," Julian said. "It's got to be exactly what he wants."

"Are all archers like that?" I asked.

Julian gathered up the two plastic boxes holding the arrowheads and set them beside the cash register. "Sometimes. Kids aren't too picky about arrows. They lose them so frequently they can't afford to be picky. But someone like Dean, or even Rebecca Winthrop? They take the time to get the best."

"Rebecca? The pediatrician?" I asked.

"She's a great shot," Julian said proudly. "She shoots targets only. But that girl has a real natural ability."

"Sort of like Dean," I said.

Julian stopped, and I saw his lips twitching. "Not exactly."

"I thought Dean was a good archer," I said. "That's what everyone has always told me."

Julian took the two arrows over to the electric saw and started to clamp one into place. "Dean is sort of in a whole other level of good."

"I've only seen him do a practice shot into a field," I said.

Julian started cutting the first arrow. "Did he lose an arrow when he did it?"

"He lost two. That's why I'm in here. He did it as a favor for me," I said, confessing.

Julian appraised me carefully. "He must think a lot of you, then."

"Does everyone in Killdeer get their archery gear in here?" I asked.

"Everyone who doesn't want to drive all the way over to Parkman and pay twice as much at the Gordon's Hunting Supply," he said.

"Did you ever sell any arrows to Hooper?"

Julian's face twisted up with disgust. "I sold him a dozen, about four months ago. He's a lousy shot. And I don't like to say that about customers."

"What kind of arrows does someone like Hooper buy? I suppose they are cheap."

"Cheap and junk. He wanted to go elk hunting. Can you imagine Hooper bow hunting for elk? You ought to have to pass a test first or something. He couldn't hit his own foot, never practiced that I knew of, and mostly I think he was a display hunter."

"What's a display hunter?"

Julian looked slightly embarrassed to be snitching on a customer. "A display hunter is someone who carries the gear around in their truck to impress girls. Hooper kept his bow on a gun rack behind the seat of his pickup. Nice bow, too. I think he wanted the cheerleaders at Killdeer High to think he was a bow hunter. It's just cashing in on the whole Robin Hood thing."

I tried to picture Hooper as Robin Hood and got a bad taste in my mouth. "I wonder if he was trying to impress one girl in particular."

"Now that I think about it," Julian said, reaching for the second arrow. "It seemed to me like he was more worried about his wrestling buddies than any girls."

I was learning more from Julian in ten minutes than I had managed to piece together after ten hours of asking questions.

Julian started to cut the second arrow. It made an irritating grinding noise. "We've got an outdoor archery range a quarter mile from here. I rent the space from Sander's Ranch. I let the serious customers try out a bow before they buy it, because for some of the guys, it's a real investment. Hooper and his wrestling team buddies came in here together, all four of them, and he seemed like he was in some sort of hog heaven because they were all paying so much attention to him."

"Did they go to the range to test a bow?" I asked.

"Yes. Hooper wanted to get a Bowtech CPX."

His expression was grim.

"Are they expensive? I'll bet you weren't crazy about letting Hooper test one."

Julian's hands moved quickly. "The strings alone retail for sixty dollars. I sell my CPXs for twelve hundred."

He finished cutting the second arrow and gathered them both up to take to the cash register.

"I always go with a customer when they are testing a bow. And it was like Hooper hadn't even shot before. Maybe he hadn't. But his teammates were all jumping around like monkeys, going crazy and making such a big deal out of it that he was getting a bow, I think it shamed him into buying it. His aim was so poor I almost tried to talk him out of buying it."

"He paid $1,200 for a bow?" I asked. That was probably as much as my car repairs would cost.

"You would have thought the kid had just won the Nobel Peace

Prize or something, the way his teammates were carrying on."

"Did any of the other kids shoot the bow?" I asked.

Julian grimaced. "Just Hooper. None of the others wanted to try it. Shame really, because any one of them would have probably been a better shot. But in the end, Hooper shelled out the cash for it. Practically broke my heart."

"Why is that?" I asked, thinking that it must have been bad for him to consider losing a $1,200 sale.

Julian's face fell with regret. "Hooper was an accident waiting to happen. He was the most careless guy I had ever seen when it came to handling a bow. I don't like to put weapons into the hands of someone who is so inept. But, I've got a business to run."

"Business must be pretty good," I said.

"It's good enough. I like my toys, and I'll be able to afford a nice wedding for Patty this New Year's Eve."

"Where did you say you and Patty were going?" I asked.

"Sedona. She wants a traditional Native wedding, even though she's about the least traditional gal you could ever meet," he said with a grin. "Patty is half Cherokee, but you wouldn't know it. She likes the idea that she is just a regular girl and doesn't go in for all that ceremonial stuff unless it's something really important like a baby's birth or a wedding."

"Sedona is beautiful, from the pictures I've seen," I said, cringing as Julian hovered over the cash register. I sighed and waited to hear the grand total. "It can't be very cheap to fly down there and get married."

"It's not. But nothing is too good for my Patty," he said.

"Well, what's my contribution to the Julian and Patty wedding fund going to be?" I asked.

Julian rang up the arrows and the arrowheads. "Seventy-nine, even."

I dug out my checkbook from my coat pocket and wrote out the amount. Next time I wanted Dean to lose a couple of arrows in a lousy experiment, I would come up here and buy something cheap and disposable.

"Thanks, Julian. You've really helped me a lot."

Julian took the check from my hand. "So, what's the word around town about what happened to Little Joe?"

He looked grim. That was understandable; after all, he had inadvertently sold Hooper the murder weapon.

"The word is that Hooper is an idiot, but not a criminal," I said, replacing my checkbook. "He got released, and it looks like Loy and Nick are satisfied it was an accident. I guess he wanted to show up his wrestling buddies, and they didn't bother to check and see if anyone was out in the pasture where they were shooting their arrows."

"What a shame," Julian said, his head bent.

"Wilma told me Little Joe was going to Bozeman to study astronomy. She said he loved math, enjoyed school, and it sounds like he was pretty good at it. He had so much going for him."

"And because of the carelessness of one stupid kid, he won't ever get the chance."

"Maybe," I said, thinking. "Maybe it was carelessness, but maybe not."

He glanced up at me. "You think it wasn't an accident?"

I wasn't entirely sure what I thought. "Do you know how unlikely it is that those boys could have hit a target as small as a person with just two arrows?"

He shook his head. "But that's what the sheriff thinks happened, isn't it?"

"He tries not to talk to me about it," I said. "But to tell you the truth, Julian, I think that one of those boys knows a hell of a lot more than he's telling."

Julian was watching my hands, his eyes hooded, like he was appraising me. "You know, you should try shooting sometime. We've got a beginner range that is only twenty yards, and I think you would do well."

"Thanks. But I don't think I can afford this hobby."

He slid the check inside the register. "Sure, sure. You think that Finn will ever try it? Usually he just comes in for bullets."

I suppressed a stab of pain, forcing my expression to stay neutral. "We broke up. I'm not sure what he is up to lately."

Julian glanced at his counter quickly. "That's too bad. I think Finn would make a pretty good archer."

"What's your longest target over at the range?" I asked, shifting the topic.

"It's about sixty yards. Much further than that, and the guys end up shooting their arrows into the trees. Most of them think they are a lot better than they really are."

"Is that a long way for an archer to shoot and still be accurate?"

"Yes. Most guys are comfortable between thirty yards and seventy yards. The good ones can shoot ninety yards and stay accurate."

"How far can Dean shoot and still be accurate?" I asked, more from idle curiosity than anything else.

"He can hit a mouse at 110 yards," Julian said without hesitation.

I doubted I could hit a mouse if I was standing directly over it and holding a cinder block.

"Wow."

He handed me my receipt. "Anyone who has ever seen him shoot tends to say that a lot."

Julian placed the arrows and the arrowheads lovingly inside a bag. He handled everything he touched with care.

"Hey, Julian," I said, gathering up my bag. "What kind of arrows did Hooper buy that day?"

He scratched his dark hair roughly. "Let's see. I'm not really sure. Sometimes they just grab them out of the mismatched bin."

He went to his arrow box. It was waist high, and he ran his fingers over the dozens of types of arrows standing up in divided holders inside the box. The container holding all of his arrows was about the same size as a couple of grocery carts.

"These," he said, pulling up an arrow and showing it to me. "The Gold Tip Lightning White. I sold him a dozen of these for twenty-six bucks. They bend real easy because they are made out of aluminum."

I touched the tip. "But this is just a round point. It doesn't have a—what are they called? It doesn't have a broadhead with those razorblades on it."

"No, these are your basic bullet point. But they screw off, see? I'm pretty sure Hooper bought a couple packs of broadheads he could put on them. Cheap arrows, sexy looking points. Like I said, he was all about show, not about accuracy."

He twisted the end and took off the point, showing me how easily they detached.

"But this would still do a lot of damage, wouldn't it?" I asked.

"Not really. I know a guy who wanted to get rid of a porcupine that was eating his apple trees. He put four blunt-tip arrows into the animal, and it still survived."

"Four? How could anything survive that?" I asked.

"Because this type of tip doesn't cut. It's not for hunting. It's for target shooting. If you want to use a tip that will be effective, you have to use a broadhead, because they cut as they go in."

I swallowed, thinking about Little Joe. "So, a broadhead is what hunters use?"

"If they want to actually kill what they are shooting at, yes. It's not ethical to bow hunt with equipment you know won't do the job."

I tucked my bag under my arm. "Thanks, Julian. I'll see you later."

He left me and went to help a young backpacker who was struggling with the labels on the high-altitude sleeping bags.

As I left the store, I noticed the truck that Julian drove, and since I was a bit more familiar with expensive vehicles now I could see that it was not a cheap ride. Gold letters stood out on the tailgate. The insignia on the back said, "Ram Laramie Longhorn." The top half gleamed jet black, and the bottom half faded into a stylish light gold trim. It made my Honda look like road kill in comparison. It might not be a bad idea to apply for a job at Julian's sporting goods. His business was obviously doing fine, in spite of the recession.

As I was about to unlock my door, Sheriff Shucraft pulled into the parking lot beside me. He stared at me for a moment before killing his engine and climbing out of his truck.

"Hun, what are you doing up here?"

"Doing my part to stimulate the American economy," I said, holding up the bag.

"You aren't buying me a new shotgun for Christmas, by chance?" he asked.

I smirked. "No, I had to replace a couple of arrows. Dean lost two doing me a favor."

"Maybe December isn't the best time to practice archery," he said, standing beside me.

"I asked him to shoot two arrows into our pasture to see what the chances were that Hooper could have accidentally killed Little Joe."

"I can't believe I am asking you this, but what did you find out?" he asked.

"That the chances Hooper could have done it are next to impossible. About twenty million to one."

"I see impossible things every day," he told me. "Why do you think I have an ulcer?"

"It is so unlikely that I think it's next to impossible," I said.

He wrestled his big hands into a pair of gloves. "I do too," he said.

That surprised me. "Really?"

"I can't talk about this in any detail," he told me as he watched a magpie settle in the trees across the road. "But I don't necessarily think Hooper did it."

"Neither do I."

He gave me a lopsided grin. "So, we do have something in common after all."

"Do you still think it was Dean?" I asked, cringing.

He rubbed his hands together. "I think it might be."

I let out a disgusted sigh. "There is no way it was him. What kind of arrow was used to kill Joseph? I'll tell you. It was a Gold Tip Lightning White, and it was a piece of junk. Maybe Hooper swapped out the tip for a broadhead, but that was the only part of the arrow that was any good. Dean would never shoot something that low of quality."

Loy turned his gaze on me in disbelief. "How did you…?"

"Dean shoots something called an Easton Epic. It's carbon, not aluminum."

"Marley, I want you to be really careful here," he said, facing me squarely. "How did you get this information?"

I shrugged. "Julian told me. Didn't you go talk to him?"

"I talked to him. He said that his customers' sales records were confidential, and I would need to get a warrant if I wanted any information about what kind of gear they used. Why was he so willing to talk to you?"

"I had to get a couple of arrows for Dean, to replace the ones he shot into the pasture. Julian told me that Hooper uses the white arrows."

"I don't think Julian likes cops," he said. "It's going to be a while until I can verify he sold Hooper a dozen for his quiver. When we get that information we might be a step closer to figuring out what happened. I came up here today to try and talk to him again, but I don't think I will have much luck."

I stamped my feet to warm them. "Well, it wasn't Dean. I know it."

"And I don't think it was Hooper. Even if the kid believes he did it."

"I heard he confessed," I said.

"He thinks he's going to hell for all eternity. I have never seen someone so god-awful miserable about an accident before. I didn't take my gun into the interrogation room in case he got a crazy idea to pull it and shoot himself. The kid is devastated."

"And he was believable?"

Loy grimaced. "He doesn't remember much. Hooper was so drunk that night, all he really remembers is the moment he saw Joe lying in the pasture with that arrow sticking out of his chest. He became miraculously sober in about twelve seconds. At least, sober enough to panic and flee the scene."

I felt the breeze chill my neck and wished that I had worn a scarf. Something occurred to me.

"How did he know it was his arrow?" I asked.

Loy's face pinched with confusion. "What do you mean how did he know?"

"Well, if Hooper and another boy were both shooting into the field, how did he know it was his arrow that killed Little Joe?"

Loy didn't reply. He avoided my gaze. "Like I said. I can't talk about it," he told me.

I decided it was time to have the conversation with him that I had been dreading. I knew he would not be happy, but there was no avoiding it.

"I went to talk to Wilma after you had spoken with her. She told me something that embarrassed her, something that she probably didn't say to you."

I had his attention now. "Go on," he said.

"She told me that the night Joe was killed, he made a remark. It was odd, so I thought you should know what he'd said."

"Was it about watching someone in the shower?" he asked.

"Yes," I said. "She actually talked to you about that?"

He held up his hand and studied me. "This stays between us, Marley. I'm serious. You clear?"

I nodded. "Of course."

He pulled the zipper of his brown sheriff's coat up until it was hugging his chin. "Wilma didn't tell me," he said.

"Then who did?" I asked.

Loy struggled for a moment, torn between duty and a desire to fish for the truth. Finally he gave in and leaned towards me.

"Mr. Compton, the wrestling coach at the high school."

I had to mentally shift gears. "The wrestling coach?"

Loy held up a hand to quiet me down. "Yes, and could you not broadcast it, please?"

"But how did he know about that?" I asked, lowering my voice.

"He said a week ago, Joe came to talk to Matthew at a practice match. He said that Hooper and Connor were hovering around the two of them like horseflies and that after Little Joe left they were both on fire."

"They were angry? About what?" I asked.

"The coach said, as he understood it, the boys were upset because one of them thought Joe had said he wanted to watch the twins in the shower, and Hooper got it in his head that Joe was talking about watching Meg."

I felt the color drain out of my face. "Oh no. So they thought..."

Loy nodded. "Hooper and Connor thought that Joseph had just asked Matthew if he could watch his sister take a shower."

"That's not good," I said.

"This whole situation is not good," Loy replied.

"That doesn't help straighten any of this out. It only makes it worse," I said.

"Tell me about it," Loy said.

I felt the hairs on the back of my neck stand on end. "Loy, you have got to figure out who killed Little Joe. And you have got to do it fast."

He plunged his hands inside his coat pockets, like he'd find the answers buried there.

"I'm working on it, Hun. I'm working on it. Now if I can just get Julian to tell me all the information he was willing to tell you, it might put me a step closer to doing that."

I watched the burly sheriff head towards the front door of the sporting goods store. A flicker of movement caught my eye, and I spotted Julian standing in the window watching us. He didn't look very happy to see Loy coming in his store, and his expression was a surprise. Julian didn't look angry that the sheriff was there. He looked worried.

Before I could make sense out of why he would be concerned, Julian turned away from the window and vanished from view.

Maybe I shouldn't have said anything about the fact that I thought it was unlikely that what had happened to Little Joe was an accident.

223

I chided myself for opening my big mouth. Not only was my speculation making me paranoid, it seemed that it was having the same effect on everybody else around me.

It was time to go talk to someone who might be able to put my fears to rest. And this time I vowed to keep my opinions to myself.

CHAPTER 18

"**B**rain damage."

"Excuse me?" I asked.

A woman wearing a peach-colored dress, her blond hair a bird's nest of fluff and barrettes, was standing beside me. She was watching the boys warm up for the wrestling match, her arms folded in a knot across her chest and her face prim with disapproval.

"Those kids hit each other so hard that they give each other brain damage," she said.

I didn't know what to say, so I didn't say anything. She turned to look me over.

"You're Marley, aren't you?" she asked.

"I am. And you are?"

She took my hand and shook it hard. I almost lost my balance.

"I'm Beverly Christy. I teach art."

"Oh, it's nice to meet you. I came by to see if I could talk to the coach, Mr. Compton. I didn't know there was a wrestling match today."

The gym was full of excited parents, jostling and wrangling for seats in the small row of risers that had been brought in for the wrestling match. Perhaps a dozen boys milled around the gym, hauling heavy bags of gear and already looking sweaty.

"Mr. Compton encourages them," Beverly told me. She sniffed.

"Isn't that what a coach is supposed to do?" I asked.

She looked away from me, uninterested now that she had determined I was not going to be a sympathetic audience.

"It's primeval claptrap," she said. "Someday one of these kids is going to get hurt. Why does the school devote its budget to sports when art is so much more productive and fulfilling?"

"Do you know which coach is Mr. Compton?" I asked. He was the one teacher at Killdeer High I wasn't entirely sure I knew by sight.

She let her eyes drift in my direction as she tried to decide if she would help me or not. I gave her a sunny smile.

"He's the tall scarecrow with the comb-over," she said, pointing with her chin. "And tell him this gym has to be empty by six thirty tonight because if we can't get started on the decorations by then, the school Christmas party will just have to go on without balloons."

"Ah, sure. I'll tell him," I said. It never ceased to surprise me what people chose to get upset about.

I navigated the squirrelly crowd, pushing my way past the Parkman Bears, the opposing team, and found the warm-up area for the Killdeer wrestling team. Only three wrestlers were representing Killdeer High today. Hooper was conspicuously absent.

Mr. Compton was busy filling out forms on a clipboard. He didn't acknowledge me when I stopped to stand beside him. His small band of wrestlers was subdued, but they looked determined. They were practicing take-down moves with each other while they waited for the match to get started.

"Miss Christy sends her regards," I said.

Mr. Compton's pencil lead shattered. "Drat."

He fumbled in his shirt pocket for a pen and carefully slid the broken pencil into the groove on the top of the clipboard. "I'll bet she does," he remarked.

I watched the Killdeer wrestlers warming up, marveling that boys who were only seventeen could be so developed.

"They look a lot bigger than the boys did back when I was a junior in high school," I said. "They don't even look like kids to me."

Mr. Compton beamed when he surveyed his team. "Matt wrestles 171. He's our team captain. The kid's in fantastic shape, and he has great stamina."

"Who's your weakest link?" I asked. I was simply trying to get the conversation rolling. I didn't know a thing about wrestling.

The coach answered at once, not critical of his team, simply honest in assessing them. "Connor. He wrestles 152. He'd be a lot better if he applied himself, but he's just too lazy to ever go anywhere."

I studied Connor. He was a smaller version of Hooper, with a squint.

"What about Hooper? I don't see him today." I recognized Connor and Matt, but not the other boy.

The coach grimaced. "We thought it would be distracting if he was to participate today."

I could imagine. "Is he any good?" I asked.

"Hooper? He's average. But he's our heavyweight. Hooper wrestles 189. Sometimes he wins; sometimes he loses. He does it because he likes the camaraderie."

"Hooper looks up to his teammates, doesn't he?" I asked.

"Who are you again?" Mr. Compton asked.

"Marley Dearcorn," I said, extending my hand.

The coach didn't shake it, but stared at me for a moment as recognition dawned. "Oh. Dearcorn. I know who you are now."

I didn't want to give him a chance to escape. "Your team is pretty tight, aren't they?" I asked.

"As a drum. Those boys are a credit to the sport. They look out for each other."

I waited while he scribbled a few items on the sheet.

"How are they coping under all the pressure?" I asked. "After what happened, I mean."

The coach stopped writing and let the clipboard hang at his side. "As well as can be expected. I can't believe that Matt let this happen."

"Matt?" I asked. "But it was an accident."

"Yes. But it was reckless, and it shouldn't have ever gotten so out of hand," he said.

"So was Matt at the bonfire party that night?" I asked.

"They all were, for a short time. The party started to get wild, and Hooper came up with the idea for the arrow contest. Matt feels terrible. Says he should have told the boys to forget about it."

"He's got that much influence over the others?" I asked.

Mr. Compton watched his team. "Matt's a natural leader. They all look up to him. He's solid as a rock."

I considered that. As I watched the three boys warming up, I could see that Matthew did seem like he was calling the shots, offering direction and generally in charge of the action. "He must be a good wrestler," I said.

"He's driven," the coach said. "Matt never wins by decision, he always wins by fall."

"I'm not sure I know what that means," I told him.

"It means that he always takes his opponent down and pins them, and never relies on the judges to determine if he has out-maneuvered them. He always wins by fall, so there is never any doubt about who is the superior wrestler. His only weakness is that if he thinks he can't win a match, he hesitates and hangs back. Matt doesn't ever let himself get pinned."

"He seems pretty protective of his sister," I said, trying to ease into my next question.

The coach seemed eager to talk about anything other than the accident. "Meg? Oh, sure. He watches out for her, always challenging her to do better at school and try harder. He's a natural leader, like I said."

"What did he make of Little Joe having a friendship with Meg?" I asked.

The coach's cheeks flushed. "I don't really get into the kids' personal lives."

"I'm sure it was mostly harmless, anyway," I said, baiting him.

"Harmless? Sure, if you call distracting Meg from homework and getting her busted for ditching school 'harmless.'"

I was surprised by that. "Joe and Meg were caught ditching school? When?"

"A couple of weeks ago," he said, shoving his pen back in his shirt pocket. He'd forgotten to click it shut, and a blue spot started to appear on the fabric.

"Why were they ditching school?" I asked. This sounded like one of those details that was important, but nobody recognized it as such.

"They drove over to West Yellowstone and went to that IMAX theater to see some documentary," he said, clearly astonished. "Like that is worth ditching school for."

"But that's a four-hour drive one way," I said.

"And they got busted," he said. "They didn't get back into town until well after dark. Mr. and Mrs. Chan were not too happy that Little Joe would convince Meg to run off and do something that irresponsible. I understand that they instructed their son to keep a better eye on his sister from then on."

"And I suppose Matt wasn't too happy about Little Joe hitting on Meg, either," I said casually.

The coach flushed even more. "It wasn't exactly like that."

I kept my eyes on the boys while they practiced escape moves. They were all well out of earshot. "What do you mean by not exactly?"

Mr. Compton shouted at Connor to stop dropping his right elbow. He looked like he wanted to walk away, but eventually he answered my question. Sometimes I figured that people just needed to talk, and I always seemed to have a knack for getting them to do it.

"Little Joe came to talk to Matt last week at a practice. I didn't hear what he said. But Hooper and Connor went ballistic. They said they heard Joe telling Matt he wanted to watch Meg in the shower, or something. Matt told them both to forget about it, and Joe left, looking really unhappy."

"What happened after Joe left? Did Hooper follow him?" I asked.

"No way. Matt told him to let it go. And, as far as I know, Hooper let it go," he said.

I was listening, but I was also searching the crowd for Meg Chan. It was lucky a wrestling match was going on because if I could locate Meg, I'd get a chance to talk to her without her brother hovering around. But as I searched through the crowd of noisy parents and bouncing kids, it was clear that Meg wasn't there.

"Mr. Compton, did Hooper ever talk about the accident to you? Did he ever tell you what he remembered about that night?" I asked.

"Why don't you ask him yourself?" the coach said.

I thought he was blowing me off, until I followed his gaze and saw Hooper Bukowski finding a seat in the bleachers.

"Great balls of fire," I said. He was the last person I expected to see in the gym.

The coach didn't bother with excusing himself and simply walked away. He headed towards his team to offer last-minute tips before the match started.

If Meg wasn't able to fill in a few blanks from that night, maybe Hooper would be. I strolled over to the risers and caught Hooper's eye.

He shifted and squirmed when he saw me coming towards him, and when I stopped beside the bleachers, he tried to pretend that I wasn't there.

I held my ground. Eventually he gave in and acknowledged me.

"What are you looking at?" he asked.

"I was hoping I could ask you something?"

He glanced around, noticing that several of the people seated on the bleachers were staring at him openly. Hooper was discovering the perils of infamous celebrity.

He fidgeted from the unwanted attention. "Parking lot," he said, rising and heading for the door. Apparently, talking to me was less painful than being scrutinized by the mob.

I had to hurry to keep up, but I followed him outside and came to a stop beside him. He propped himself against the bumper of his battered white pickup.

I noticed that the truck still had a gun rack on the back window, but no compound bow rested in the hooks.

His head bobbed back and forth as he watched the people hurrying to the match. They avoided his gaze.

"So—what? What do you want?" he asked.

"I was hoping you could tell me what you remember about that night," I asked as evenly as I could. I didn't want to sound like I was accusing him of anything.

"Why do you care?" he asked.

"Wilma Flies Low wanted to know what really happened, and

I said I would tell her," I explained.

Hooper's eyes instantly became a flash flood. Tears fell off his broad cheeks, and he wiped them away with an angry hand. "Nothing. I don't remember nothing," he said.

I had never seen someone cry so easily. He looked absolutely wretched. His eyes were bloodshot, and I doubted very much that he was wrestling 189 anymore. He'd dropped at least ten pounds since I'd last seen him.

"You really don't remember?" I asked.

His Adam's apple worked up and down as he fought to swallow back the tide of tears. "I told everyone. I don't remember much that happened that night. I just remember seeing Joe laying in the field with my...with my goddamned arrow...with my arrow..."

He hung his head, his lips pulled apart with pain.

This was going to be a lot harder than I'd first thought. I resisted the impulse to put a hand on his shoulder. I doubted very much that he needed any pity gestures.

"But how did you know it was your arrow? Didn't you have a contest to see who could shoot the farthest? You weren't the only one who was out there that night," I said.

He swallowed a few times, struggling to keep control of himself. Hooper was a boy trapped in a man's body. He was the size of a professional athlete, but he had the emotional development of a teenager.

The bigger they are, the harder they fall apart.

"Take your time," I said.

He wiped his face off again, staring at the ground with hollow eyes. "Connor put a piece of duct tape on the end of his arrow, right in front of the feathers, so we would know which one was his and which one was mine. Nobody else wanted to shoot, so it was just him and me," Hooper said.

"And when you got to the field, the arrow you saw in Little Joe didn't have any duct tape on it," I said.

"Yeah." He sniffed loudly.

"It was Connor who challenged you to the contest?" I said.

Hooper wiped his nose on his letter jacket. "I just remember Connor saying he could probably shoot farther than me, and Matt saying that he couldn't."

Movement caught my eye, and I looked up when I saw someone jogging towards us. It was Matthew Chan, dressed in his wrestling suit.

He stopped on the sidewalk in front of us, giving me a puzzled look. He clapped Hooper on the shoulder. "Hey, man. Thanks for coming by to show your support for the team. It means a lot to us."

Hooper looked up at his team captain, and I could see tears starting to form again. "Yeah. Yeah, no problem."

"How are you?" Matthew asked. He was breathless, even though he hadn't run very far.

Hooper shrugged. It looked like it took all his strength. "I'm holding up."

"Why don't you come sit with us on the bench?" Matthew said. His dark eyes were filled with concern.

"Really?" Hooper said, hopeful and surprised. "Yeah. I'd like that."

Matt slapped Hooper on the shoulder again and nodded towards the door. "Go on. I'll catch up."

As Hooper headed for the gym, Matthew let his chin drop. His expression was set with disappointment.

"This must be hard on all of you," I said. I felt sorry for them, to my surprise. Even big, dumb jocks had feelings, so it seemed.

"It's a lot harder on him than it is on me," Matt said. "Hooper wasn't ever going to make much of himself. But now? His future is ruined."

"You really think this could ruin his life?" I asked.

Matthew rolled a shoulder, speculating. "I guess it depends on what he decides to do from now on. He could give up, feel sorry for himself, and let it eat him alive. Or he could try to find something good to put his energy towards. If it was anyone else other than Hooper I'd say they could find a way to get past it. But he's not smart enough to do anything other than spend the rest of his life beating himself up."

For a high school kid, Matthew seemed pretty jaded. It was a cold assessment of the situation.

"I don't know about Hooper, but if I had accidentally killed one of my classmates it would take me years to get over it," I said.

Matthew chuckled. "That's because you're weak."

"Having compassion doesn't make someone weak," I said, a little surprised at his response.

He glanced back towards the door. "Whatever." He started to walk away.

"Can I ask you something?" I said.

"I don't have a lot of time. I should be in there now," he said hastily.

"I was just wondering if you knew why Joe was out in our pasture that night. Did he say anything to you about going to the party?"

Matthew seemed to be thinking back. "No. I don't think he did. Well, he never said anything to me about going. And we didn't invite him. I think he knew that if he was alone with Hooper and there was a lot of beer, that it would be a bad night for everyone. Hooper is a lousy drunk, and he didn't like Little Joe."

"Did Meg say she was going to the party?" I asked.

"Meg's grounded. I've got to go," he said. He gave me a curt nod and jogged away.

I watched him dart back inside the gym. "What a jerk."

It was a mystery to me why Coach Compton would appoint Matthew to be the team captain. The kid had about as much sympathy as a tax assessor.

The car was ice cold again when I climbed inside. When I caught sight of the arrows that I had bought for Dean still resting on the seat inside the bag, I resolved to take them to Dean now before they slipped my mind.

There was a chance that he was still loitering over at the Rock Stop Inn playing video games with Will and Seth, and I drove over hoping to catch him.

I parked in the parking lot and sat in my car, watching the light fade behind the shadow of the mountain. Try as I might I couldn't think of any reason why Joseph would have been out in the pasture, other than to spy on the wrestlers at the party, or in the vain hope that he could have seen Meg. Maybe Joe didn't know that Meg had been grounded and was living in a maximum-security house. I doubted that she could have snuck out without being missed, and I was sure that after she'd driven off to West Yellowstone to see a movie, her parents would be watching her much more closely.

I felt the start of a headache and gathered up Dean's arrows. I saw the battered truck Will and Seth drove parked in front of room number twelve, and I marveled at how similar the truck actually looked to a coal bed methane roustabout's rig. It was a very effective disguise, until Will and Seth opened their mouths, that is.

I knocked on the door of room twelve, and almost at once Seth jerked it open. He had a bag of Doritos in one hand and wore a pair of floppy reindeer antlers. They had tiny bells on the end.

"Oh, hey. It's you," he said, his head making tinkling noises. "Ah…M-Mary?"

"Marley," I said helpfully.

"Marley, right."

He leaned back and shouted for Dean into the gloom of the hotel room. I could see Dean and Will sitting cross-legged on the floor next to each other in front of the television. Dean was frantically fingering a game control. The sounds of gunfire and screams were deafening.

"What have you done to him?" I asked.

"He's fine," Seth said. "There won't be any permanent damage."

I wasn't so sure about that. When Dean pulled himself up and came to the door, he had a glazed expression.

"I brought you some arrows," I said, handing him the bag.

He looked over the contents and frowned. "You didn't have to do that."

"I told you that I would replace them."

He took the bag and tucked it under an arm. "Thank you. That was nice."

"It's the least I can do. I didn't know that those arrows you use are so expensive. I feel bad now, knowing that you lost those other two just to do me a favor."

"I'll get them in the spring," he said. His mouth was ringed with unnatural yellow powder. The boys must have introduced him to the cheese puff.

"If you can find them," I said. "It's a big field. You might not ever see those arrows again.

"I'll find them. The snow won't hide them forever," he told me with a calm smile. "Arrows can't get up and walk."

I had a really hard time believing what my father had said

236

about Dean attacking another man simply because he'd made a pass at a girl Dean fancied. The story about the fight between him and a ranch hand of Tatiana's had to be some sort of tall tale.

I toed the ground, nudging a few stones with my boot. They were frozen and didn't budge.

"Hey, Dean. Did you really choke a ranch hand with a lead rope?" I asked. I had no idea why I needed to know if it was true or not, but I did.

"A ranch hand?" he asked.

"I heard that you got angry at one of Tatiana's workers in the tack and saddle shop and choked him with a lead rope," I said. It sounded silly even to me.

"No. It wasn't like that at all," he said.

Relief settled over me. "Sure. I didn't think so."

He ran a hand through his rumpled hair. "It was a bullwhip."

CHAPTER 19

"It's a documentary called *Bears*," said the chipper female voice on the other end of the phone.

"*Bears?*" I asked. That didn't seem right to me.

"Yeah, its about bears," she said helpfully.

I thought for a moment. "What movies were playing two weeks ago? Is this bear movie new?" I asked.

I was talking to the West Yellowstone IMAX theater, and not getting the answers I was looking for. I doubted that Meg and Joseph would have ditched out of school to go see a bear documentary.

"Let's see," said the girl. "Um."

I could hear her rummaging through papers, and she partially covered the receiver with one hand.

"Kyle? What was playing two weeks ago?"

She paused. "I don't know, some lady," she said.

I waited, drumming my fingers on the counter. I was sitting in Leif's kitchen, the cordless phone tucked under my chin while I tried to satisfy my curiosity.

"Kyle says that it was called *Destiny in Space*," she said at last.

"What was it about?" I asked.

"Um, space I think," she said.

"Don't you have a poster still up or something?" I asked.

"It's my first day," she said. "I'm not even supposed to be answering the phones yet, but the manager said his nephew quit and even if he hadn't quit he'd have gotten fired, so it was probably better that way, but…it's just my first day," she said. Her tone was apologetic.

"Thanks. That's all I needed to know," I said.

I hung up the phone and propped my chin in my palm. I knew from what Wilma had told me that Little Joe was planning to go to Bozeman and study astronomy, so it made sense that he would ditch school to go see a movie about space. It made more sense than him ditching to go see a bear documentary.

In Killdeer if you wanted to see a documentary about bears all you had to do was look out your back window and watch your garbage cans for a couple of hours.

My stomach growled, and I realized I hadn't eaten all day. Since it was edging towards evening, I decided I had better get a plan to feed myself. Leif was gone, a note telling me he'd be back much later in the evening, so I was on my own for supper, and Lil's was sounding better and better the more I thought about it.

My shoulder gave me a twinge of pain, just to remind me that I was nearly, but not quite recovered from my broken collarbone. The doctor said it was normal to expect the occasional pain. The day after I'd trudged down the mountain with my father and Dean, I'd gotten more than that; it had been sore and inflamed the next day. Today it was better. I thought about the assistant librarian position that my father had told me would be opening up soon in the Fable branch library, and I wondered if they would require me to do any heavy lifting.

The phone rang, and since it was sitting beside my elbow I answered it on the first ring.

"Marley? You had better come down here."

"Wendy?" I said, a cold shiver going down my back. "What's wrong now?"

"There are a bunch of Indians on my deck," she said. Her voice came out like a squeak.

"What? What are they doing?" I asked.

"I think they are trying to set the house on fire."

"I'll be right there."

I hung up the phone and scooped up the car keys as I headed for the door. The only person it could possibly be was Martin Flies Low. I doubted very much he was in a reasonable state of mind.

I jumped into the black SUV and was heading towards the caretaker's house before it occurred to me that I hadn't called Loy. As I drove down the snow-packed road I hoped that Wendy at least had the good sense to do that much.

It was dark, and I flicked on the high beams, driving faster than I should have on the slick surface. The SUV dug in, and some invisible mechanism must have engaged the four-wheel drive because I was able to keep my speed up even around the corners. I drove straight by the ranch house driveway and on towards the caretaker's house without stopping. I was sure Martin would argue with my father, but he might not be so confrontational with a woman.

I came to a stop in the driveway, and I could see Wendy peering out of the living room window nervously. A dozen men crowded the driveway, their cars and trucks parked randomly. One man stood on the deck, holding a wooden bowl that billowed grey smoke. It was a burning sage bundle. He was dressed in blue jeans and a heavy parka, but he wore a dark head scarf, and his long hair dangled in two braids that fell to his waist. I could see that his face was painted white, but two red trails of paint fell from his eyes like tears. He held a feather fan in his left hand, and he was blessing the porch with the smoke from the bowl. His hands were wrinkled with age. I could see plainly that he was a Crow medicine man and that I had just interrupted a ceremony. All of my bluster vanished in an instant.

Martin stood at the bottom step, watching me walk towards him, impassive and glaring.

I looked at the faces of the men who stood in a lose circle around the deck. They were far from combative; they were solemn. Two of the men held hand drums. I'd come expecting a fight, and I'd blundered my way into a man's private moment of grieving.

"Did you come to pay your respects?" Martin asked, his tone heavy with bitter sarcasm. He looked emotionally wounded and sounded defensive.

I wished that I had been a bit more restrained when I'd driven up. I stopped in front of Martin and at least came to my senses enough to lower my voice respectfully.

"Is this a ceremony for Joseph?" I asked quietly.

Martin didn't answer. He watched me, suspicious, with arms folded and chin jutted forward. "Are you going to tell me to get off your land?"

I wanted to crawl under a rock, but I'd barged into this, and I would have to extract myself.

"No, I'm not going to ask you to leave," I said. "But I wish you would have contacted us before you came down here."

"Why? So you and your father could say no?" he asked.

"Martin, my father wouldn't say no to this," I said. I knew that was true, at least.

He looked on the verge of disagreeing, but he hadn't come to this place to make trouble, and I could see that he was struggling to keep his defiance under control.

A single owl called from the trees, and I saw the medicine man turn towards it with a knowing and sad expression. He looked back at me as if waiting for something.

"I'm sorry I interrupted," I said. They had no idea how much I truly meant those words.

"Is it all right with you," Martin asked with an edge to his voice, "if I say goodbye to my dead son now?"

Each of the men stood around me in silent protest, waiting for me to challenge Martin. They seemed to expect it.

"It's all right," I told him.

"We won't trouble you for very long," he said. "I wanted to see the place where Joseph was killed and make an offering to his place of rest."

"He was found here, but he was killed in the pasture," I said.

Martin frowned deeply. "I know. But I will make an offering here because the snow covers the place he died in the field. We won't find it until the spring. I will make an offering where he was killed when the time is right."

"I'm very sorry, Martin. You can come to the pasture any time you wish to do that," I said.

He nearly said, "Thank you," but he couldn't bring himself to utter the words and simply gave me a quick nod of his head.

I backed away from the circle of men and left them to complete the ceremony. As I walked towards the backdoor of the cottage, they began to sing a song of mourning. It sounded less like singing and more like wailing, it was so filled with sorrow.

I knocked on the backdoor and Wendy pulled it open like she had been hiding on the other side.

"What are they doing?" she asked.

"It's only a ceremony. I don't think they will be here for more than an hour or so. Did you call Loy?" I asked.

"Yes. He was in Parkman and said he would be here as soon as he could," she said. She was hugging herself against the bitter cold air seeping inside the open door.

Wendy didn't have an ounce of fat, and I figured that it would take about a minute for her to freeze to death standing there. I decided not to keep her.

"Don't worry about Martin. I think they will be gone before Loy even shows up. I gave them permission to do the ceremony, and I don't think they will give you any trouble at all. Just stay inside and let them have a little privacy," I said.

Wendy looked uncertain, but I reassured her that the men standing around her deck were not interested in making trouble. They were interested in putting trouble to rest.

She reluctantly closed her door against the cold, and I went back to the SUV, giving the group of grieving men a wide berth. Little Joe obviously had more friends than anyone knew about. Maybe these men were relatives or friends of Martin's, who had come to support him. I noticed that only two or three were Martin's age. The other men were far older. It was possible I was looking at the majority of the Crow Tribal Council.

I sensed no maliciousness from them as I climbed inside my vehicle and pulled away. This gathering lacked venom. It was calm and sad. I did see an expression of bitter resolve on Martin's face as my headlights flashed over him.

My windshield fogged with mist as I drove into town. It was humid, cold, and I found myself parking in the lot at Lil's automatically, and I went inside feeling morose.

When I sat down on my usual stool, Irene leveled a steady gaze on my expression and wordlessly plunked a piece of cherry pie on the counter in front of me. She pulled a can of whipped cream from a small cooler at the end of the counter and sprayed a fat cloud of cream on top of the pie.

"Thanks," I said.

"They buried Little Joe yesterday on the Reservation," she told me.

I took my first bite of pie. It wasn't as sweet as usual.

"Martin is having a ceremony over at the caretaker's cottage right now," I said.

She pulled out her stool and leaned a leg on the lip. "I'm sorry about you and Finn."

I felt my stomach twinge. "Did Loy tell you?"

"That, and I had a feeling you two wouldn't be that permanent," she admitted.

"Oh?" I asked. I had no right to feel irritated, but I was. "What gave you that feeling?"

"Finn did," she said. "He was too absent."

I hadn't thought it was possible for me to feel worse at the moment, but I was wrong. "So, I wasn't the only one who noticed that?"

"No, you weren't. He was not too interested in making himself available. Honestly, I'm surprised he stuck around as long as he did," she said.

Stephen, the flirty waiter, was sitting at the end of the counter with the cook. They were bent over the newspaper together and reading the comic section, looking bored.

I glanced around the café and saw that it was empty aside from two exhausted-looking snowmobilers who had finished dinner and were nursing a couple of cups of coffee. They still wore most of their snow gear, having stripped down just enough to accommodate eating. Their snowsuits were bunched up at their waists, and gloves and hats were strewn on the chairs beside them.

"It's quiet tonight," I said.

"It's the snow," she said. "It's too much work to go out if you don't have to. We've been closing early the last two nights."

I took another bite of pie. "Irene. You wouldn't happen to have seen my father lately, have you?"

She suppressed a grin, but I saw it before she could hide it.

"You have," I said.

"Maybe," she told me.

"Are you two…?"

"Maybe," she said.

I dropped my fork.

Irene hastily put a hand over my forearm. "Is it okay with you, Honey? Your dad is beside himself. He can't find a way to tell you about it, but he asked me on a date a couple of weeks ago and we had a really nice time. But I need to know, are you fine with me seeing your father?"

"Am I fine?" I asked.

Her expression shifted to panic.

"Irene," I said, trying to reassure her quickly. "Of course I am fine with it. I think it's probably the best thing that could happen to him."

She leaned forward and gave me a crushing hug over the counter, getting a huge dollop of whipped cream on the front of her red blouse. "Really? Oh, you have no idea what a relief that is. I've been trying to come up with the right way to let you know about us."

I was surprised, but after the horrible week I'd had this was welcome news. Irene was my best friend, and knowing that she was dating my father would come with its own set of complications. But those were surmountable. The important thing was that my father was happy, and if his demeanor lately was any indication, Irene seemed to be pretty good for him.

"What's his sign?" asked Stephen from the end of the counter.

"His sign?" I asked.

Stephen and the cook were still bent over the newspaper.

"Sure. Is he a Leo? Because, Miss Baker is a Leo, and two Leos shouldn't date. But if he is a Taurus, they will be great together," said Stephen cheerfully.

The cook, a chubby-faced man named Andy, nodded agreement. "You can't have two Leos."

"His birthday is November 24," I said.

Stephen scanned the newspaper. "He's a Sagittarius, the centaur. You are good, Miss Baker. You can date Mr. Dearcorn."

"Well I can't tell you what a relief that is," Irene said, rolling her eyes.

"What's your sign?" Andy asked. His plump fingers were laced across his round belly. When I looked at him, he grinned. "I heard you broke up with your boyfriend," he said.

"She's a Scorpio. She isn't compatible with anyone," Irene said.

"Too bad," Andy said, a bit too wistfully. "I'm a Gemini. I'm compatible with everyone."

"Don't sexually harass the customers," Irene told him.

Andy looked hurt. "But, Stephen sexually harasses the customers all the time, and you never say anything about it."

"That's because they like it when he does it," she said.

I had finished my pie, and I tucked some cash underneath the empty plate.

"Marley, I am glad you are fine with me and your father dating," she said. She gave me what was, for Irene, a warm smile.

"I am better than fine," I said. "I'm happy for you both."

She scooped up the plate and pocketed the cash. It was usually a toss-up whether or not I paid for my dinner at Lil's. She always refused money when she was experimenting on me with a new dish. Taking my money tonight was Irene's way of showing me that things wouldn't change between her and me simply because of this new relationship she had with my father. It was a small gesture, but I appreciated it anyway.

I stood up and pulled on my coat, preparing to face the chill air. "Are you coming by the ranch house for dinner on Christmas, by any chance?" I asked.

"I am," she said happily.

"I'll see you then," I told her. We shared another smile, and I turned towards the door.

I put my palm on the handle and stopped to glance back at Andy and Stephen, who were arguing about who would have to load the café dishwasher when the snowmobilers left.

"Hey, Andy," I said.

He slid his gaze towards me.

"What's the symbol for Gemini?" I asked. Something was nagging me, buzzing inside my head like a persistent fly.

"Why? You change your mind and want my phone number after all?" he asked.

"I don't deserve you," I said, deadpan.

He chuckled and spun a lazy circle on his stool. "Probably true."

"So, what's the symbol?" I asked again.

Andy watched as the two snowmobilers gathered their gear and headed for the door. They squeezed past me, leaving their table littered with dirty dishes that needed to be picked up. Reluctantly, Andy pushed himself to his feet and grabbed a grey tub to collect the dishes, so they could shut down the café for the evening.

I waited for him to answer me, putting a hand back on the door. I could feel the cold seeping in from outside, chilling my fingers. I thought I already knew what he would say, but I had to be sure. My thoughts were climbing over each other, all trying to race to the finish line at once.

248

Andy breezed past me towards the table, the tub propped on one hip bone. He started tossing dishes into it, giving me half of his attention. When he finished loading the tub, he started for the kitchen door, seemed to remember what I'd asked him, and finally glanced back at me, answering almost as an afterthought.

"The symbol for Gemini is the Twins."

He disappeared inside the kitchen, leaving me standing there, feeling as if the floor had just dropped out from underneath my feet.

CHAPTER 20

When the librarian at the Fable branch library pulled into the parking lot, I was sitting in the black SUV waiting for her. She looked a bit surprised that someone would be lurking there already, shoved her thick glasses back up her nose with one finger after locking her car, and walked past me into the building. She glanced back a few times as if she were trying to place me in her memory. I knew she wouldn't open the front door for business until nine, and since it was only eight thirty I would be sitting out in the cold parking lot like an idiot for half an hour, but I didn't care. It would give me time to think.

The symbol for the astrological sign of Gemini was the Twins, and Joe loved astronomy. Wilma had told me Little Joe was planning to attend Bozeman in order to study astronomy, and I felt stupid I hadn't seen the connection before. I had been so distracted by the notion that Little Joe might have wanted to crash a party that I had been blind to the truth of the situation.

The day Little Joe had talked to Matthew in the gym his words had been misunderstood. He hadn't literally meant "take a shower," Joseph had been talking about something else entirely.

I sat inside the SUV with the heater off. The windows were

already icing over, and I could see my breath even inside the car. But I was just angry at myself enough that I felt warm.

The Fable branch library was small, maybe the size of a roadside filling station, but it was beautiful. It looked more like a quaint log cabin than a library. I'd seen the inside a few times, and from what I remembered of the place, it was as groomed and organized on the inside as it was on the outside. It wasn't able to house many titles because of a lack of space, but the shelves were always neat and tidy, the hardwood floors always clean.

When nine a.m. arrived, the librarian flipped on the lights inside the library and unlocked the door. She stood watching me for a moment to see if I would race inside to escape the cold. As soon as she turned the open sign around, I didn't disappoint her.

"Good morning," she said as I pushed open the door. "What can I help you find today?"

Her name badge indicated she was Rose, the manager.

She was short, maybe five one, but her small frame was packed with focused energy. She had a quick expression and bright eyes. She was close to my age or a couple years older, maybe thirty-five or so. Her hair was wild, to say the least. It was long and mostly blond, but streaks of hot pink had been painted on here and there haphazardly, and if I hadn't seen her with her name badge, I'd have never guessed she was the branch manager. I'd have pegged her for the assistant.

She walked behind a small pine desk that sat across from the main counter, and took a seat behind her computer screen, her hands ready to type. I could see she knew at once I was looking for information, and I got the impression she was intrigued.

"I was afraid you would be closed, it being Christmas Eve and all," I said, taking a seat in the heavy pine chair across from her desk.

"We close at two today," she told me. "So what are you looking for today?"

"Well, first I need to know if the astrological sign Gemini has an astronomical correspondent," I said.

She smiled faintly. Her fingers flew over the keyboard. I was relieved that she obviously knew the difference between astronomy and astrology. "Yes," she said.

I waited for her to finish answering. I could see she was just getting warmed up.

She studied the screen for a moment, condensing the paragraphs of information I saw reflected in her glasses to one sentence. "The astrological sign Gemini is Latin for 'the twins,' and there is a constellation called Gemini that is also associated with the Greek mythological figures of Castor and Pollux, also known as the Gemini Twins."

She held her hands over the keyboard, ready for another question. Her expression seemed to say, "Come on, give me something hard."

"Okay," I said. This was the tricky part. "Is the Gemini constellation visible at night in December in our hemisphere?"

She smiled a little wider, and her fingers danced over the keyboard. "No. It's only visible in our hemisphere in January and February, and then again in April and May. Not in December."

I sat back in the pine chair and thought. "What about meteor showers? Are there any meteor showers that are visible in December here in Killdeer?"

She typed, humming to herself. "Yes."

I hadn't noticed it, but I'd been holding my breath. "What's it called?" I asked.

She scanned her computer screen. "It's a doozy. Supposed to be one of the biggest showers of the year. The peak night for viewing this shower was on December 14, at midnight. That was a Tuesday."

"Why midnight?" I asked.

"Because the moon was one-quarter full and didn't set until 12:02 that night. So before that, it would have been too bright to see the meteors. But after midnight it would be perfect for viewing."

I took a very slow, deep breath. "What was the name of that meteor shower?"

She looked at me over the top of her thick glasses. "The Geminid. Also known as the Twins Shower."

I smacked myself on the forehead hard enough to leave a red mark.

Rose blinked, but she seemed more curious than put off by my gesture.

I leaned forward in the chair. "Okay. I don't know if you can tell me this or not. But what was the weather forecast on Tuesday the fourteenth? Was it clear, or was it cloudy?"

She typed and hummed. "It was clear," she said, her fingers pausing. "Clear and warm. Unseasonably warm."

I rubbed my tired eyes. I hadn't gotten much sleep the night before. "Anybody with a computer could get this information, couldn't they?" I asked.

"Well, not anybody," she said. "You would have to know what you were looking for. It isn't as if something like a meteor shower gets air time on the nightly news. But if you were into astronomy, you could find this information without any problem."

It all fell into place with a click in my head. Little Joe had gone to our pasture to watch a meteor shower; that was the only logical explanation. When he had told his grandmother he was going to go out that night to "watch the Twins Shower," she had misunderstood him completely. Everyone had misunderstood him.

Now it was clear to me what had really happened that night.

Rose tilted her head to the side. "Is there anything else?"

I let out a deep sigh and nodded. "Yes. Can you get me the address for someone living on the Reservation over at Crow Agency? I need to know if I can find the residence of Martin Flies Low."

Again with the tapping. "It's 45 Mapata Road."

"How did you find that so fast?" I asked.

She waggled her eyebrows at me. "Super-secret librarian powers."

"Do you have to go to school to learn that?" I asked, maybe a tad bit hopefully.

She laughed. "It's not absolutely necessary. A library degree is preferred if you are in the profession, but my undergraduate degree is in history."

"I have an associate of general science," I said.

Her face brightened. "That's not a bad degree. It's a good stepping-stone for all sorts of undergrad programs."

So far, all my associate's degree had ever gotten me was useless trivia about the natural world and the ability to say that I at least had a degree in something.

"I have thought about going back to school, but working full time, it's not an easy thing to do," I admitted.

"If you work full time, what are you doing up here on a Friday morning?" She looked immediately apologetic. "I'm sorry, that was snoopy," she said quickly.

"I was a landscaper, but I got injured, and I couldn't work at that anymore," I told her. "I'm supposed to stay out of the workforce until next week. That's when my doctor will release me to jump back in and be a productive member of society again."

Her face went through the gymnastics I was used to seeing when people registered who I was.

"Oh, you are Marley," she said, the story unfolding in her mind. Everyone in Killdeer knew about my getting shot.

I couldn't tell if she was one of those who fell into the category of shocked and titillated.

Rose didn't say anything either way concerning her opinions about me, but she did lift a pencil in her hand and tap it on the blotter, showing that she was thinking.

"I heard that you might lose your assistant up here." I winced inside, hoping I wasn't overstepping my bounds, but I hadn't worked for nearly eight weeks, and I was getting desperate.

Rose hadn't taken her eyes off me the entire time. "It's not official yet."

"Officially, I'm not supposed to go back to work again until Friday of next week," I said.

Was this a job interview?

"Friday, it will be official that we have a position open," Rose said carefully.

"I've never worked as a librarian, but I worked as an office manager in Helena for nine years for the Fish and Wildlife Service at their little branch office," I said, trying to sound casual. "It wasn't the main office, which is like a small city, but I had some interesting responsibilities."

She raised her head at that, pondering. "You know spread-sheets?"

"Inside and out," I said.

She hummed again, the pencil rapping on the blotter. "The pay won't be that great. It's only sixteen hours a week."

I kept my face as neutral as I possibly could. "Any job is better than no job at all."

"It can be boring sometimes."

"Have you ever had to input fifteen hundred sage grouse sighting reports into a database?" I asked.

"Game wardens recorded fifteen hundred sage grouse sightings?" she asked.

"Biologists," I said. "And after a couple of days putting in the data I started to think that they had just seen the same sage grouse fifteen hundred times."

She laughed and tossed the pencil on the blotter, having made up her mind. "Listen, I'm not supposed to do this, and if anyone asks, we never had this conversation. But, I'm planning on filling this position on a first-come-first-serve basis. I'm listing the job in the paper Friday after next, and you know how the *Killdeer Press* is. It doesn't really hit the stands until around three in the afternoon. So, if someone was to have their resume up here and in my hand on that Thursday morning, it's not my fault that nobody else gets a crack at it. I posted the job, so my obligations are fulfilled. Right?"

"Right," I said.

"The side door has a mail slot," she told me. She pushed her glasses back up on her nose.

"My resume will be waiting for you when you get to work that day," I said.

She tapped a key on her keyboard, and a printer on a small side table behind her chirped to life. It spit out a single piece of paper, and she handed it to me.

"This is the job description."

I took it and carefully folded it in half, slid it into my coat pocket, and stood up. "Thank you for your help."

"I hope I told you the information you needed," she said.

I borrowed a pen from the desk, pulled a sticky note off a stack of the yellow slips, and jotted Martin's address down while it was still fresh in my memory. "You told me exactly what I needed to know. I appreciate all of your help."

She propped a foot on the corner of her desk, her beige slacks riding up her ankle, revealing hot pink socks. Rose was not like any manager I had ever seen before. Maybe librarians were unique in that respect.

"I have a feeling you will," she said.

I left the Fable branch library, not daring to hope that I would soon have a job working there, and felt my mood pick up a notch.

As I drove back towards Killdeer, I thought the pieces of the puzzle had finally all fallen into place at last.

Little Joe had gone out to our field on the night he was killed to watch the meteor shower. He had arranged to meet Meg, so they could enjoy it together. She had never showed.

He must have felt so disappointed, but he had stayed to watch the meteors anyway, probably figuring that it would be the last chance he would get to see a show as spectacular as the Geminid shower for a while.

What was the best way to watch the night sky? Go to an isolated area with no lights around. In Killdeer valley, you couldn't get much more isolated than the Dearcorn pasture. So, it was as simple as that. Little Joe had chosen our pasture because it was close to town, but far enough away to give him a good view of the sky. Everyone who had overheard him talking about watching the Twins Shower had jumped to the wrong conclusion. Even me.

Finally, I'd managed to solve the mystery. Little Joe's death had been an accident after all.

A part of me was relieved to finally know what had really happened, but a part of me was heartsick too. Even though it was Christmas Eve, I didn't feel very festive. The Flies Low family would be celebrating without Joseph this year. It made me grateful that my father and I had each other.

As I drove through downtown Fable, which consisted of a block and a half of tiny retail shops and Julian's sporting goods store, I could see that it was completely deserted. A light snow started to fall, salting my windshield with crystal flakes. The air was crisp with cold, and I flipped on the seat warmer, reveling in the decadent feeling.

A car came into view as I rounded a tight corner, and I slowed down to peer at it through the dusting of snowflakes.

It was an older, silver Volvo, exactly like the one Meg and Matthew Chan drove to school every day.

I tapped my brakes, watching the Volvo with growing concern. The car was parked in the middle of the street, the taillights facing me, and the engine running. Smoke drifted from the tailpipe, but as I pulled up closer to the car I could see that the driver's side door was open.

"What the hell?" Parking in the street behind the car, a feeling of dread started to creep over me. I climbed out of my SUV and hurried over to the Volvo.

The front, right tire was twisted, and the bumper had been torn off. Glass crunched under my feet, and as I bent down to peer inside the car, I could see that the passenger side window had been smashed and glass peppered the seats. The Volvo looked like it had been rammed by a dump truck. I expected to see Matthew Chan slumped over on the seat, but the car was empty.

Panic started to fill my chest. I stepped back quickly and searched the ground. I was making a mess of it, my own footprints smudging the tracks that were dotted on the road, but I could clearly see that someone had jumped from the car.

I scanned the ground and saw footprints heading away from the Volvo and moving towards the tree line. Someone wearing sneakers, about the size of a tall teenage boy's, had run from the Volvo, across the road, and had deliberately gone into the thick trees.

I cupped my hands around my mouth and called out. "Matthew! Can you hear me? Where are you?"

No answer. Not a sound could be heard from the forest. I trotted across the roadway, following the tracks as best I could. When I got to the edge of the road, the trees grew so thick it was difficult to see anything. But even I could tell almost at once that Matthew Chan had left his car and had run across the road and straight down towards the forest. The tracks led down the steep drop towards the valley, and after following them for a few yards into the thick brush and trees, I could plainly see that he was moving at a dead sprint. The tracks were spaced too far apart for him to be walking. He was running.

As I searched the ground, Matthew's tracks were not the only thing that I saw.

Full-blown panic set in, and I did the only thing that I could.

Sprinting back to my SUV, I dove for the driver's seat and slammed the door closed as I threw the car in gear. I gunned the engine and turned my car around as fast as I could, pushed the gas pedal to the floor, and drove up the road deeper into the twisting labyrinth of Fable.

As I reached the house I was looking for, I slammed on the brakes just before shooting by the driveway, spun the wheel, and brought the SUV to a sliding stop at the door.

When I jumped out of the car, Dean Tisdale was standing in his doorway looking at me with surprise.

I ran to him, out of breath. "I need you. Matthew Chan is lost in the forest. I need you to track him."

Any other man would have wanted an explanation, wanting more facts, and would have given me the fifth degree before making a move. But not Dean. Wordlessly, he went back inside, and I could see him reaching for his boots and his coat.

I leaned against the door frame, trying to catch my breath. "Dean," I said, my voice ragged. "Bring your bow."

He reached for his coat, lifted his longbow from a wooden stock by the door, and looped a quiver of arrows over his shoulder.

We ran for the car, and as soon as he was inside, I threw it in reverse and drove him back towards the center of town.

"Why do I need my bow?" he asked, looking at me with concern.

"Because," I said, ignoring the warning chime from my unbuckled seat belt. "Matthew is in serious trouble."

"How do you know that?" he asked.

I kept my eyes on the road so that I wouldn't roll the car and kill us both.

I gripped the steering wheel so tightly my hands were turning white. "Matthew's tracks weren't the only ones I saw going into the forest."

The engine roared as it shifted gears.

CHAPTER 21

My SUV slid to a stop beside the silver Volvo, and I threw open my door. Dean was already out, leaning down and looking at the ground while he strung his bow with one smooth motion. He slung his quiver over his shoulder, putting the arrows in the quick-draw position I'd seen him use up on the mountain.

As I stepped closer to the abandoned Volvo, it started to snow in earnest. Tiny flakes like specks of dust gave way to larger, fuller clumps of white the size of cotton balls. I knew the tracks in the forest wouldn't last much longer.

"Miss Marley, please don't walk there," he said, waving me back with his free hand.

I jumped back, giving him room to study the tracks. He glanced briefly at the inside of the Volvo, his expert eyes seeing things that I hadn't.

"Blood," he said, crouching beside the car door.

I had missed it entirely, but two tiny, round drops dotted the road beside the car tire. He cocked his head to the side, and it looked to me like he was reading the tracks and drawing a picture in his mind of what had occurred.

His pale eyes lifted to the tree line, and he squinted through the grey forest.

Without a word Dean started walking towards the trees, determined.

"Wait," I said, reaching for his arm. "What do you want me to do? How can I help?"

He blinked once, looking at me with an expressionless face. "Don't follow me," he said, his voice stern.

With that, Dean disappeared into the trees.

I stood in the middle of the road for a full minute, trying to make sense of what had just happened.

In my blind panic I'd neglected to slow down and think about what the tracks in the snow were telling me. I took a deep breath and studied the roadway and the tracks carefully.

Fable rested on a rough plateau at the crest of the mountain. If Matthew kept running straight down the slope and did not veer off in another direction, then he would come out of the trees in the valley not very far from my father's ranch.

So would whoever was chasing him. But maybe I could get to Matthew first.

My adrenaline forced me to climb back in my car. I couldn't stand around hoping for the best. I had to do something.

My mind raced as I hugged the tight corners, the tires barely managing to keep traction on the slippery road.

Who could possibly want to hurt Matthew Chan? Somehow that didn't seem as important as getting to the boy before they did. I could sort out the reason behind it later.

As I drove the twisting turns, feeling the wheels spin and try to bite the slippery roadway, I kept my eyes focused on the side of the road. Maybe Matthew had managed to evade whoever was chasing him and had been able to find the road again?

But as I kept my steady pace down the mountain, I could see

that wasn't likely. The closer I got to the valley the more perspective I gained, and it became apparent where Matthew's path would take him. About halfway down the steep slope, the even ground shifted into a deep channel that drained spring runoff, and the flat track became a narrow cut in the landscape. The terrain on either side of the drainage was tough going, and more than likely Matthew would follow the channel all the way. The drainage came out at the bottom in one very specific place.

"The culvert," I said out loud. I hit the gas.

The wheels spun, but managed to keep enough traction to keep me on the road. I ignored the leaning stop sign at the bottom of the hill and sped through it towards my father's ranch.

I pulled up along the fence line beside our pasture at last, parked, and stood on the roadway, searching the sloping hillside and watching for any sort of movement. Nothing. Not even the ground could help me now. All traces of activity were being erased by the fat snowflakes falling from above. If Matthew had run through here recently, I wouldn't be able to tell. The snow had covered everything with a fresh coat of white.

As I searched the ground in vain, the only thing left to do was check the culvert to see if he had made it that far down the mountain.

I trotted across the road and headed for the culvert, thinking that I could at least check inside the twisted hulk to see if Matthew was hiding inside. I knew the kid was in fantastic physical shape, according to his coach. By cutting through the woods and coming straight down, I guessed that it wouldn't take him more than a half an hour to reach the bottom.

As I ran up the shoulder of the road towards the culvert I noticed a vehicle parked behind a stand of trees, and my heart skipped a beat. I could just see the back bumper of the vehicle, but

I couldn't see what it was. It looked black.

I slid down the sharp drop that led across the barrow ditch towards the culvert, and had to dig in with both feet to stop sliding on the slick snow. I was closer to the vehicle now. All I could see through the trees was one taillight, but I couldn't see anything else. It was a dark vehicle, but not completely black as it had first appeared.

Wet snow crunched and popped under my feet.

I walked towards the vehicle, leaning to the right as far as I could, trying to see what it was. When I was only a dozen yards away the shape of the vehicle came into view at last, revealing its outline. Black and gold paint, high aluminum wheels, and a mirror shine showed me it was a Laramie Longhorn.

It was Julian's truck. What was he doing down here?

I walked closer to see if I could spot him and crouched down to peer through the bent culvert. I saw a shadow move on the other side of the twisted tube.

"Julian?" I called. "It's Marley."

Julian didn't answer me. I frowned and took another step towards the culvert, stopping to rest one hand on the lip. The metal was ice cold, and I pulled my fingers away. "Hey, Julian?"

"What are you doing here?" he called back.

He was standing at the opposite end, peering back at me, hands at his sides.

"Matthew Chan might have gotten lost in the forest and might come down this way. Have you seen anyone?"

He shook his head, his hands flexing. "No. But there is something back here that I think you should take a look at."

"What is it?" I asked. I took a step inside the culvert and crouched a bit lower to see if I could spot what he was talking about. I could see his outline but not his face.

266

"Come this way," he said. "There is something strange here. You should take a look and tell me what you think."

I moved further inside the culvert. The roof was twisted, but it was still in sound enough shape that I could crab-walk through the center.

"What did you find?" I asked as I inched my way along.

"I'm not sure. It could be important," he said.

I had to lift my hands and steady myself using the sides of the culvert as I went through. I stumbled on a burned-out stick of wood that must have been left over from a bonfire, and I had to catch myself to keep from falling. Sticks and half-burnt branches littered the inside.

I was almost to the end when Julian took a few steps towards me. He gave me a warm smile and jerked his head towards the other end.

"It's really odd," he said. "Come take a look."

"What is it?" I asked, confused.

He didn't answer, but lifted his right arm and draped it over my shoulder, helping to steady me.

"Let me give you a hand," he said, tucking me under his arm. "It's pretty slick down here."

He started to pull me through the end of the culvert when I heard a loud snap. A shadow flickered across my vision, and I felt a rush of wind. Something wet and warm splashed my cheek, and I pulled away.

In the blink of an eye Julian went rigid beside me and his arm fell from my shoulder.

I turned towards him, my mind trying to make sense of what I was seeing. Julian teetered on his heels, his entire body suddenly limp, and he fell forward out the end of the culvert.

The shaft of a dark arrow gleamed black from Julian's blood.

A razor sharp arrowhead protruded from the back of his head and red oozed from the wound onto the fresh snow.

He twitched once and fell still.

My legs gave out and I had to lean against the side of the culvert to keep from falling over. Stars swam in my vision. Through the haze of shock, I saw a shadow moving fast through the trees. Someone was running towards me, sprinting out of the tree line off in the distance.

It was a man, and he was holding a bow.

He moved like a cat and covered the distance so quickly it was a blur.

I scrambled backwards trying to make my feet move. All I could manage was a pathetic shuffle, and I couldn't make it to the other side of the culvert before he caught me. Fear and anger surged through me when he ducked down and came inside the culvert.

Dean's face came into focus, and my legs completely collapsed when I saw him.

"Dean! What did you do?"

"Are you all right?" he asked. He was gasping for air, like he had just been running for his life.

I couldn't believe what I'd seen. I turned back and saw Julian lying motionless on the ground, blood leaking from the back of his head and pooling beside his still body. The dark arrow had cut cleanly through his eye and protruded from the back of his skull as if the bone had offered little resistance. He had been killed instantly.

"Why?" I yelled. "Why did you do that? He was showing me something. He didn't want me to fall down. He wasn't groping me!"

Dean was watching me, his expression calm. He set his bow aside and leaned over me, wrapping a hand under my arm. I inched away until my back was against the culvert wall and shoved at his shoulders.

"Don't you touch me!"

I struggled as he tried to lift me again and aimed a wild punch at his jaw. He ducked me easily and pinned my arms.

His voice was gentle. "Miss Marley," he said softly. "Stop."

"You let me go," I said between clenched teeth, trying in vain to shove him away.

"There's something you should see," he told me.

I swung my fist again as hard as I could but he shrugged the blow aside. "I told you to let me go!"

His expression was blank. He shook my shoulders, hard. "Miss Marley!" he said. Then he lowered his voice. "There is something you *need* to see."

He released my shoulders and stood up as much as he could. He walked out the back of the culvert and stopped, waiting for me.

My head felt thick and it was so difficult to focus I could barely stand. Dean beckoned to me, holding up one hand. I managed to stumble out of the culvert, and my throat tightened as Julian's body came into view. He lay sprawled at the end of the culvert not more than a few feet from where I stood.

I swallowed, my mouth bone dry. I tore my eyes away from Julian and fixed them on Dean just so I wouldn't have to look at the lifeless body any longer. Dean lifted one hand and pointed to the right.

I followed his hand and then I saw what he had been trying to show me.

Matthew Chan was on the ground, face down. His head leaked blood from a gash above his eye and dried blood was crusted around his nose.

Realization dawned like an avalanche.

I had surprised Julian in the act of assaulting Matthew, and he had come close to killing me. The only reason I was still alive was because of Dean.

I dropped to the ground beside Matthew, shoving his dark hair out of the way so I could check the wound on his head. His forehead bore a deep gash, but I couldn't see any bone in the wound. Blood flowed from it liberally.

"Matt, can you hear me?"

I forced my shaking hands to be still long enough to check for a pulse, and I covered the big gash with my hands. I looked up at Dean, shock giving way to relief. I swallowed hard, regret and gratitude washing over me.

Dean simply watched me with an unreadable expression.

My voice came out like a gasp. "He's alive."

CHAPTER 22

"The doctor says it might be days before he wakes up," Loy said.

The burly sheriff sat across from me at my father's kitchen table, one big hand wrapped around a mug of steaming coffee and the other rubbing his tired eyes.

He yawned and leaned back in the chair, looking exhausted.

Three days had gone by since Matthew had been taken to the emergency room in Parkman, and this was the first news I'd had of his condition.

"It must have been a very bad head injury," I said.

"By rights, it should have been fatal. Julian very nearly got the job done, but you kept him from finishing it."

My hands felt cold, and I tucked them inside my blue sweatshirt to keep them warm. My father sat to my right at the table, nursing his own mug of black coffee and watching the sheriff with a sympathetic eye.

Loy groaned and stretched his arms. "It just doesn't make any goddamned sense. Nick and I have been able to figure out one thing that connects Little Joe to Julian Hartmann, but only one."

"Wilma's glaucoma medicine," I said.

Loy stopped stretching and stared at me. "That's right."

I wasn't about to tell him that Wilma had slipped up and inadvertently mentioned it to me. I had finally recalled she had said that Little Joe was able to get her eye medicine from the *heart man* up in Fable. After putting some thought into it, I realized she hadn't been talking about a doctor or a pharmacist. She'd been talking about Julian. Julian Hartmann. And the eye medicine she had mentioned wasn't prescription. That was why Wilma had suggested her son Martin wouldn't want to go pick it up for her any longer. It wasn't exactly legal to purchase.

I shrugged when he continued to stare. "Small town."

He rubbed his chin and gave me a speculative look. "Uh huh."

My father shook his head at Loy. "Glaucoma?"

Loy sighed. "Wilma smoked marijuana. A lot."

I chimed in. "You know how her house always smelled like burning sage? She used it to mask the smell of pot."

My father made a noise like a grunt. "I thought she burned it all the time because she was a very spiritual person."

"Amen," Loy said, taking a long draw on his coffee.

"So Little Joe was buying marijuana for his grandmother from Julian?" my father asked.

"Probably for years. It was the only thing we could find that connected the two of them. But knowing that doesn't do a damn bit of good. It doesn't explain anything else that happened," Loy said, looking miserable. "There's the connection between Joe and Julian. But the rest of it makes no sense at all. We cannot find a single thing connecting Matthew to Julian. Other than the fact that Little Joe knew them both, there isn't even a hint about why Julian would have it in for Matthew."

"Kiddo, why are you bugging the sheriff today?" my father asked. "He looks like he could use about a month's worth of sleep."

I'd had three long days to think about the events of Christmas

Eve, and after the thoughts had buzzed in my head like angry hornets until I was pretty sure I'd go crazy, something finally clicked into place. When I had come to the realization that Little Joe was a long-time customer of Julian's, that he had been buying marijuana from him for an extended period, then everything else finally fell together. I'd been blinded by my sympathy for Dean to the point that I hadn't been able to see the whole picture. I'd been so focused on proving that Dean was innocent, the rest of the facts hadn't sunk in completely. But after I'd had a few days to really think about everything, the answer was obvious.

"I'm pretty sure I know what happened the night Joseph died," I said, keeping my voice level.

Loy's jaw jutted forward and he sat up. "Marley, I've got a kid in a coma, a kid that's been murdered, and the only guy who can shed any light on the subject is lying on a slab at the funeral home thanks to the efforts of your good buddy Tisdale. I don't have the time, or the patience, to hear your personal theory about how my town suddenly went crazy."

"It would have been a lot worse if Dean hadn't been there," my father pointed out, his expression hard.

Loy held up a hand. "Granted, he did the right thing, no question. But couldn't you tell me about your theory after I get this all sorted out?"

"I didn't want to waste time telling you," I said.

Almost as if on cue, there was a knock at the door. I stood up and pulled it open. "So I thought I would show you instead."

Hooper Bukowski, Connor Schultz, and Meg Chan stood in the doorway. Hooper's battered white pickup truck was parked outside the ranch house.

Meg had knocked, and when she saw me she gave a thin smile, her slender hand dropping to her side. "Hi, um. Is this the right time?"

"The perfect time," I said.

Loy shot me a suspicious look. I held up one hand. "Bear with me. We need to go for a drive down to the pasture. Why don't I drive the kids down there, and you can meet us?"

The sheriff stood up, hitched up his gun belt and made a face like he'd just stepped on a tack. But he grumbled, pulled out his keys, and waved a dramatic gesture to the door. "After you."

"What do you want us to go over there for?" asked Hooper. He was still thin and pale.

"I think it will be easier to explain if we are actually there," I said.

After squeezing the high school kids into my SUV, my father insisting that he wanted to be included and ending up in the front seat with me, the five of us left the ranch house and headed down to the pasture. We met Loy on the road, parked, and everyone climbed out.

It was a crystal-clear winter morning. Flecks of snow tumbled across the frozen ground, swirling in gentle circles across the landscape like tiny dust devils made of ice. The air was chilled and silent.

As the sheriff stepped out of his brown truck and adjusted his hat, he gave me a warning look, indicating with his unhappy expression that he would participate in my little exercise only for so long.

Hooper was the first to speak. "It's freezing. How long do we have to stand out here? This place gives me the creeps."

"Can we hurry up? My parents think I'm at the grocery store," Meg said, her long black coat looking like a raven's wing against the snow.

Bracing myself for impact, I turned to the boys first.

"Hooper, whose idea was it to have a bonfire party on that Tuesday night?"

He frowned, his heavy brow working hard. "I don't know.

Connor told me about it."

"I thought it was your idea," Connor said.

I looked back and forth between them. "I think it was Matthew's idea."

They both shuffled their feet. Connor shrugged. "Maybe. It sort of just happened."

Meg was looking at me with an unhappy expression. She started to say something, but I cut her off.

"Whose idea was it to have the contest with the bow?"

Hooper shot a worried glance at the sheriff, but he didn't say anything.

"Do you remember?" I asked, prompting him.

"Marley, we have been through this," Loy said.

"I don't remember," Hooper admitted. "For honest to God, I don't remember."

"Connor?" I asked.

The smaller boy hunched his shoulders. "I thought it was Hooper's idea."

"I think it was Matt's," I said, ignoring the searing look that Meg was giving me.

"Why is this important?" Connor asked.

"How many arrows did you shoot?" I asked.

Neither boy hesitated at all.

"Two," said Connor.

"Two. I shot one; Connor shot one," Hooper said, not a shadow of doubt in his voice.

"Okay," I said. "So what happened to the third arrow?"

Everyone grew quiet suddenly.

"Third arrow?" my father said, glancing out at the pasture.

I held up my fingers. "Connor shot one; Hooper shot one. But I don't think that Little Joe was killed by either one of them. The chances that a person could be hit with an arrow out in a pasture of this size are remote. I think that Julian Hartmann killed Joe with an arrow that was identical to the other two."

Even Loy was regarding me with an appraising look.

"But, why would Julian want to kill Joseph?" Meg asked.

"I'll get to that. But first of all, I know this is not exactly procedure, Loy, but did the arrow you found in the pasture have any duct tape on it?"

The sheriff cleared his throat. "I think I will keep that information to myself. For now."

"I'm going to assume that it didn't," I told him. "Hooper, you told me that Connor put duct tape around the shaft of his arrow so that you could tell them apart in the pasture. That's how you knew it was your arrow that killed Little Joe."

"It was that heavy silver kind," Connor admitted. "We put in on the end, right in front of the feathers."

"But the arrow in the pasture didn't have any tape on it," I said, looking at the sheriff. "And neither did the one used to kill Little Joe. So, what happened to it? Where did the arrow with the duct tape go?"

Meg was looking confused and unhappy. "But what does this have to do with what happened to my brother?"

I'd been dreading this part. But it was no time to be timid. "Meg, the night that Joseph went to our pasture, you were supposed to meet him there. You were going to watch the Geminid meteor shower with him, weren't you?"

She stammered and started to wring her hands. "I—I'm not supposed to talk about it. Matthew said he didn't want me mixed up in it."

Loy leaned closer to Meg, his voice a mixture of surprise and anger. "Is that the case, young lady? You were supposed to meet

Little Joe out there to watch the stars?"

"Please don't lie," I said. "I know that the two of you had plans to watch the meteor shower. But I also know you got caught trying to sneak out and have been grounded since then."

She looked stricken, but she nodded. "The best time to view the meteors was a little after midnight. I was going to pick up Joseph before midnight, and we wanted to be there before the moon set, so we could find a good spot. But my parents were so mad I didn't want to get in even more trouble. Matt told me it would be better for me to just stay home. But I never got a chance to tell Joseph I wouldn't be there. I thought he went looking for me over at the bonfire party and that's why he got killed. We were going to drive out there together but I couldn't go."

"Someone else gave Joseph a ride that night," I said. "I think it was Matthew."

Meg's eyes flashed. "You don't know that."

"I think I do. Wilma's neighbor across the street said that your Volvo was always coming and going. If she saw the car the night Joseph died, she wouldn't have thought twice about it. But it wasn't you driving it that night. It was your brother."

"Why? Why would Matt go to the trouble to give Joe a ride to the pasture?" Loy asked.

"Because it was all a part of his plan," I told them.

No one spoke. Hooper's face was a mass of emotions. If it was possible, he looked paler than he ever had.

"See where the bonfire is?" I asked the group.

Everyone pivoted around.

"You can't, can you?" I asked.

"So?" Meg demanded.

"We know where it is, but from here, from this spot, you can't quite see it because it's too far back in the trees. The only thing we can see from the road is the very end of the culvert. So, Matthew could have brought Little Joe to the pasture, dropped him off, and nobody at the bonfire would have ever known it."

"This doesn't make any sense at all," Meg said.

"We need to go for another quick drive," I told everyone. "We need to go up to Julian's sporting goods. I think that I know why Matthew was up in Fable the day Julian tried to kill him."

This time, the sheriff didn't grumble or hesitate, and the kids had all grown very quiet. We clambered back inside the SUV, Loy started his truck, and we drove up to the sporting goods store in tandem.

Once there, everyone milled in the parking lot; nervous glances and mumbled questions flew back and forth.

When Loy stepped out of his truck, I nodded towards the store. "The day that Julian tried to kill Matthew, the sporting goods store was broken into, wasn't it?"

"How did you know that?" he asked.

"Because Julian said that his alarm system on the store was tied to his telephone at home, and that it alerted him when someone broke into the store. Unfortunately for Matthew, I don't think he knew that."

"Why would my brother break into Julian's store?" Meg said. "There's nothing in there he would want to steal."

"He wasn't taking something," I told her. "He was leaving something."

Everyone started talking at once, asking questions and arguing with what I had just said. But Hooper was quiet and subdued. The sheriff was focused.

"Marley, what's your thinking on this?" my father asked, holding up his hands to quiet everyone down.

"Can we go inside?" I asked the sheriff. "I promise you, it will be worth the trouble."

"We can't all go inside," Loy said. "Tell me what you are looking for, and I'll see what I can do."

I was willing to compromise at this point. "Hooper, me, and you. The rest can wait outside."

"Why do you need me for?" asked Hooper.

"You'll see," I told him. "It will only take a moment."

The sheriff led the two of us around to the backdoor of the store. The small window had been broken out on the top of the door, and a piece of cardboard had been taped in place over the missing pane of glass to keep out the snow. The door handle was nothing more than a thick steel bar bent in a crescent shape that had been screwed right into the wood frame. A heavy chain and padlock were looped through the handle and had also been looped through an iron ring bolted on the side of the building. It was crude, but effective.

"We put up this chain until Patty can come back and get the glass replaced," Loy explained.

He used a small key to open the padlock and ushered Hooper and me inside.

The sheriff flipped on the lights, and I led them both through the storage area in the back and out onto the main floor of the store.

I stopped beside the big arrow box in front of the counter and started searching through them.

"What are you doing?" Loy asked.

"Just a minute."

Hooper stood beside me, peering over my shoulder.

After a diligent search, I finally found what I had dearly hoped would be there.

With two fingers, I gingerly grasped an arrow inside the mismatched bin and lifted it out by the plastic tip.

I held it up to the light so that Hooper could see it clearly. It was a gold-tipped, aluminum Lightning White arrow, identical to the one used to kill Little Joe. The bullet tip had been unscrewed from the end and a brand new broadhead was in its place. Just in front of the feathers, wrapped around the shaft clumsily, was a piece of silver duct tape.

"That's Connor's arrow," Hooper said instantly. "That's the tape we used. What the hell is it doing in here?"

Loy took it from me at once, using his fingertips and being careful not to touch the shaft. "Are you sure?"

"Positive," Hooper said. "I'm positive."

The sheriff went behind the counter and pulled out a plastic bag. He carefully placed the arrow inside and wrapped it up.

"We can go back outside now," I said. "This tells me everything we need to know."

After Loy had secured the store's backdoor once more, the three of us joined the others in the parking lot.

"What did you find?" Meg asked. She was nervous, but curious.

"We found the reason that Julian tried to kill your brother," I said.

Meg put a hand over her mouth, her eyes welling with sudden tears. "Was it the drugs? Was Matt buying drugs from him? I sometimes gave Joseph a ride up here to get pot for his grandma."

The sheriff had tucked the arrow inside his truck and locked the door. He came back, stood in front of me, and folded his arms. "All right. I'm listening."

I took a deep breath. "Meg. Your brother didn't like the fact that you were friends with Little Joe, did he?"

Her lower lip trembled, but she shook her head and managed to answer. "He told me that I shouldn't hang out with Joseph because he was holding me back, distracting me from school, ruining my reputation. But that's not the way it was. Joseph and I were just friends. There wasn't any more to it than that."

"But Matthew thought there was more," I said.

Loy wasn't looking at me any longer. He was listening to Meg very carefully.

She sniffed and wiped a hand across her nose. "Maybe. I don't know. He got really mad when we ditched school to go to the movie. He told me that I couldn't ever see Joseph again after that."

"You told him that you would stay friends with Little Joe in spite of that, didn't you?" I said.

"We wanted to go to Bozeman and study astronomy," she said desperately.

"Your brother wanted you to forget about that," I said.

Loy was letting his eyes play across the cold ground. His expression was grim, and I could see that he was starting to put it together in his mind.

I held up three fingers and ticked off my points one by one to Meg. "Only three people knew that Joseph would be in the pasture on that Tuesday night, that he would be alone, and that he would be there at exactly midnight. You, Joe, and your brother."

She started to cry in earnest. Fat tears dropped from her dark eyes and froze as soon as they hit the ground.

"It was so convoluted, I didn't see it at first," I said to Loy. "But I think it went something like this."

I took a moment to gather my thoughts. When I was ready, I spoke to Loy, laying it out as carefully as I could.

"Matthew hated the fact that his sister was friends with a kid from the Rez. He tried to convince her to stay away from Little Joe, but she wouldn't. I think that when the two of them ditched school and ran off to West Yellowstone to watch a movie, it was sort of the last straw as far as he was concerned. When Matthew found out that Julian had been selling pot to Little Joe for his grandmother's glaucoma, he thought he might be able to figure out a way to use that information somehow to make trouble for Joe so he would stay away from Meg. Well, he figured out a way to do it, all right. He started hanging out up at the sporting goods store, convinced Hooper to buy a bow, and at some point, he probably deliberately told Julian that Little Joe was talking about turning him in for selling pot."

"Hold on, hold on," Loy said. "We never found any marijuana in Julian's shop. Or his house. We couldn't definitively say he was dealing."

I'd thought of that too. "I think he was getting out of the business because he was about to get married to Patty. I think that Julian wanted to start over and put his past behind him, but Matthew somehow managed to convince him that Little Joe was going to turn him in. Everything he wanted was about to be snatched away."

"It was Matt who told him where Little Joe would be that night?" Connor asked.

"And he told him that if Julian used a bow, used arrows that were identical to Hooper's, that he would make it look like it was just an accident."

"You're wrong," Meg said. "My brother would never do that."

Loy looked incredulous. "All Julian had to do was wait for Little Joe to show up in the pasture that night, shoot him, and walk away."

"I don't believe you," Meg said wretchedly. She glared at me openly.

"Hooper, who walked out into the pasture to see who won the contest?" I asked.

"All three of us did," he said. "When we saw Little Joe, Matt told us it was just an accident, not to say anything, and nobody would ever know what happened."

"Did you all leave together?"

Connor was staring at the sheriff with open fear. "I know we should have called someone. But he was already dead, and Matt told us to just get the hell out of there so I took off running."

"What about you, Hooper?" I asked.

"I think I went right after Connor. It was dark. I couldn't see a damn thing, and I didn't make it back to my truck as quick because I think when I did Connor was already gone."

"Didn't you take a flashlight to look for the arrows?" I asked.

Both boys exchanged a look.

"Matt had the flashlight," Hooper said.

"Stop it," Meg said. She covered her ears with her hands. "Just stop it."

"So he could find the third arrow," I told Loy.

The sheriff looked disgusted. "Which is exactly what he did. He picked up the third arrow and took it with him."

"I'm afraid that it might be my fault that Matthew tried to break into the store," I said. Regret washed over me.

"Your fault?" my father said.

"I told Julian that I thought Little Joe might have been killed on purpose. I think he started to panic, and he probably confronted Matthew about what had happened. I think that's when Matt decided to take the third arrow up to Julian's store and plant it there."

"That's impossible," Meg said.

"I'm sorry, Meg. But the day Julian tried to kill your brother, it was because he caught Matt breaking into his store, and he knew that he was being framed."

"Little Joe's getting killed, it wasn't my fault?" Hooper said, his mouth agape. Realization had just crashed down on him, and he let out a hysterical laugh.

"Matt didn't know about the alarm system on the store," Loy said. He shook his head. "Otherwise, he might have got away with it."

"That just isn't true," Meg said, refusing to believe it.

"We found Connor's arrow. It was in the arrow box inside," I said.

"Hooper identified it," Loy told Meg regretfully.

Meg's knees wobbled, and she looked around like she didn't know what to do. She looked up at Loy, her voice like a frightened child. "I want to go home."

Loy gave me a strained look. "I'll take her back."

The sheriff cupped Meg's elbow and led her towards his truck slowly. Meg was past being able to cry and had simply shut down. Her eyes looked hollow.

Hooper was walking circles in the parking lot, staring at his hands and choking back his own tears. "I didn't do it. I didn't kill anyone."

I had just uncovered the truth, but it was a bittersweet victory. Hooper Bukowski had just gotten a new lease on life, whereas Meg's life had just been shattered. Whether she idolized her brother, feared him, or a little bit of both, Meg's world would never be the same again.

My father draped an arm around my shoulders and gave me a hug. "I don't know how you did it, Kiddo. But that was pretty good work."

I hugged him back, watching Loy key his truck radio to contact his deputy so they could secure the sporting goods store. It was a crime scene after all.

Meg sat inside the sheriff's truck with her shoulders slumped so low it looked like she was a melting candle. I could only imagine the betrayal she felt.

"I never thought I would say this," I said, looking up at my father, "but for once in my life, I wish I had been wrong."

CHAPTER 23

I sat across from Wilma on a lumpy sofa, noticing that this house smelled a little less like sage smoke and a little more like beef stew than her home in Killdeer had. I could see a crock-pot on the counter in the kitchen, bubbling away.

I had come to Wilma and Martin's home on the Reservation because it seemed only right that she should hear the events from someone she was familiar with. I was careful to keep my involvement out of the story as much as possible.

"It was Julian Hartmann all along," I said, "but Matthew was the one who convinced him to kill your grandson."

Wilma sat in the worn leather recliner, her cloudy eyes fixed to the floor while she took in everything I had said. Her son lurked behind her, looking sad but not as filled with animosity as he had been the last time I'd seen him.

"What will happen to the Chan boy now?" Martin asked. He walked around her chair and sat on the sofa beside me, elbows propped on his knees. He was leaning forward, listening to every word.

"I don't know," I said. "He woke up this morning, and he will have to face the consequences for what he did. I can't tell you what the punishment will be, but there will be one."

Wilma shook her head. "Why did he hate my Joseph so much?"

I didn't know how to answer that.

"It was because of the sister," Martin said.

I didn't say anything, but I thought it was a bit more complicated than that.

Wilma was silent for a moment, and I could see her trying to find her balance in this new reality.

"Why would the Hartmann be afraid of Joseph?" Wilma asked.

"I believe he was trying to quit his business. He was getting married and wanted to start a new life. Matthew Chan convinced Julian that your grandson was going to tell the police about his business of selling drugs to people. I think that's what happened."

Martin looked angry and disgusted. Wilma looked stricken. "Did Joseph die because he bought my eye medicine for me?"

I was quick to answer. "No, no. He died because Matthew was a bad person. It wasn't your fault."

"And what's going to happen to Bukowski?" Martin asked. He was still leaning forward intently.

"Hooper? He didn't do anything wrong," I said.

"He should have turned himself in when he thought he'd killed my son," Martin said. "He should have come forward."

"He made a terrible mistake," I said.

Martin stood up and went towards the front door. I understood that it was time for me to leave.

I went to Wilma's chair and gave her hand a gentle squeeze. "I'm very sorry. Your grandson will be missed."

She didn't squeeze my hand back, and I couldn't blame her. She was too tired from grief.

I pulled the door open and felt it grow stiff in my hand. I glanced over and saw Martin standing beside me holding onto it.

Martin was too proud to say the words, but in his eyes I saw a look of something akin to gratitude. He looked less angry than I remembered ever seeing him.

"My son was a valuable person," he said. "It is good that the man who took his life is gone now."

"I'm sorry, Martin." I didn't know what else to say.

I let myself out of the house and climbed inside the black SUV to head back to Killdeer. As I drove, it occurred to me that things might have been different had Joseph not been from the Rez. Would Matthew have still nurtured so much resentment and hatred for a boy who was white? I had to accept the fact that nobody would ever know the answer to that question.

When I pulled up to the driveway at Leif's house, I was startled to see Finn's black Jeep blocking the driveway. I parked in front of the house and when I stepped out of the car, Finn was coming down the steps towards me.

He hastily slid on his sunglasses.

"Finn, what are you doing here?" I asked.

He took a moment to answer, trying to form the words. "I wanted to check on you."

I gave a small laugh. "My run-in with Julian was days ago, and Killdeer isn't that big. You knew I was all right."

"I'm not talking about what happened at the culvert," he said.

"What then?" I asked.

Finn turned to look back at the house. "Him."

I saw Leif watching us from the living room window. He was sipping a cup of something hot, fogging up the glass, and giving me a warm smile.

"I'm not sure I understand," I said.

"It's not like he has a normal job," Finn said.

"He's just a businessman," I told him, a bit defensively. "Leif told me he is the president of a couple companies. He's got a pretty normal job, except I think he might be a CPA."

"Sure. A CPA who does freelance work for Homeland Security every now and then," Finn said.

I was confused, and I started to argue, but he held up his hand. "Marley. It's fine. He's a good man."

"You came all the way over here to find out if my landlord is a good man?" I asked.

Finn tilted his head down low enough that I could see his eyes over the top of his sunglasses. "Yes. I did."

In spite of everything that had happened between us, I felt my heart wrench with regret. "Thank you, then."

He was about to answer, but he stopped himself and closed his mouth, letting his expression shift back to the usual thousand-mile stare. He pulled out his keys and walked past me without another word.

I watched him drive away, and although it hurt to see him leaving, I knew letting him go was the right thing to do.

I turned back towards the house and saw Leif standing by the door, holding it open patiently.

I walked up the front steps and stopped in front of him. I noticed that he seemed particularly cheerful. What had he and Finn really talked about?

Leif was not simply my landlord. It was time I knew where I stood with this man.

"I've got a job interview tomorrow," I said. "I'll be able to start paying you rent if you like."

He took a sip from his mug, one corner of his mouth turned up with amusement. "You know you don't need to pay rent."

"And the car? It can't be cheap to operate a car like that. How can I help with that expense?" I asked.

He shook his head. "I can afford to take care of the car, too."

I braced myself internally. He was not an easy man to pin down. Even if he wouldn't volunteer where he stood with me, I needed him to know where I stood.

"You can't buy me, Leif. I'm not for sale."

He chuckled. "That's what I like about you. And I'm not trying to buy you. I only want you to see what life could be like."

"You're letting all the warm air out," I said.

"Just waiting until you are ready to come in. I don't ever want you to feel like I am pushing you into anything."

"What could you possibly see in me?" I asked.

Considering the vast gap between us financially, the difference in our ages, and the fact that he was an international businessman and I was just a girl from a small town, I had to admit I was not entirely convinced that Leif would ever be able to see me as an equal. I wasn't sure I could ever get over the thought that he was simply playing with me until a sophisticated and wealthy woman came along to complement his life.

He watched me stand in the doorway, wrestling with myself.

"What do I see in you?" he asked. "I'll tell you. I see a woman who doesn't fall apart when life gets messy. I'm not sure you can appreciate what an attractive quality that is."

"I have never known life to be anything other than messy," I said.

He stepped aside and pulled the door open a bit wider. "How would you like to be with a man who can clean up after himself?" he asked.

I had to admit that an offer like that sounded pretty good. For the sake of Leif's heating bill, I walked inside and let him shut the door behind us.

ABOUT THE AUTHOR

JESSICA McCLELLAND is a fourth generation Wyoming native raised on a cattle farm twenty-five miles from the Montana border. She is a librarian, avid archer and has explored the Australian outback around Brisbane, performed with the New York Philharmonic orchestra in a guest chorale production, and spent a decade hunting dinosaurs in the Jurassic formations of Johnson county, Wyoming. She is the author of the Marley Dearcorn novels, and a graduate of the University of Wyoming. She and her husband divide their time between Colorado and Wyoming.

CPSIA information can be obtained at www.ICGtesting.com
Printed in the USA
LVOW08s0855110414

381277LV00004B/745/P